IN THE TICK OF TIME

IN THE TICK OF TIME

P.D. WORKMAN

ISBN: 9781988390154 (IS Hardcover)

ISBN: 9781988390147 (IS Paperback)

ISBN: 9781926500690 (KDP Paperback)

ISBN: 9781926500706 (Kindle)

ISBN: 9781926500713 (ePub)

ALSO BY P.D. WORKMAN

Zachary Goldman Mysteries

She Wore Mourning

His Hands Were Quiet

She Was Dying Anyway

He Was Walking Alone

They Thought He was Safe

He Was Not There

Her Work Was Everything

She Told a Lie

He Never Forgot

She Was At Risk

Kenzie Kirsch Medical Thrillers

Unlawful Harvest

Doctored Death (Coming soon)

Dosed to Death (Coming soon)

Gentle Angel (Coming soon)

Reg Rawlins, Psychic Detective

What the Cat Knew

A Psychic with Catitude

A Catastrophic Theft

Night of Nine Tails

Telepathy of Gardens

Delusions of the Past

Fairy Blade Unmade

Web of Nightmares

A Whisker's Breadth

Skunk Man Swamp

Magic Ain't A Game

Without Foresight

Careful of Thy Wishes (Coming Soon)

Time to Your Elf (Coming Soon)

Undiscovered Tomb (Coming Soon)

Auntie Clem's Bakery

Gluten-Free Murder

Dairy-Free Death

Allergen-Free Assignation

Witch-Free Halloween (Halloween Short)

Dog-Free Dinner (Christmas Short)

Stirring Up Murder

Brewing Death

Coup de Glace

Sour Cherry Turnover

Apple-achian Treasure

Vegan Baked Alaska

Muffins Masks Murder

Tai Chi and Chai Tea

Santa Shortbread

Cold as Ice Cream

Changing Fortune Cookies

Hot on the Trail Mix

Recipes from Auntie Clem's Bakery

AND MORE AT PDWORKMAN.COM

1

M att, wake up! Are you okay? Matt!"

Matt pried his eyes open. His head whirled in confusion. He pressed his hands over his eyes, trying to block out the bright light slicing into his brain like a knife.

"Ow. Oh… what happened?"

He felt the back of his head. He'd been hit. He remembered he'd been hit during an investigation. He'd been talking to one of the infected men, lying in a hospital bed and the other man must have gotten up behind him. Matt remembered the crushing blows. Crashing to the dingy tiled floor in a heap. There was yelling and noise and chaos around him.

But it was quiet now. They must have transferred him to the hospital. He'd been all stitched up and bandaged, loaded up with painkillers, and he was in recovery now. Waiting to go home.

Except he was pretty sure there were no painkillers. Not with the way the white light hurt his head.

There was no bandage on his head, as he explored his short brown hair with careful fingers.

"I was hit," he mumbled. "I know where I am. I'm okay."

"Matt," the voice insisted again, still shaking him. The movement nauseated him. They should be more gentle. He'd just been assaulted. "Wake up, Matt."

"I was hit," he repeated.

"Yes, you were. But that was weeks ago."

The words didn't make any sense to him. Weeks ago? What was weeks ago? Matt scrubbed at his eyes, trying to clear his blurred vision to look around the hospital. What was he doing in hospital if it wasn't because of the assault?

He must have a concussion. That's why he was so disoriented.

"Matt. You need to wake up. Mavis is coming around and if she finds you asleep again…"

"What?"

Blinking and rubbing his eyes some more, Matt pulled his head up and sat up straight. Or mostly straight. He canted to one side and had to steady himself with his hands.

There was a pool of saliva on his desk where his head had been lying. There were papers on the floor. There was a long series of M's across the computer screen, wrapping for several lines.

He was at work. Matt cleared his throat, frowning and looking around.

"You okay, man?" Jared asked.

Jared was boyish and slim, and his eyes protruded slightly, making him always look a little surprised and uncertain. He let go of Matt's shoulder slowly, making sure Matt was going to stay upright.

"Yeah." Matt rubbed the back of his head slowly. He could still feel the shorter hair, where they had shaved him. But the wound and the stitches were long gone. There was a little knot of tissue that was tender if he rubbed it too hard. He could feel a sort of a seam where they had repaired the skull fracture. "I just… I guess I fell asleep."

Jared nodded. "Again." He straightened his light brown uniform shirt, which all the lab techs wore.

"Again?"

How many times had he fallen asleep at work over the past few weeks? It was all a little foggy. Matt could feel it coming back if he thought about it hard enough. It was getting sharper the longer he focused on it. He plucked a tissue out of the box on his desk to mop up the spittle and wiped his cheek with the back of his hand.

"I guess I just stayed up a bit late last night. I'm fine."

"Mavis would really give you hell."

"Yeah." Matt rubbed the bridge of his nose with both index fingers. He slid his hands down his face making sure everything was still in place. The assault had been so sudden and violent; everything felt knocked out of place. Nothing had been the same since.

But when he looked in the mirror, he still looked the same. As if he was still the same person he had been before being hit. Matt Malloy. Investigator for the Department of Public Health and Environment.

"Coffee," Carol suggested with a smile, putting a large mug in front of Matt. "You'd better get down as much as you can."

"Thanks."

She lingered there for a moment as if she expected more. Her long, dark blond hair curled in spirals down to her shoulder. She was allowed to wear it loose, because she worked at a computer like Matt, not at a lab bench where it would be a potential contaminant. Matt's brain was still stuttering. Still trying to warm up like a car engine on a cold morning. He didn't know what else he should say to her. Carol walked away. Matt picked up the cup and had a drink, willing the caffeine to do its job and bring him back to life.

"What time is it?" Matt tried to squint at the corner of his screen where the system clock ticked the minutes away. But it was too small or too far away and he couldn't sort out the shapes.

"It's two o'clock," Jared said, looking at his phone. "That's quite the post-prandial crash. What exactly did you drink with your lunch?"

Matt rubbed one eye at a time, juggling the coffee cup and taking a couple more sips.

"I haven't been drinking."

He was pretty sure he hadn't been drinking. He would know if he had been drinking. He was just tired.

"What day is it? How long ago..." Matt chewed on the inside of his cheek. "How long ago was I hit?"

The wound was healed. He was back at work. It was long in the past.

"That was May," Jared said, enunciating the words like Matt was hard of hearing. "It's the end of June now."

"Right." Matt looked at his desk calendar. "It's June." He ventured a smile. "Just testing you."

Jared walked away without any change of expression. He didn't roll his eyes or shake his head or grin at the joke. Just walked back to his lab bench and sat down to continue with his work.

Matt groaned and swigged down the rest of the coffee.

"Okay," he said aloud. "Back to work."

He deleted the lines of M's on his screen and read back to see what he had been typing before he had nodded off.

———

Duane really hated his job.

If he could have done something else, he would have. But he couldn't live on the wages he would make at a fast food joint. He had been lucky to be taken on by Bug Bee Gone. As Duncan kept reminding him. Duane had been lucky to land the job, and he shouldn't complain about it.

The stupid truck was bad enough. *Eye-catching* was what management called it. Duane felt like an idiot every time he drove it. Everyone looked and pointed as he drove down the street. The brilliant orange half ton was eye-catching enough. What really clinched it was the huge dead cockroach lying on its back on the top of the cab. Duane's face flushed warm as he looked at it, his clipboard of orders in hand.

"What are you waiting for?" Brad needled. "It's not going to get any brighter." He snorted. "Just like you!" He guffawed, slapping Duane on the back.

Duane jerked away from Brad, lips tightening. He tried to focus on the truck and to block Brad out of his consciousness. If there were any new scratches or dents on the truck at the end of his shift that he didn't note on his walkaround sheet at the beginning of his shift, his pay would be docked to cover the repairs. And they never kept track of the dents and scratches on each truck and rarely actually repaired them. Duane was pretty sure the company was paid ten times over for each ding. They sucked the lifeblood out of their employees. Just like a damn tick. They were vampires, draining each of their employees until they were lifeless, soulless husks.

"What's the matter?" Brad challenged. "I'm just playing with you, Duane." He said *Duane* like it was an insult. Like the name itself was a symbol of how much he despised his coworker. "I'm just being friendly. Don't you want a friend?"

Duane shook his head and climbed up into the cab of the truck without bothering with the walkaround.

"Duane the bathtub, he's dwowning," Brad mocked. "What a sniveling wuss you are, Duane. You know that, don't you?"

"I'm not a wuss," Duane snapped back. His face was a tight mask, and his voice shook. It was like prison all over again. All the taunting. All the stupid macho positioning. Guys like Brad trying to assert themselves as the alpha male. Humiliating the smaller, less violent cons like Duane. Short in stature and too skinny, Duane had struggled to keep his head above water. He'd constantly been pushed to the bottom. Pushed by the guards. Stomped on by the cons. And worst of all, walked all over by Menendez, the cellmate he could not escape.

"Don't cwy, Duane!"

Duane heard a bark of laughter from one of the other exterminators. He struggled to keep his face impassive. To pretend he hadn't heard. He was a rock. Nothing could move him. Duane didn't need Brad's approval.

Duane pulled the truck door shut with a slam and looked at the first address on the clipboard. He pretended he couldn't hear the falsetto Brad adopted as he continued to mock Duane before his audience.

———

Matt's eyes were blurring, and his eyelids kept fluttering shut. He looked at his empty coffee cup. If he kept drinking coffee, he was just going to have to run to the bathroom all afternoon. Mavis wouldn't be much more impressed with that than with Matt falling asleep at his desk.

He decided to go out to the vending machines. An energy drink, or maybe a couple of them, would pack a lot more caffeine than coffee, with less excess fluid. Hopefully, it would be enough to keep him awake.

Matt pushed himself to his feet and rubbed his eyes. The closest vending machine was a couple of hallways away. He got there and felt his pockets before realizing he had no change for the machine. He kept a change tin in his drawer for just such emergencies because he didn't like carrying it around with him.

The coins weren't doing him much good in the drawer of his desk.

Matt turned around and traipsed back to the lab.

Carol raised an eyebrow at Matt as he poked through the change in his tin.

"You getting something?"

"Yeah. Can I pick you up something too?"

She pursed her lips, considering. "Why not? Just… one of those little bags of pretzels? Hang on, I'll get you some money for it."

Matt waited while she rummaged through her purse and pockets to scrape up enough change for the snack. She put it into his hand and Matt headed back over to the vending machine.

He had seen television commercials lately about not driving tired. Studies showed it was worse than driving drunk or on drugs. Matt was so tired he felt like he was already half asleep just walking to the machine. It was a good thing there was no foot traffic or he might have had a head-on collision. As it was, when he got to the vending machine, he stood there for a moment, letting his eyes close. In an instant, he could feel himself diving into sleep. He couldn't help himself. He was *that* tired.

Matt leaned his head against the vending machine while he looked down at the money in his hand. Put the money into the slot. Make his selection. It was only two steps, but it wasn't only two steps. He had to shift his weight, keep his eyes open, grasp the coins one at a time and feed them into the slot without dropping them. He had to see how much money the energy drinks were and watch for the counter on the vending machine display to get up to that amount. Then he had to note the correct letter-number code beneath the energy drink and select it on the number pad. Lastly, he had to pull the energy drink out without overbalancing and falling flat on his face. And then make it back to his desk.

His eyes closed again, and the next thing Matt knew, the money in his hand was clattering across the floor, released from his slack hand as he fell asleep on his feet. Matt swore to himself and dropped to his knees, trying to corral it before it could spread too far. He picked up the coins with clumsy fingers. Despite his efforts, they had rolled across the hallway, down the length of the hallway and under the vending machine. He was certain to have lost half of it in the process.

Eventually, Matt stood in front of the machine again. He went through the painstaking process of feeding the coins into the slot and selecting his drink. He had been planning on buying a couple of drinks, but looking down at the coins remaining in his hand, he didn't think that he had enough left to buy another. Not if he was going to buy Carol a snack as well. She had given him money for a treat.

Matt's brain hadn't registered what snack she wanted him to get her. He stared at the money in his hand, calculating how much he had left. He tried to will himself to recall what she had asked for. Or at least, what her usual snack was.

What had he seen Carol eat?

They had worked side by side for a couple of years. He must have seen her eat dozens of snacks.

What did she like?

After staring through the window of the vending machine for a long time, Matt finally settled on peanuts. He was sure Carol would like peanuts. She wasn't allergic. He'd seen her eat them before. And most of all, they were the cheapest thing in the machine and he didn't have much money left.

With a stifled sigh, Matt fed the rest of the change into the machine and pushed the button for the peanuts. Nothing happened. He pressed again and still nothing happened. Matt rubbed his eyes, staring at the labels below the merchandise and realized he was pressing the button for the shelf above the peanuts. He tried again, and, this time was rewarded by a whir as the machine pushed the peanuts forward and dropped them into the slot for Matt to retrieve.

"About time," Matt grumbled.

His words were soon to be repeated by Mavis, who was waiting in the lab for Matt. Matt had opened his energy drink on the way back and had already consumed half of the contents. Carol's peanuts were all but forgotten in his pocket.

"Just going for a snack run," Matt explained, forcing a cheerful tone. He raised the canned energy drink a little higher. "Have to stay alert. No mid-afternoon slump around here."

He saw Jared's head go up at this comment, and Jared grinned. No, no mid-afternoon slump. A complete mid-afternoon blackout on his desk, but no mid-afternoon slump. Jared raised his hand to his mouth to hide the smile, then went on seriously adding droplets to test tubes with his blue-gloved hands.

"No," Mavis said dryly. "We wouldn't want any more of that, would we?"

Matt nodded, holding his head high and confident. She wouldn't know from his attitude that he was lying to her. He had taken care of the problem already; so it wasn't really a lie.

"You owe me some reports, Mr. Malloy."

"Yes, I was just proofing them before sending them to you." Matt gestured to his computer, where he hoped they were all queued up and ready to go. "You'll have them this afternoon."

"Good. I look forward to seeing them. Once that is done, I need you to update the website FAQs."

She handed him a sheaf of papers. Matt looked down at them. Questions submitted through their website 'contact us' form by the public.

"Sure. No problem."

"Don't get creative. Remember to keep them brief and clear. Don't include anything not blessed by the CDC."

Matt cleared his throat. "No problem," he repeated. "I'll see to it."

2

———

Duane scanned the vehicles parked in the lot. Most of the other workers had returned before him. Which meant he was probably late, and Steve would accuse him of trying to get paid for unauthorized overtime. He wasn't. He was just trying to do the job he was paid to do. But it sometimes took him longer than it took the more experienced exterminators.

Brad's usual vehicle had already been returned. Duane wondered whether he would be inside, or whether he had already left for the day. He hoped Brad had already clocked out, and Duane wouldn't have to put up with any more torment. Duane had thought when he left school, he would be leaving all the testosterone-driven bullying behind. He had not been happy to discover adults still got bullied too. Workplace bullying was a commonplace occurrence. At least, it had been for him. Duane had not had very good luck in any of the places he had spent time the last few years. Wherever he went, there was always a bigger dog determined to force him into submission.

Duane locked up his truck and took his kit with him into the building.

"Clocking out," he informed the gangly supervisor. Steve was a pimply youth who barely looked old enough to be out of high school. But he had earned a degree already, a prerequisite for being able to order people around at Bug Bee Gone.

"You're late. Anything I should know about?"

Duane shook his head. "Just took longer than it should have. And traffic. You know traffic…"

Duane swiped his prox card across the sensor three times before it green-lighted and gave him the two-toned 'dee doo,' confirming it had recorded his time. A couple of times, Duane had made the assumption it had worked without actually seeing the green light or hearing the duplex tone. Which meant either his clock kept running all night, tallying up unearned overtime, or his start time wasn't entered, and he had no time booked for the day. Either way, it had to be manually overridden and the time fixed, irritating the powers-that-be.

"I've got samples," Duane informed Steve.

"Everyone's got samples," Steve muttered.

Brad had put his kit on the floor and was wrestling with a sticky latch. Duane put his down on the counter, even though he knew Steve didn't like it where it might scratch the finish.

As Duane took the first sample tube out of his kit, he jumped. One of the bugs was on the outside of the glass instead of the inside.

He couldn't let Steve see he had made a mistake. Somehow a tick had fallen into his kit while he wasn't looking, or he had managed to transfer one from the collection cloth onto the outside of the tube instead of down into the inside. Either way, Duane had made a mistake, and he didn't want to own up to it. He gave the tube a little shake before handing it across to Steve. The tick fell off.

Duane didn't see where it went, but he realized too late he had just shaken the tube over Brad's head. Another mistake. He swallowed. Should he tell Brad what he had just done?

Not yet. Not in front of Steve. Duane would wait until they were both outside, going back to their own vehicles, and then he would explain to Brad what had happened.

Duane gave Steve the log sheet that went with the sample tube. Steve ran his eyes over it, squinting at Duane's chicken scratch.

"Where did you collect it?" he asked.

"The last appointment," Duane said and looked at his call sheet. He read out the address. Steve printed in heavy strokes over Duane's writing, clarifying the address. Duane felt a wave of heat go over his face. He prickled over this demonstration of how useless he was.

Brad straightened up and put his samples and log sheets firmly down on the counter. He looked at Duane's sheet and snickered.

"Better send you back to school to learn how to write. My five-year-old niece has better printing."

Duane looked sideways at him, saying nothing.

"Maybe little Duane could retake kindergarten at night school!"

"All right, Brad. That's enough," Steve said.

Brad opened his mouth and didn't say anything, choked over being told by a kid how to behave. But that kid was his boss, and he couldn't do anything about it. He swallowed his ire, and Duane and Brad waited, silent, side by side, as Steve examined the log sheets and copies of the invoices and receipts for the day's work. Two school boys waiting for the approval of their teacher.

When Steve finished, they left their kits in the locker room and changed out of their uniforms in silence. Back in the parking lot, it was time for Duane to tell Brad what happened inside. He tried several times to explain, but every time he opened his mouth, the word stuck in his throat. Brad didn't look at him. There was no small talk. The two of them never talked; they had nothing in common other than the job.

Maybe it wasn't such a bad thing that the tick had fallen into Brad's hair. Maybe Duane didn't care if Brad had gotten himself bitten by a tick.

Duane let himself into his car. It was his last chance to tell Brad what had happened. If he didn't say anything now, he couldn't. He watched Brad get into his big red truck and drive away.

Duane wondered if Brad would get sick. Ticks carried a lot of diseases. Rocky Mountain spotted fever. Tularemia. Even Lyme disease.

Duane knew all about Lyme disease.

It wouldn't be such a bad thing if Brad got a tick-borne disease. Duane wouldn't mind seeing him taken down a peg.

He wouldn't mind at all.

———

Matt sat down at his computer. He leafed through the sheets of papers and sorted the questions into different piles. He stopped to chug down more of the energy drink. He blinked his eyes. He was feeling wider awake after the caffeine boost. But he was still tired. It felt like he was trying to work at midnight instead of the middle of the afternoon. At least the caffeine put legs under him for a while.

He looked through the questions, trying to figure out which ones would need updated answers on the FAQ. A lot of questions were repeated over and over. He noted there was more this time about person-to-person communication of Lyme disease. Matt started composing comprehensive questions and answers.

Question: My husband has been diagnosed with Lyme disease. Can I catch it from him?

Answer: There is no evidence Lyme disease can be transmitted from person to person. You cannot get infected from touching, kissing, or having sex with a person who has Lyme disease. You do not need to worry about getting it from your husband.

Matt knew it wasn't a complete answer. But Mavis only wanted him to include information that would be approved by the CDC. Matt knew there was research showing live spirochetes could be found in human saliva, blood, urine, and semen. There was no *proof* Lyme disease could be transmitted through contact with bodily fluids, but there was some evidence to suggest it was a possibility. The studies were too small and human experiments transmitting Lyme disease were unethical. There was evidence that Lyme disease could be passed from mother to child, but Matt didn't want to open that can of worms either.

Question: Is there Lyme disease in Colorado?

Answer: You can't get much safer than Colorado. The only state with fewer confirmed cases of Lyme disease is Hawaii. Colorado has only had three reported cases of Lyme disease in the last decade. None of those cases were proven to be contracted in Colorado, but were imported from other states.

Again, that was all Matt could safely say. There was a lot more he would have liked to put in his answer. For example, there were many Lyme-like diseases in Colorado and the other States. There was STARI in the southern states. There were other vector-borne diseases that started with a rash, fever, and achy joints. As far as the CDC was concerned, there was no Lyme disease outside of the northeast. And if the CDC said there was no Lyme disease in Colorado, Matt couldn't say there was. He couldn't report on the questionable cases he had seen. They had all tested negative for Lyme disease. But the testing they did wasn't comprehensive, and Lyme was notoriously hard to get a positive result for.

Question: I have seen on the Internet you can get Lyme disease from other insects, not just from ticks.

Answer: There is no convincing evidence insects such as mosquitoes, flies, or fleas can transmit Lyme disease. In fact, you can't even get Lyme disease from all ticks. You can only get Lyme disease from black-legged ticks. And not all black-legged ticks are infected with the bacteria that can transmit Lyme disease.

At least Matt believed this statement to be true one hundred percent. There was a lot of chatter on the Internet suggesting you might get Lyme disease from mosquitoes. But Matt believed if you could get Lyme disease from mosquitoes, Lyme disease would be a heck of a lot more common. Sure, there were a lot of cases where someone diagnosed with Lyme disease couldn't remember ever being bitten by a tick. But that didn't mean they *hadn't* been bitten by a tick. Many people never knew they had been bitten. A tick bite didn't hurt. It might itch a little bit at first. But if the bite was well-hidden in hair or an armpit, the person might never know they had been bitten. After the tick had fed and was engorged with blood, it would drop off. And the subject would never know it had been there in the first place. Lyme disease didn't always start with the bull's-eye rash around the bite. So many people didn't even know they had been bitten.

Question: Is it true that nothing can be done about Lyme disease unless it is diagnosed right away?

Answer: No. That is false. Even months later, Lyme disease can be treated with a round of antibiotics. While Lyme disease can be devastating, it is easily treated once properly diagnosed.

Matt didn't write there would be no after-effects. While the Lyme infection could be cured, there were a lot of cases where the patient still had ongoing symptoms years later. The longer Lyme disease went without being treated, the worse the long-term damage was. But people didn't want to read that on the Department of Health website.

He wasn't sure why he was spending so much time answering questions about Lyme disease when, as far as his office was concerned, it did not even exist in Colorado.

Matt rubbed his eyes and took another swallow of his drink. Carol hovered near his desk, looking at him uncertainly.

"Yes?" Matt asked.

"Uh, I was just wondering, whether you had picked up some pretzels for me," Carol said. "From the vending machine."

"Oh!" Matt slapped his forehead. "Yes, of course, I got you…" He reached into his pocket and pulled out the package. "Uh… a package of peanuts."

Carol quickly masked her disappointment.

"Yes, peanuts. That's great. I just needed something salty to munch on this afternoon. Thanks!"

"I… probably owe you some change. What's the difference in price from the pretzels?"

"Oh, don't worry about it," Carol said. "It's nothing."

She took the package of peanuts from him and opened it, offering him a few. Matt shook his head.

"No, that's okay, thanks."

Carol nodded. She looked over the papers strewn on his desk. "So how's it going? Are you feeling better?"

"Yeah, I'm fine." Matt made a motion, waving away her concern. "I don't know what happened. I guess I just stayed up a little too late last night. You know, with Rebecca."

"Ah." Carol nodded. "Sure, of course. That's great." She turned slightly to go back to her desk. "I just worry, you know. You haven't been quite yourself since the accident."

"The accident?" Matt repeated. "Oh… yeah… I don't know if I'd really call it an accident, though. It was… intentional…"

Carol shifted. "Right. Well, since… getting whacked over the head."

Matt grinned. "Yeah. Don't worry about it. Really. I'm fine."

She returned to her desk. Matt saw Dewey turning back to his lab bench. He had obviously been following the conversation closely, but now he pushed up his dark-rimmed glasses and pretended he had been working all along.

"I really am fine," Matt reiterated to him.

Dewey made a small shrug with his hands and nodded. "You're fine," he echoed.

Matt shuffled through the papers to see what other questions might need to be answered.

————

Duane looked around the locker room as he picked up his uniform, kit, and truck keys. He was running a little late, but there were still a couple of trucks left in the lot. At least if Duane were in trouble, someone else would be in more trouble.

He punched in at the front desk and picked up his work orders.

"You're late," Steve pointed out.

"Just by a minute. I'm not the latest."

"Berkley called in sick. You *are* the latest."

"Brad is sick?" Even if Duane was late, at least he had shown up. Did Brad have the flu, or was he hung over or had he slept in after a late night? Duane tried to hide the smile stretching at the corners of his mouth, contemplating the trouble Brad would be in. He didn't need to worry, Steve didn't even look at him.

"Better get on your way," the manager growled, typing furiously on his computer.

Duane went out to the truck to do his walkaround and start the day, a spring in his step.

————

Duane bit his lip, thinking while he clocked out. In the days since the accidental dumping of a tick into Brad's hair or down his neck, Duane had hoped it had just been shaken off, or Brad had found it and disposed of it before it had a chance to feed. As the days had passed, Duane had convinced himself this was the case. But now word was out that Brad was down with a rash, fever, and aching joints. His neurological symptoms were bad enough he couldn't walk and had been admitted to the hospital to see if he'd had a stroke. He was still there now.

"Sounds like Lyme disease," Marg declared as they handed in their reports at the desk. "I bet he got bitten on a job."

Steve glared at her. "There's no Lyme disease in Colorado. He did *not* get it on the job."

"It could be another tick-borne disease," Klaus threw out as they returned to the locker room. He stripped off his uniform without regard to the fact Marg was standing right there. Duane waited. There was no way he was going to undress in front of Marg.

He hated the uniform. It reminded him too much of the coveralls he had worn for the previous two years. That uniform did not bring back fond memories.

"We've got Colorado Tick Fever, Rocky Mountain Spotted Fever," Klaus went on, listing them off on his fingers. "Tularemia. Could even be STARI, if it was a lone star tick."

Duane eyed Marg, waiting for her to leave the locker room. She still needed to change herself, and she wouldn't do it in front of the men. She'd use the private bathroom across the hall.

"How do you tell a lone star tick from a black-legged tick?" Marg asked.

Klaus rolled his eyes at this. "Because the female has a single white spot on its back, instead of black legs," he suggested.

"That's fine if it's big and female," Marg pointed out. "But some of these babies are barely the size of a speck. Until they bite you and fill up with blood. So how would you know?"

"Doesn't matter," Duane contributed. "We don't get either one in Colorado."

Everyone turned to look at him, and Duane felt his face flush red. He didn't usually participate in the back-and-forth banter of the locker room. He barely ever opened his mouth, even to respond to Brad's needling.

"We've got Rocky Mountain wood ticks and dog ticks," Duane explained, feeling his ears flaming red, "but not lone star or black-legged."

"How do you know that?" Marg demanded.

Duane shrugged uncomfortably. "I've just read it," he lied.

Klaus gave a little snicker. "Who would have guessed beanpole could even read?"

Duane turned away to put his kit in his locker. He pretended he was getting ready to change out of his coveralls. He wasn't about to get into the details. He wasn't going to tell them he had learned about them the hard way. Like Brad, by experiencing tick-borne disease himself.

The researchers in other countries said other kinds of ticks could carry Lyme, but in North America, they wouldn't admit to anything other than the black-legged tick carrying it. And then only in the northeast. Southern ticks apparently had different palates.

Whatever the illness was and whatever kind of bug carried it, Duane wouldn't wish it on his worst enemy.

Or… maybe he would. Smiling into his locker, Duane considered this new line of thought. He couldn't claim to be devastated Brad was now going through something similar to what Duane had suffered. Duane wouldn't feel particularly bad if Klaus got it too. Or even Marg, for that matter. She might not torment Duane like Brad did, but it wasn't like she ever defended him.

Duane found Marg irritating. The only female in their number, Marg got under his skin. Always in the way when he wanted to change. He felt like he had to let her go first if they arrived at the same time to clock in or out. He always felt awkward when they approached a door and he wondered if she expected him to hold it for her. And it just wasn't normal for a woman to be so comfortable around bugs and other vermin. She didn't squeal or shrink at the sight of creepy-crawlies. In fact, she seemed to be far less bothered by them than Duane himself was. And that just wasn't normal.

He wouldn't really mind if any of them got Lyme disease or any other tick-borne disease.

And that included smarmy supervisor Steve. Duane wouldn't mind seeing him taken down a notch or two by a nasty case of bug-borne illness.

3

Matt knew someone was trying to wake him. And he knew he couldn't wake up. He was too far under, his brain too exhausted. He was in bed, and that meant it was okay to sleep, no matter if someone else thought he should be getting up. Eventually, the insistent hands and distant voice went away, and he was able to swim deeper into the darkness, snuggling down in the blankets.

When Matt eventually woke on his own, the room was dark. He didn't feel like he had gotten enough sleep, but his brain was restless, and he remembered someone had been trying to wake him up earlier.

He crawled out of bed and staggered to the bathroom to wash the foul taste out of his mouth and use the john. He rubbed his eyes and splashed water on his face, then went to look for Rebecca. Of course, that was who had been trying to wake him up. Who else would even be in his apartment?

She was sitting in front of the TV on the couch, curled up in the corner with a blanket and with her journal propped in her lap. Matt's eyes traveled appreciatively over her smooth brown face and mass of twisted black curls, tinted a light reddish-brown on the ends. Her slim curves were hidden under the blanket, which it was really too warm to be using in the summer weather. But despite her Jersey birth and upbringing, she seemed to have inherited from her ancestors a preference for much hotter weather than they ever experienced in Colorado.

Rebecca had been intent on writing in her journal, but she suddenly became aware of Matt, her eyes flicking up from the page. Her lips curved up in a smile.

"Well, he lives!"

"Hey." Matt wiped his mouth with the back of his hand. "What time is it?"

She glanced toward the TV. "Ten o'clock."

"Sheesh." Matt scratched his head. "I'm sorry, Bec. I was just too wiped out. Are you going to be up for a little longer yet?"

"I have to be at work in the morning. So… maybe another hour. Then I really have to hit the sack."

He crossed the room and sat down on the couch beside her. She stretched her feet out into his lap, and he obliged by massaging them.

"How was your day?" Matt inquired.

"You need to call Sharon." Rebecca's eyes went to the clock again. "You'd better do it now. She'll be heading to bed soon too."

"I'll call her tomorrow. I need to spend some time with you."

"She was really worried. Especially when I couldn't wake you up. She needs to hear you're okay."

Matt sighed in exasperation. "She can't wait?"

"Just a quick call to let her know how you're doing."

Matt patted his pockets, but he must have emptied them before lying down to sleep. He groaned as he climbed to his feet. He knew he was acting grumpy about having to call his sister. She was just concerned. She wasn't trying to interfere in his life. Put it down to being chronically short on sleep since the assault. He traipsed back to the bedroom and picked up his phone. He sat on the side of the bed while he called Sharon.

"Matt?"

Rebecca was right. Even one syllable from Sharon raised his blood pressure. She sounded worried, angry, and on the edge of panic all at once. And all she'd said was his name.

"Hi, baby sister," Matt made an effort to sound cheerful and normal. "Becca said you were looking for me."

"She said you were asleep."

"Yeah. Sorry. She did try to wake me up, but I was right out."

"If you want to get back onto a normal sleep schedule, you can't be conking out after work. You won't be able to get back to sleep at bedtime."

Matt rubbed the back of his head, his fingers automatically seeking out the spot shaved a little shorter. The seam in his skull. He rubbed it, wincing slightly.

"It doesn't work that way," he told Sharon. "I've tried keeping to a schedule, but my body won't let me. I can barely get through work without falling asleep. There's no way I can keep myself awake once I'm home."

"You just need to find physical things to do. Clean house. Ride a stationary bike. Get out and get some sunshine."

"Okay."

They both knew he only agreed because he didn't want to have an argument. He didn't actually intend to follow her advice. There was silence for a few moments while Sharon considered his statement, apparently working out the next prong of her attack.

"How's your head?" she asked in a more conciliatory tone.

"It's not *hurting*."

"Well, that's good. That's an improvement, isn't it?"

Matt grunted, noncommittal. "So what did you want? Why did you call?"

"Can't I call just to visit with my big brother?"

"Sure. But if you wanted Rebecca to wake me up, then I assume you wanted more than just to say hello."

"Not really. I just wanted to make sure you were okay."

"Don't tell her to wake me up."

There was a moment of silence. "Okay," Sharon agreed. "I'm sorry."

Matt felt a little bad for getting after her. But he needed his sleep, and he couldn't let her think it was okay to wake him up without any pressing reason. "How about you?" he asked, turning the conversation back on her. "What's up with you lately?"

With a sigh, Rebecca folded the blanket into a neat rectangle and laid it over the arm of the couch. She stood up and straightened the cushions. Her journal went into the little drawer of the side table. She turned off the TV and the lamp and walked down the dark hall to the bedroom.

There was a lamp on and for an instant, she dared hope Matt was still awake, on the phone with Sharon or completing some reports he had brought home from work. Or even playing a game on his phone.

Anything other than sleeping.

But there he was. Not under the covers this time. He was crossways across the bed, his feet still on the floor. His phone rested loosely in his hand, on the bed, near his ear. Rebecca wondered whether he had finished the call with Sharon and hung up, or whether he had fallen asleep in the middle of the call.

She took the phone out of his hand and plugged it in on the bedside table. She picked up his feet and swiveled them onto the bed. Matt moved in his sleep, turning and straightening out on instinct, so he was in his proper place. She pulled a blanket over him.

Rebecca got herself ready for bed and lay down beside him. She cuddled up to his body, nestling her curves into his form, and found her sweet spot for sleep.

———

An hour later, Matt was kicking restlessly. Rebecca drew back from him, waiting for him to settle again. Matt tossed from one side to the other. Rebecca could hear him muttering and cursing under his breath. His movements grew increasingly erratic.

"Shh," Rebecca tried to calm him back down. Even though she knew it was hopeless. Once he was wound up, nothing she could say or do was going to get him back on track. "It's okay, Matt. Go back to sleep."

"I can't go back to sleep," Matt growled. He swore. "Don't you think I would if I could?"

"If you'd just stay calm and not get all angry…"

He swore again and bounded out of bed.

"Matt—"

"Go back to sleep. I won't bother you."

"But I want—"

Too late, he was out the door and gone.

Rebecca snuggled back down under the covers and tried to find sleep again.

4

———

M rs. Shirley Stemple had the kind of body Duane would normally have been attracted to. Shorter than he was. Nicely built. She had long spiraling blond curls falling to her shoulders in ringlets. Her features and makeup were flawless, but when she looked at him, her perfect little mouth twisted into an ugly sneer. She folded her arms across her chest.

"How long is this going to take?"

Duane looked around the property, estimating the size and how long it would take to spray the grounds.

"Maybe… a couple hours," he suggested.

She sighed in exasperation and shook her head. "You were supposed to be here at ten."

"I got held up at a previous appointment," Duane explained. "Sorry…"

"They could have at least called me to say you would be late."

"Yeah. I guess."

"It would be nice to know these things. I don't have all day to wait around for… pest control."

Duane was getting angry about having to look at her face and listen to her complaints. She wasn't a very nice person. He turned to get his equipment off the truck, then looked back at her.

"Mind if I use your facilities before I get started, ma'am?"

Her nose wrinkled. "No, you may not. I'm not in the habit of opening up my home to all sorts of... service people."

Duane stared at her. He shifted his stance, uncomfortable. It was a long time since he'd downed an extra large java. Most people were gracious when he asked to use the bathroom.

"There's a gas station down the street," Mrs. Stemple said with a sniff. "But I expect you to do your job first. You are already late."

Duane shook his head. "I can't wait until the job is done. So unless you want me to water your trees, you're going to have to wait until after I run down to the gas station."

She scowled at this. "I will be making a complaint to your supervisor," she snapped. "This sort of behavior is completely unacceptable."

"Yes, ma'am," Duane said, forcing himself to be polite the way he had been trained. The customer might not always be right, but the customer was to be treated courteously at all times. He tried to keep the anger and sarcasm from entering into his voice. "I'll be back as quickly as possible."

She harrumphed, sniffed again, and turned on her heel to go back into her house. Duane took a long, slow breath, and headed back to his truck.

———

"Morning, Matt," Carol sang out as he entered the lab.

Matt nodded at her, doing his best to smile and look chipper like she did. "Morning, Carol."

"Did you sleep better last night?"

Matt grimaced. His favorite topic of discussion. "Yes."

Carol's face brightened hopefully.

"Until about midnight."

Her expression fell again, and Matt felt a little cruel for getting her hopes up.

"I dunno. Seems like that's the only time of day I'm wide awake. Did some reports, read a book, watched some early-morning shows..."

"You've got your day and night reversed," Dewey observed. "I had an aunt like that. No matter what she did, she couldn't go to sleep at night and be awake during the day."

He looked back down at his bench, absorbed in his work. Carol and

Matt looked at him, waiting for more, but it appeared Dewey's contribution to the discussion was finished.

"What did she do?" Carol prodded.

Dewey didn't look back up.

"Dewey. Dewey!"

Dewey looked up again, his expression vague. "Eh?"

Carol and Matt exchanged glances.

"What did your aunt do?" Carol repeated.

"My aunt?" It took a few seconds for the penny to drop. "Oh. You mean the one who had day and night reversed."

"Yes. What did she do?"

Dewey considered for a minute. "Everyone said she should try to adjust her schedule by going to bed fifteen minutes earlier every night."

Matt had frequently heard the same advice. And it was totally useless.

"That didn't work," Dewey acknowledged. "She saw a specialist who told her she had to do the opposite. Instead of trying to go to bed earlier every night, she was supposed to follow her natural sleep cycle to start out with, and then she was supposed to stay up an hour later each night until she was back around the clock to where she should be."

Matt could see the attraction of staying up later instead of trying to go to bed earlier. "Did it work?"

"For a while," Dewey said obliquely.

Again, they waited for more information from him, but he didn't offer anything.

"For a while," Matt repeated to Carol.

She shrugged. "Might be worth a try."

Matt nodded. "The trouble is starting out by following my natural schedule. The job isn't exactly conducive to sleeping during the afternoon."

"You should talk to Mavis about it. Maybe if the administration understands what you are trying to do, they'll be flexible for a while. Let you work it out like Dewey's aunt."

Matt shrugged. He got himself a cup of coffee and headed for his desk, giving Jared a little wave on his way there.

———

It had been a long, hot day and Duane was glad to be home. Even if home was just a ratty little basement apartment with a box fan and no air conditioner. At least there was a fridge and an adjustable easy chair in front of the TV. Heaven compared to the last couple of years.

He had barely returned home and was just contemplating what to do for some supper when there was a knock on a door. Not just the routine knock of a door-to-door solicitor, but a sharp, self-important knock he recognized only too well.

Duane ignored it.

After a minute, the hammering was repeated.

"Open up, Duane," Duncan yelled through the door. "I saw you come in, there's no point in pretending not to be home!"

He pounded on it again.

Duane conceded, walking over to the door and throwing the bolt. He didn't actually open the door. Duncan took the initiative and opened it himself, barging into the room.

"Took you long enough. I expect you to answer the first time instead of hiding in here like a shy schoolgirl," he bullied. Several inches taller than Duane and a good hundred pounds heavier, Duncan was slightly paunchy and doughy from lack of exercise, but big enough to dominate Duane physically. It was unfortunate that they looked so much alike. Both white, with dark brown hair, Duane's buzz-cut short and Duncan's coiffed. They both had their mother's small nose and father's jaw and ears. Duane couldn't help looking at Duncan and wondering why Duncan had won the physical lottery. Was it because he was the first-born? The favorite? Because he always got the better portion at dinner?

"It's my house, not yours," Duane pointed out.

"Yeah? Who put down the deposit and first month on it? Not you, I don't think."

"I've been paying the rent."

"Late, according to the landlord. There's no reason you can't pay it on time. And who got you the job to pay the rent, anyway?"

"I could have found something else. I didn't ask you to do it."

Duncan looked in the fridge. Duane wondered whether he was happy to see that Duane was following the rules or disappointed not to be able to help himself to a cold beer. Duncan went back to the living room and positioned himself in Duane's easy chair.

"Mom would never forgive me if I let anything happen to her little boy," Duncan said. "I have to do what I can to help out my poor baby brother."

"I can get on by myself," Duane insisted. "I don't need any help."

"Yeah, you've been doing a great job up until now, haven't you? Without someone looking after you, you got no place to live, no job, no money. You'd be back in prison in a week."

The anger heating up in Duane's chest started to boil and steam. "I would not! I'm not in prison, and I'm not going back there."

Duncan snorted. "You're a worthless, ignorant layabout. You won't ever amount to anything without someone holding your hand. Everything you've got here is from me. You'd be nothing without me looking after you, and Mom before that."

"That's not true!"

"Yeah? Name one thing you've done for yourself. Name one thing you've got because of your own efforts."

"Get out of here!" Duane shrieked. His voice was shrill in his own ears. He sounded more like a child or a girl than a man outraged. But he didn't let that stop him. "This is my home, and I didn't invite you in. You get out, or I'm calling the police!"

"What would you tell them?" Duncan challenged. "I'm a fine, upstanding citizen. You're prison trash. Who do you think they're going to believe? I'll tell them you threatened me. I caught you buying drugs. I'll tell them you've broken your parole terms, and you'll be right back in that stinking hole. How would you like that?"

Duane froze. Duncan wouldn't do that. He might threaten, but he would never do anything that would send Duane back to prison. Would he?

Duncan laughed. "If you want a roof over your head and to stay out of prison, you'd better mind your manners. I am the only one standing between you and the law. Don't you forget it."

Duane stood there looking at his brother and didn't know what to do.

"You wouldn't do that," he said finally.

"Tell me 'thank you.'"

"What?"

"If you want me to keep taking care of you and not turn you in, you tell me 'thank you.'"

Duane didn't say anything.

"Tell me 'thank you,'" Duncan insisted. "I want to hear the words. You know the only reason you're out of prison and in a place of your own is because of what I've done for you."

Duane looked at Duncan's pompous expression, the evil enjoyment in his face. Duncan was daring Duane to fight back, to take Duncan up on his challenge. Did he really want to turn Duane in? Get him put back in prison?

Duane gulped. "Thank you."

Duncan laughed. "What? I can't hear you, baby brother."

"Thank you," Duane said with more force. He choked back any objection, any vestige of pride. It was just a game for Duncan. It didn't mean anything. Duane was just playing along with the game.

Duncan continued to laugh, pushing himself up again from the chair. "You are the most pitiful, cowardly milksop I have ever met!"

Chuckling to himself, he stood there for a moment with his hand on his chest. While still a young man, in the apparent peak of health, Duncan had a bad heart. He'd had open heart surgery while barely in his twenties, replacing a couple of defective valves and repairing other issues. Duane didn't know all the details. Even with a defective heart, Duncan had been able to do more with his life than Duane. He had succeeded in all the places Duane had failed.

And he made sure Duane knew it.

5

____

"Mr. Malloy!"

Matt jerked upright in his desk, just about falling out of his chair in the process. He hadn't been completely asleep, not with his head down on the desk in a pool of saliva. But he had been drifting, his thoughts sliding in and out of reality like an otter. Even as he blinked and focused on Mavis, the elastic feeling of unreality clung to his brain cells, and he knew he wasn't quite present.

"Mavis. Ms. Booker. What can I do for you?" he asked politely.

"What can you do for me? You could do your job, for once," she snapped.

Matt took a sip of coffee, blinking his eyes rapidly while he was facing away from her. He put the cup back down again, centering it carefully on the coaster he always used to avoid marring the desktop.

"I'm here," he pointed out. "I'm doing my job."

He glanced at his computer screen. No long string of letters pressed in his sleep today. Everything looked to be in order until he got to the last few words across the bottom of the page.

Under inside where moon

Okay, that wasn't quite kosher. He'd obviously been drifting off when his fingers had tapped out the random string. It had made sense at the time. But Mavis couldn't see his computer screen from where she was

29

standing. Matt used control-backspace to quickly delete the offending words in case she should come around and look at his screen.

"I was just thinking through the next paragraph," he explained. Which was true. That was how it had started. That was why he had closed his eyes in the first place. "So what can I do for you?"

"Where is the updated FAQ? You were supposed to have it to me days ago."

Matt's brows drew down as he squinted his eyes and thought about it. He knew he had processed the big stack of questions and updated the FAQ. It should have been back on Mavis' desk.

"Somebody must have taken it out of the interoffice mail," Matt said slowly. He looked at his out basket, which was empty. "I finished it and sent it off to you. You never got it?"

"Would I be here if I had received it?"

"No, I guess you wouldn't. Unless... no, of course not." Matt looked again at his out basket. "Why isn't there anything in there? Who took my mail?" His voice rose without him meaning it to. The others stopped what they were doing to see what was going on. Matt tried to remember what should be in his out basket. Who would come and take things out of the basket? How much of his work had disappeared over the last few weeks? It was no wonder he was getting in trouble all the time now.

Somebody was sabotaging him.

Mavis was frowning, her brows drawing close together.

"Matt?" She looked confused and concerned instead of angry.

Jared had left his lab bench. He approached Matt's desk.

"Hey, Matt. What's wrong? What's going on?"

"Did you take them?" Matt demanded.

"Take what?"

"You know what I'm talking about. The FAQ. Did you take the FAQ?"

"Nobody took the FAQ. You gave it to Carol for proofing."

"Oh."

Matt's face flushed hot.

He didn't remember giving it to Carol. He wondered whether Jared was telling the truth, or if he was covering for Matt, trying to save face in front of Mavis.

Mavis looked back and forth between Matt and Jared and she looked over to Carol's desk.

"Well then, I guess I better talk to Miss Stern."

With another odd look at Matt, she walked over to Carol's desk to talk to her.

Matt looked at Jared.

"I finished that FAQ ages ago," he said. "Does Carol really have it?"

"You dumped it on her couple of days ago," Jared said. "She's got too much to do. She probably hasn't had time to look at it yet."

Matt's skin crawled, and he scratched at his arms. Try as he might, he couldn't remember giving the FAQ to Carol. He knew how busy she was. Why would he put something else on her? Mavis could proof it just as easily as Carol. Why get two people to do what one could?

Matt looked down at his arm, scratching harder. As he looked, the veins seemed to throb and writhe like worms. He pulled his hand back from his arm in shock.

"What?" Jared looked down at Matt's arm. He frowned. "What's wrong?"

"It's... didn't you see that? There's something under the skin! I've got something in there."

Jared studied Matt's arm and then his face.

"It's okay," he soothed. "Let's just take a minute here..."

"Take a minute? But there's worms under my skin. Bugs. How did they get there?"

"Worms aren't bugs," Jared said, the corner of his mouth lifting in a smile. "You know that."

Matt's rising panic stuttered to a halt.

Of course worms weren't bugs. How many people had he lectured over the years about the proper use of words like bug and insect? People thought every creepy crawly was a bug. When in reality, the pests they dealt with came from many different branches of the animal kingdom.

Mavis walked away from Carol's desk, her high heels marking her pace with sharp clicks. Matt's eyes followed her out of the room. Then Carol was beside his desk, and Dewey hovered nearby, not quite abandoning his bench, but coming much closer to Matt's desk than he normally would in the middle of the work day.

"Is he okay?" Carol asked in a low voice.

"I don't know," Jared said.

"I'm right here," Matt pointed out. But neither one of them paid any attention.

"He's hallucinating," Jared said. "Demonstrating paranoia."

"When's the last time you had a good sleep?" Carol asked Matt, giving his shoulder a soothing rub. "Do you have a fever?" Her hand went briefly to his forehead, touching it with the backs of her fingers. She shook her head. "Seems normal. Matt? How much sleep have you gotten this week?"

Everything seemed to be moving too fast. Matt couldn't understand what they were all talking about. They were all so intense and concerned all of a sudden.

"I haven't slept all this week," Matt said. "Any amount, anyway."

"Should we take him to the hospital?" Carol asked.

"I don't know. Are they going to be able to do anything to help him? Besides giving him a pill to help him sleep?"

"Have you seen the doctor, Matt?"

"Have I seen a doctor about what? About not being able to sleep?"

"Maybe we'd better," Jared offered.

Carol looked at her watch. "Do you think we can wait until the end of the day?"

"If he stays stable. How are you feeling, Matt?"

"I'm fine," Matt assured them.

"We'll keep an eye on him," Jared said. He looked back at his desk, and Carol looked back at hers.

"Why don't you put your head down on the desk for a while?" Carol suggested. "I don't think Mavis is going to be coming back here again tonight. She's made enough trouble, and she's got work to keep her busy the rest of the day."

"I should finish this," Matt protested, gesturing to his screen.

"Just save it and put your head down," Carol said. "You can finish it tomorrow when you're fresh. You're about ready to drop now, aren't you?"

Matt couldn't deny it. Staying awake during the afternoon was next to impossible. He was going to get in real trouble if he didn't manage to get his days and nights worked out. He'd be fired without ever being given a chance to explain. Mavis had always been a little hard-headed, but Matt had always been able to produce for her before. Now, that had all changed. How was he going to survive if he lost his job? He would lose his apartment. Rebecca was still paying for her own, even though she usually slept at his. She wouldn't be able to help him out much with the bills. And he would never ask her to.

Matt rested his forehead in his hands, elbows braced against the desk. Maybe a trip to the hospital was a good idea. He needed to figure out what was going on.

He was going insane. The empty out basket and worms under his skin just proved it. He was losing his mind. He had heard a person could die from not getting enough sleep. Going without sleep for weeks or months, they would go insane, and eventually, they would die. That was what was happening to Matt.

His mind drifted to vector diseases. Sleeping sickness was a vector, wasn't it? But that was sleeping too much, not being unable to sleep. Dying from being unable to sleep was called… fatal insomnia? Was it vector-borne? He had a feeling it was genetic, somehow. But that didn't mean a new disease couldn't make an appearance. Just because fatal insomnia didn't show up in Matt's family tree, that didn't mean he couldn't get it from something else. A mosquito bite, maybe.

"Matt. Matt, can you wake up?"

Carol's hand on his shoulder was always gentle, even when he didn't wake up right away. But this time, he wasn't asleep. He was drifting, dozing a little, but not unconscious. There didn't seem to really be any difference between sleeping and waking lately. Both were sort of fuzzy.

"I'm awake," he told her.

"Okay, good. Open your eyes. Jared and I are going to take you to the hospital now, okay? Get up."

"You and Jared?" Matt repeated muzzily. "I don't need two sitters."

Jared was chuckling nearby. "Don't be so sure, bro. If you fall asleep in the car, I don't think either one of us is going to be able to get you out on our own. It's okay. Neither of us has anywhere we need to be right now. We've got the time."

"Awful nice of you," Matt slurred.

"Come on, Matt. On your feet."

Matt rubbed his eyes and got to his feet, where he swayed for a few seconds before he was sure he could walk without falling back down again. The three of them moved in a row, in tandem, across the lab. Matt turned his head toward Dewey.

"Dewey? You coming?"

He caught the quizzical look Dewey threw him. They had never been friends, but Matt was always polite to him. They weren't enemies. But Dewey clearly didn't expect to have to take Matt to the hospital with the others.

"We'll make it a party," Matt said. "You'd like to come to a party, wouldn't you?"

"Leave Dewey alone," Carol said. "He doesn't need to come."

Dewey gave a shake of his head. "I don't like parties," he said.

"It's okay," Carol said. "I don't think Matt really wants you to come. He's just a little loopy."

"He's not sick, is he?" Dewey asked. They were walking away from him, and he had to raise his voice to ensure he was heard. "He doesn't have anything, does he?"

"He'll be fine." Carol laughed. "I don't think you need to worry it's contagious. Not unless you're planning to go out to DOC and get hit in the head anytime soon."

"Don't do it," Matt advised Dewey. "It's really not worth it."

Jared and Carol laughed. Matt stumbled, tripping over a crack in the floor where there was none. Carol took his arm lightly and tried to keep him steady.

"Hang in there, Matt."

There was some discussion in the parking lot as to whose car they were going to take. There was no overnight parking allowed in the lot, so before the night was out, all three of their vehicles would have to be removed. Carol and Jared decided Carol's van was the best option. She had to move seats and equipment around, and they all got into the van as Carol apologized for the mess it was in.

"You camp?" Matt asked as they started out.

But if she answered, he didn't hear her.

———

"Dropped off like a tired toddler," Jared said cheerfully.

Matt wasn't sure whether this comment was aimed at his ears or whether Jared was talking to Carol or someone else nearby. But it wasn't true. Matt was unable to sleep, even though his eyes were closed and he was listening to the quiet drone of the engine, expecting the vibration of the road to instantly drop him into Neverland.

"Let's get you out of there," Jared encouraged, gripping Matt's arm.

Matt thought if they kept waking him up every ten minutes, he really *was* going to go insane. They shouldn't have brought him to the hospital. They should have just taken him home where he could sleep soundly. Or left him at his desk at the office. Trying to wake him up over and over again was playing havoc with his head.

"Come on," Jared persisted.

Matt fumbled for the seatbelt latch, but found it had already been unbuckled. He levered himself out of the seat and held onto the sides of the van as he climbed out, unable to feel his legs under him and not at all sure they would hold. Jared and Carol each took an arm, and walked him into the hospital. There were a couple of curbs to negotiate.

"We don't negotiate with terrorists," Matt murmured.

Carol laughed. Finally, they got to the emergency room, and Carol and Jared lowered Matt into an uncomfortable plastic chair. Resting his elbows on his knees, Matt put his face in his hands and closed his eyes.

"You go ahead and rest now," Carol encouraged. "I'll talk to triage."

Matt was aware of the nurse who came over to examine him, asking him brisk questions and hooking him up to a machine to check his pulse and blood pressure.

"You need to wake up and pay attention to my questions," she insisted.

"I need to go to sleep," Matt countered. "But I can't."

He didn't know what time it was. Afternoon or evening or night. The time crept by and all Matt could focus on was his inability to either get out of the haze or to sink deeper into sleep. He was caught in the twilight between sleep and waking.

They hooked him up to machines. There were leads on his chest and his head. They asked him infinite questions. He did the best he could to answer them, but it seemed like they were just asking the same things over and over again. He was certain he had given the same answers a hundred times.

"We're going to have your friends drive you home, Mr. Malloy." A doctor was sitting on a stool beside his hospital bed, close to his face, commanding his attention. "They're going to give you something to help you sleep through the night in your own bed, so you can wake up feeling refreshed in the morning."

"Sure," Matt agreed. That sounded heavenly. To actually be able to sleep at night and wake up in the morning. And to be rested. It was an impossible dream.

"It really isn't unusual to have problems sleeping after a head injury. Almost everyone does. It seems to be taking you longer than usual to get back into an acceptable sleep schedule, but it will come. Your body will normalize. You need to practice good sleep hygiene. That means going to bed at the same time every night, and getting up at the same time every morning. Not watching TV or computer screens before bed. No caffeine after noon. I'll give you a list of dos and don'ts. You follow the instructions, and you'll be on track before you know it. Okay?"

Matt looked at him. Did the doctor think he hadn't tried all of those things already? The very first internet searches Matt had done for insomnia had turned up long lists of things to do to help yourself get to sleep. Everything from what to eat and drink at what time of day, to not using your bed for anything but sleeping or sex, to getting lots of sun in the afternoon.

"You do that, Mr. Malloy, and I guarantee we'll have you back up to snuff in no time."

"Can you give him a note for work?" Carol suggested. "Something saying he needs a few days off? Maybe if he has a few days to recover... he didn't really take much time after he got hit over the head. He was back at work before the stitches were out."

The doctor frowned at her, then finally he shrugged and pulled out a prescription notepad, where he scribbled out an excuse note and handed it to Matt. Carol took it out of Matt's hand.

"I'll give that to Mavis. You take it easy."

6

Duane methodically started the propane and lit the pilot on the small tabletop barbecue. He closed the lid and left it to heat up while he went back into the house and got a cold bottle of lemonade and the burgers from the freezer. When he went back out to the back yard, Rich Adams was sniffing around the barbecue. He looked up as Duane walked back into the yard.

"Taking advantage of the warm weather?" Adams observed.

Duane nodded.

Adams looked at the little hibachi. His lip curled, and he shook his head. "Hardly seems worth it with that little thing. Looks like a little girl's Easy Bake Oven." He laughed at his own joke.

Duane's smile was forced and frozen. He knew better than to give away his feelings to a bully like Adams, but at the same time, he refused to laugh at himself. He waited for Adams to give up and walk away.

"You see mine?" Adams demanded. He walked over to the enormous barbecue and pulled the cover off. It was shiny stainless steel and looked brand new. It was the size of a small car, not just a grill but an entire outdoor kitchen. There were two big propane tanks, and Duane couldn't identify what all the grills and cubbies were for. "Now *that's* a man's grill! You can cook half a side of beef! That's a real barbecue. Not a little girl's toy," he sneered at Duane's grill.

"It's nice," Duane agreed. "Very handy."

He opened the package of burgers.

"What kind of meat is that?" Adams demanded. "Chicken?" He laughed.

Duane glanced at Adams, feeling his face flush in response to the teasing. "No… veggie burgers."

"Veggie burgers?" Adams laughed uproariously, slapping Duane on the shoulder with a loud, stinging slap. "Veggie burgers in an Easy Bake Oven! Of course! And lemonade! Are you having all your girlfriends over for a slumber party? You can paint each other's nails."

Duane didn't respond. He laid a couple of veggie burgers on the grill.

"You're a vegetarian?" Adams demanded. "That figures!"

"Yes."

Adams snorted. "Real men eat meat, Duane. Red meat. Lots of it."

Duane didn't explain. He stood there staring at his little barbecue in silence.

"I'll get you some venison next week," Adams promised. "Me and the boys are going out hunting. You try that, and you'll forget all about being vegetarian. We'll have a cookout right here." He slapped his huge cooker affectionately. "You'll see."

Duane grunted, refusing to take the bait. Rich covered up his grill again.

"Enjoy your vegetables, little girl."

———

The sleeping pills Matt had gotten at the hospital did their job. He swallowed them dry and slid into bed and was deep asleep within the hour. He knew Carol would take the doctor's note in to work for him so that he could sleep however long he needed to. Maybe he could do what Dewey had suggested, finding his natural sleep schedule and trying to adjust it by going to bed a little later each day. But to start with, there was no natural sleep rhythm to find. The sleeping pills knocked him out, and he slept like the dead.

It was Sharon who woke him up. She had a key from when Matt lived alone so she could check on things if he were away.

"Mattie. Come on, Matt, it's time to get up. Wake up."

Matt groaned. "Sharon, I told you not to wake me up."

"Well actually, you told me not to tell Rebecca to wake you up. You didn't tell me not to wake you up."

"Sharon…"

"I'm sorry. I had to. I'm your emergency contact for work, and they want to know when you're going back."

Matt rubbed his eyes. "I had a doctor's note for a few days. It's only been one."

"It's been three," Sharon said crisply. "And they want to know how long it's going to be."

"It hasn't been three. I went to the hospital yesterday. What day is it?"

"Thursday. You went to the hospital after work on Monday."

"It's not Thursday."

"Sorry, Mattie, but it is."

"Whoa." Matt sat up slowly, looking at the window to see whether it was light or dark out. It was light. Maybe he could stay awake for a few hours, and then go to sleep when it was dark, his days and nights fixed again. Ignoring Sharon for the moment, he shuffled to the bathroom, and then out to the kitchen, where it was even brighter, the sun beating in through the windows. Matt put a pod in the coffee maker. Sharon had joined him before it was finished brewing and he made a second cup.

"Thanks."

Matt looked surreptitiously at the clock. It was three o'clock. After-noon. "Sorry, you're missing work."

"I clocked out a bit early. I'll make it up." Sharon sat on one of the bar stools along the island. "So are you okay, Matt? I'm really worried about you."

"Yeah… it's just this sleep thing. It's nothing, really."

"Sleep is important. Especially when it's affecting your work."

"I got sleeping pills from the hospital. So I'll be able to sleep now. It will be fine."

"Will you be able to wake up?"

Matt sipped at the searing hot coffee.

"I'll manage."

———

When Duane had infected Brad with the tick that had hitchhiked on the sample tube, it had been an accident.

Brad was still out of work. He was no longer in hospital, but he wasn't well enough to return to duty. There was talk of long-term disability.

Making the decision to take things another step further was daunting. Duane didn't admit even to himself what was lurking in the back of his mind. Instead, he lied to himself about what he was doing.

He'd always wanted a pet. When they were growing up, Duncan had had a dog. In the early days, Duane had longed to have one of his own. He envisioned himself with a cuddly playmate, inseparable, loyal, always happy to see him. But over time, Cerberus had become the stuff of night-mares rather than dreams. Duncan was a cruel master, as vicious with the dog as he was with his younger brother, and the dog had, in turn, changed from a cuddly puppy to a fearsome enemy.

Now Duane couldn't even walk past a leashed dog on the sidewalk without fear squeezing his heart. Cats were aloof and had never inter-ested him. But rabbits… he had secretly longed for a sleek, soft rabbit since boyhood.

After performing a thorough sweep to pick up as many ticks and other blood-thirsty vermin as he could, Duane took his newly-acquired Flopsy Bunny out for a turn around the back yard on a leash and harness. The rabbit was inquisitive and didn't seem to mind the leash. It stopped for an occasional nibble of grass or a flower from the border. Its droppings were small and inconspicuous and would make good compost for the grass.

"No way!" Duane jumped at Adams' booming voice. Adams had seen Duane before Duane had seen him. "Get the hell out!" Adams laughed. "Now fairy boy's got a bunny? On a leash?" He chortled to an imaginary audience. "Next he's going to be wearing makeup and a dress!"

Duane turned his face slightly to look at Adams. "I'm not… I'm not *that*," he said, feeling his face flaring red. "It's just a rabbit. A pet rabbit. Lots of people have pets."

"Lots of little girls," Adams agreed. "Look at you mincing around the yard. Who do you think you're kidding?"

Duane gave the leash a little tug, encouraging Flopsy to turn around, back toward the house. Adams stood there drinking a can of beer and watching them approach.

As they walked by, Flopsy brushed against Adams' bare legs.

7

———

Matt pulled up the chart of his sleep/wake times and looked at the blue blocks running diagonally across the page. It had not been easy, but he had managed to gradually adjust his natural sleep times, so they were at least after work. In a few more days, he would be going to sleep at a natural hour. Everything would be back to normal, and he would be able to do his job well-rested.

"Is that your sleep chart?" Rebecca asked, stifling a big yawn as she walked by him to get a coffee.

"Yes. Just checking it out."

"Still looking good?"

"Pretty soon, I'll be on the same schedule as you. Everything will be back to normal."

"Well, you certainly seemed to feel a lot better since you started charting it."

Matt nodded. He sipped at the dregs of coffee left in his cup. "You'd be amazed how much better you feel once you start sleeping like your body wants to."

She poured another half cup of coffee for him and tickled the skin of his neck under his ear. "I'll be very glad when we're sleeping together again!"

Matt shivered at the pleasant goosebumps she raised all the way down his back. "Nothing to say we can't still… sleep… at other times of the day." He caught her wrist lightly and raised one eyebrow.

"It's good to see you've got some gas back in the tank. But I have to get to work. So you are going to have to wait until a more opportune time."

Matt sighed. "Okay. Tonight, maybe."

"Hold that thought." Rebecca separated from him to have her morning shower and get ready.

When she was done, she grabbed a cereal bar on her way out the door, blew Matt a kiss, and was gone.

Matt carefully folded his sleep chart and put it away. It was time for him to start getting ready for work as well.

———

Matt sat down at his desk and tried to sort through the papers stacked up in his in basket.

"Feeling a little swamped?" Carol asked.

Matt nodded without looking up. "Yeah… I can't believe how fast things pile up around here."

"I know. Anything I can help with?"

"No, thanks. I'm good." Matt knew Carol had been covering as much of his work as she could while he had been gone. And even while he had been there but unable to perform as usual. "I'll manage."

"Okay, good. Give me a shout if you need anything."

"Really, it's okay," Matt assured her. "I've got a lot to do, but I'm feeling fresh and well rested."

Carol nodded and went back to her own desk, leaving Matt to do his work. Turning to his computer, Matt could see it was probably going to take all morning just to go through his email inbox. There were new infection reports that needed to be recorded and plotted. Phone interviews that would need to be conducted to determine if possible infections needed to be followed up on. That, combined with the usual trend reports and documents in his in basket, would take several days to do. All while keeping up with anything else new that came in.

But he was feeling good now, and it would work out just fine.

———

Apartment dwellers always complained about how the walls were paper thin, and they could hear everything their neighbors were doing. Duane was finding living in a basement suite wasn't much better. He could hear every time Adams walked across the floor. He could hear what television programs were on. He could hear every telephone conversation. And of course, he could hear whenever Adams brought a girl home.

The weekend had been a sweet relief. Adams had been away with his hunting buddies. For once, the house was quiet. The only noises to be heard were Duane's own movements and his own little TV.

It made Adams' return seem that much louder. Duane grimaced listening to him pounding through the upstairs rooms like an elephant. As he had suggested he would, he grilled venison on his huge barbecue. Duane ignored the knocks on his door, nauseated just by the smell of the roasting meat.

There was no way he was going to let Adams talk him into trying any.

Adams would have to eat it all himself.

———

Adams was even sick more loudly than a person had the right to be. As much as Duane tried to ignore the sounds issuing forth from the upstairs bathroom, it was impossible to go back to sleep. Duane didn't know how much of the venison Adams had consumed. He was throwing up a lot more than a normal person should have. Duane covered his head with his pillow. He turned on the TV. He tried to go back to sleep, but it was impossible.

Adams had been throwing up for a couple of hours when he came down the stairs and knocked on Duane's door. Duane hesitated to answer. What did Adams want at that time of night? The rent wasn't yet due. Even when it was, Adams usually gave him a day or two before he began making demands. He didn't show up in the middle of the night or early hours of the morning asking for it.

After peeking at him through the peephole for a minute, Duane opened the door.

Adams looked even worse face-to-face than he did through the peephole. His normally flushed complexion was gone. He looked as pale as a ghost. Except for a number of raised red welts visible on his face and arms.

His breathing was labored. He held one hand at his throat like he was choking. Duane hoped Adams wasn't going to throw up anymore.

"Sick," Adams gasped out. "Dunno… what's wrong…"

But Duane knew exactly what was wrong. It wasn't easy to forget.

"You're allergic to something," he told Adams. "Do you have an epi-pen?"

Adams shook his head. "Not allergic…"

"Yes, you are," Duane told him. He grabbed Adams by the arm and pulled him into the living room. "Sit down. Keep breathing."

In the bedroom, Duane grabbed his phone and unplugged it from the charger. He dialed nine-one-one and headed back to the living room to monitor Adams.

"My landlord is having an allergic reaction," he told the dispatcher. "He has hives, and he's having problems breathing."

The woman on the other end assured him a first responder was being dispatched immediately.

"Does he have an autoinjector?" she asked him. "Epinephrine?"

"No, I already asked him."

"How's he doing? Is he still breathing?"

Duane was watching Adams draw in one ragged breath after another. "Yes. But he's getting worse."

"Ambulance is en route. Someone will be there soon. Just a couple of minutes out."

"Okay."

"Do you know what he's allergic to?"

Duane had an idea, but no proof. "He said he's not allergic to anything."

"Are you sure it's an allergy? Could he have taken drugs?"

"Looks like allergies."

Time stretched on. Adams was a beached fish; pale, clammy, gasping open-mouthed. Then Duane heard the ambulance pull up, siren scream-ing. The paramedics had been given directions and came pounding down the stairs, urgency in their approach.

They immediately zeroed in on Adams and went to work, talking to him and giving him an injection. They monitored his vital signs, using rapid-fire shorthand to communicate back and forth.

Adams' breathing eased.

"Thank you. Thank you, that's so much better. Oh… I can breathe again."

He took gulps of air as if still afraid he was going to suffocate. He wiped beads of sweat from his forehead.

"You saved my life," he said to Duane. "If you hadn't called for help…"

Duane gave a modest shrug.

"Thank you. And I'm sorry…" Adams trailed off.

Duane wondered exactly what Adams was sorry for.

Duane wasn't sorry. That was for sure.

————

Matt was nervous about seeing Dr. Montgomery. He knew that there was nothing to worry about, but he was still anxious about it.

Mavis or someone in administration had insisted upon Matt seeing a psychologist. Matt didn't know whether she had heard about his sleep-deprived hallucinations and thought he was totally off his rocker, if it was the nosedive in the quality of his work, or simply the fact he had a doctor's note saying he needed sleep. At any rate, they were insisting if he was to continue to be employed by the DOH, he needed to see a properly qualified doctor.

He supposed he should be grateful to those civil servants who had melted down in the past for ensuring proper mental health care was extended to all employees, whether they wanted it or not. After all the horror stories Matt had heard from friends about their employee health care, he should be thankful he had never experienced any problems getting care in the wake of the attack.

"Have a seat, Matt," Montgomery invited.

He was an older man. Experienced. White hair and a neat white beard at the bottom of a round face. He looked serious and solid and competent.

Matt sat down. No stereotypical couch, just a padded, comfy office chair. Matt ran his fingers over the arms of the chair, trying to calm his restlessness.

"So, you're having some problems settling back in after your head injury," Montgomery suggested, looking at the papers in front of him.

Matt shrugged. "Not exactly. I just haven't been able to sleep very well since then. The doctor at the hospital said that was pretty normal for head injuries."

"He's entitled to his opinion. He probably spent all of, what, ten minutes with you? We're going to take a little more time to explore the situation. Dig down into how you are really feeling. You're okay with that, aren't you?"

He couldn't exactly disagree with Montgomery. Anything he said in opposition to the doctor could have negative repercussions. He didn't want to end up on psychiatric medications, unable to work, having to go to session after endless session of counseling. If Montgomery could see he was well-balanced and healthy, Matt could go back to his life.

So Matt gave a noncommittal, non-argumentative grunt, which Montgomery could interpret as he pleased. Matt waited for the real grilling to start.

"Why don't you start by telling me about the attack?"

Matt didn't want to dive straight into it. He shifted, looking for a comfortable entry point.

"I was assigned to go out and interview a couple of patients. Roommates. And to collect swabs and blood samples. They had the hallmarks of a vector-borne illness. The doctor suggested Lyme disease, but we don't get Lyme here in Colorado."

"And what did you find when you got there?"

"The disease stage was advanced. Both men were experiencing psychosis. One believed the illness had come from a tick bite. Or bites. He'd had a number of them. I was interviewing him, getting the details of the infection. I never saw the other one coming. He snuck up behind me and hit me over the head."

"Did he knock you out?"

It was something Matt had never discussed with anyone but the admitting doctor. Everyone else had assumed he had been knocked unconscious immediately. Even Rebecca had never asked.

"Not right away. He hit me two or three times." Matt saw it replay in his mind. In slow motion, like a movie. The shock and pain of being hit, of realizing what was happening to him. He felt himself again, paralyzed, rooted to the ground, unable to turn around and stop the attack. Matt's pulse raced. "Then I fell. My head bounced off of a few things as I fell. A rolling table. The bed frame. Then the floor. That's when they managed to stop him." Matt breathed, trying to force his heart to slow down. "The first blow to the head was hard enough to fracture my skull."

"You were conscious of the entire incident?"

"Yes."

"Seeing it, but unable to stop it."

Matt rolled his eyes and nodded. Montgomery made a few notes on the file.

"How did you feel?"

"How did I feel?" Matt's voice rose, and he was unaccountably furious over the question. "I felt... hurt. Like someone was bashing me over the head. Because they were."

"Ah. You misunderstand. Not the physical sensation. The emotion."

"Hurt," Matt repeated. That was an emotion too, wasn't it? "I don't know... scared... angry... helpless."

Montgomery nodded slowly, scratching behind his ear. "Yes," he agreed. "All of those things. Who were you angry at?"

Anger rippled through Matt now. Who *was* he angry with?

"The man who attacked me."

Montgomery waited for more.

"Myself, for not being able to stop it... my boss for sending me there... anyone there for not stopping it sooner."

"Were you angry with all of them at the time? Or is that now?"

"I don't know." Matt tried to put himself back into his head at the time, back into the memory. "I really can't tell."

"Ah." The pen tapped on the desk a few times. "Who are you most angry with now?"

Matt flipped mentally through the candidates and selected the most likely. "The man who hit me," he said finally.

"Interesting. Why do you think he hit you?"

That, at least, was an easy answer. "He was psychotic. It was the infection."

"So you're angry with him for being sick?"

"No... for hitting me."

"But he hit you because he was sick. Not because of anything to do with you."

"I suppose."

Montgomery waited for any further explanation, then nodded. "Do you experience flashbacks?"

"To the assault?"

"Yes. To anything that happened around that time."

"I don't know... I guess."

"Is that keeping you from sleeping?"

"No, I don't think so... I think about it sometimes, when I'm trying to sleep... but it doesn't keep me from sleeping."

Montgomery stared at him with watery blue eyes. Matt re-examined his own statement, but couldn't find anything that needed revision. It was true. Memories of the assault were not what was keeping him from being able to sleep.

"Do you dream about the assault?"

"No."

He rarely dreamt at all. Even when he did sleep, REM sleep often eluded him.

"You haven't had any therapy to help you to deal with the trauma of the attack?"

"No. But I'm okay. It isn't bothering me."

"Let's leave that assessment to the professionals, shall we?"

Matt slumped in his seat.

"Have you lost weight?"

"A little, maybe. With my sleep schedule being thrown off... I don't really know when to be hungry. I've lost a few pounds; that's all. Nothing I couldn't afford to lose."

"Do you find yourself to be more irritable? Quicker to anger?"

"Sure. But everybody is when they're tired," Matt pointed out. "It's not because there is anything wrong with me."

"No one has said there is anything wrong with you," Montgomery soothed. "Stress is a perfectly natural reaction to a trauma like you experienced."

"But I'm not... It wasn't a trauma like that. I was hit; that's all. It's healed." He felt the small ridge in the bone at the back of his head. "It's completely gone. I don't even think about it anymore. This sleep thing is totally separate. The emergency room doctor said sometimes people have sleep problems after a head injury. It's normal."

"Of course, it's normal," Montgomery agreed. "There are a wide variety of reactions to a traum— to an incident like you suffered. You don't need to feel inferior or weak or crazy."

Matt rubbed the boney ridge of his eyebrows. "You think all these things, my sleep problems are just a reaction to being attacked. Just post-traumatic-stress."

"Not *just*. It can be debilitating."

"So what would I do about it?"

"There's no quick fix. You'll need to spend some time in counseling. There are some meds we can try for anxiety, depression, and sleep. I think with some time and effort, I can help you."

8

Duane was out in the front yard with Flopsy when a friend dropped Adams back home. The big man looked pale and drawn. Not like himself at all. Duane measured the path back into the house with his eyes, estimating whether he could retreat before Adams was able to approach him. But Adams was too close, and even sick he had a long stride that ate up the distance between them. Duane swallowed and tried to look unconcerned.

"Duane," Adams greeted, using Duane's proper name instead of an insult. That was a pleasant surprise.

"Rich."

Adams gave him a weak punch in the shoulder and opened his mouth to speak. He pressed his lips together, shaking his head slightly. Duane frowned at him, wondering what his problem was.

"Everything okay?"

"It's just… well, you're vegetarian, aren't you?"

Duane frowned. "Yes."

"I know I teased you about it before," Adams said, apparently hearing the caution in Duane's voice. His body slumped. "It's just… I guess I've developed an allergy to meat…"

Duane kept his face impassive, while inwardly exulting. He couldn't have wished for a better development.

"That's too bad," he said aloud.

"Yeah. So... I could use some tips. You know. On shopping and cooking vegetarian food."

"Sure," Duane agreed with a pleasant smile. "Why don't I bring you some veggie burgers later?"

———

Just when he thought he had the backwards sleep thing fixed, another complication arose. Matt had been successful in gradually moving his sleep phase to a more normalized schedule. Moving his 'bedtime' forward an hour every day had worked like a charm.

Until he tried to stop.

No matter what he did, his sleep time kept advancing by an hour each day.

Matt desperately tried everything he could think of. Going to bed at the same time every night. Taking the sleeping pills the ER doctor had prescribed and the medications Dr. Montgomery had prescribed. Forcing himself to get up at the same time every morning, no matter how tired he was. Walking in the sun at noon. But none of it made any difference.

His sleep schedule kept marching forward, until he was falling asleep just when he was supposed to be waking up.

———

The bus wasn't Matt's usual vehicle of choice, but with the latest development in his sleep schedule, he would have been driving to work when the urge to sleep was the strongest, and that was a recipe for disaster. So he took the bus, and he asked the driver to please wake him at his stop if he fell asleep.

The turbaned driver looked him over, one eyebrow raised. "I do not do wake-up calls."

"I know. It would just be a favor. If you could, please help me out."

The driver awoke him one stop late. Matt wondered whether that was because he had forgotten, or because he wanted to communicate to Matt he wasn't a servant about to be ordered about by his riders.

That meant Matt started his day with a brisk trot down the street arriving at his desk late and sweaty. It did help to get his heart pumping and wake him up a little, but in another hour and a half, the benefits were long gone.

"Malloy," Mavis materialized before him and slapped a stack of papers down, making Matt jump in surprise. She had opened her mouth to give him instructions, but at his undisguised shock, she closed her mouth again and narrowed her eyes at him.

"Are you high?" she demanded.

"No! Me? No!" Matt shook his head. "You just startled me, Ms. Booker."

"Are you sleeping on the job again? I thought we had that sorted out."

"No, no. I was just thinking."

"I want you to keep seeing Dr. Montgomery until this has been worked out. We don't want—" she gave a little grimace and closed her eyes for a moment to rework her sentence. "We need you to be healthy and happy, Mr. Malloy."

There was silence in the lab. Everyone else was obviously listening in. Matt cleared his throat and looked around. The others went quickly back to their individual assignments.

"I'm doing the best I can," Matt said. "I thought I had my schedule under control, but it got all— It didn't work out, everything is wrong again. I'm trying."

"And we are being as patient and flexible as we can." Mavis enunciated her words a little too crisply to be believed.

They looked at each other for a minute. Then Matt dropped his eyes to the papers she had put down on his desk. Mavis looked at them and nodded.

"These infection reports were given to you last week. You sent them to admin for filing, but when they cross-checked them, they had not been entered into the system."

Matt frowned and picked up the stack. He looked through them swiftly, but couldn't remember handling them before. He peeled off the top one and read it more carefully.

"Lyme-like infection. Unknown vector. Buffalo Head. I… I don't remember this one. But I wouldn't have given it back to admin without entering it first…"

He tapped a search into the computer and waited for it to pop up the infection report in his hand. No results. He looked at the line on the report where he should have penned the file tracking number, but it was blank.

"I don't understand it." He shook his head at Mavis. "I'm not sure what happened. There was some stuff a while back that disappeared from my desk… I don't know if the cleaners maybe… I don't know, but it was gone. Maybe interoffice picked up the documents from my in basket instead of my out basket…"

"We can't have mistakes being made. This work is vital to our department. If information does not get entered into the computer, our data will not be correct."

Matt nodded vigorously in agreement. "You're right. Of course. I'll get them in right away. Like I say, I don't know what happened. I don't remember seeing these ones before. It may be they were put into the wrong basket or routed the wrong way. I haven't seen them before, but I'll get them entered now."

Mavis sighed. "See that you do," she agreed.

She walked away.

Matt cleared the search screen in order to start entering the new reports.

———

Duane checked on the animals before going to bed. He had spent several hours with Adams—Rich, as Duane was now supposed to call him—discussing menu plans, recipes, and commercial vegetarian foods.

Rich was a changed man.

Discovering he was now allergic to meat seemed to have taken the wind right out of his sails. Always the macho 'man's man,' Rich had supposed manliness was measured by the amount of red meat consumed or iron pumped. He had never imagined something like this could happen to him. It was the equivalent of failing to perform in bed. Not being able to eat meat—who would ever have thought it could happen to him?

Rich's doctor didn't have any idea how he could suddenly have become allergic to meat. Duane did, but he didn't enlighten Rich. He mentioned the same thing had happened to him, and Rich immediately sympathized and apologized again for having teased Duane about his vegetarianism. Rich had never had a clue that it could be anything but a lifestyle choice.

Duane liked the new Rich.

———

"I need something stronger than these," Matt explained, showing the doctor the sleeping pills he had bought over the counter at the drug store. "I ran out of the ones the ER gave me and I tried switching to these, but they don't do a thing. I need something like I had from the hospital. Or stronger, because they didn't always work either."

Dr. Ramos looked at the box of sleeping pills, nodding. "You have had a sleep study done?"

"Uh… no. No sleep study. I just have insomnia. I need something that will work."

"You have been diagnosed with sleep apnea, maybe?" The small doctor raised one eyebrow.

"No. No sleep apnea. No sleep study. I just need something to help me to get to sleep at night."

"There are many different reasons people can't sleep. Sleeping pills are not one-size-fits-all. We need to first identify the reason for the sleep disturbance. Only then can we prescribe the right thing. If you have not had a sleep study or been diagnosed, then I cannot prescribe you a sleep aid."

"Oh, come on. You see them on TV all the time…"

"And do you read the fine print on the TV screen? You need a proper sleep study."

"Okay then… how do I get a sleep study?"

"We can sign you up, get you put on a waiting list. It will be a little while before we actually get to the study."

"How long is *a little while?*"

Ramos' narrow shoulders rose and fell again in an eloquent shrug. "A few months. Hard to tell."

"And in the meantime? What am I supposed to take so I can go to sleep for the next few months? I'm just supposed to not sleep until then?"

"You can take the over-the-counter pills until then," Ramos informed him tranquilly. "We cannot give you something more powerful without a proper sleep study."

9

———————

Matt rubbed his eyes to clear them and looked again at the screen. Something was wrong. He had been tracking vector-borne infections for a long time, and the cluster he was seeing on the screen just did not look right.

He couldn't explain whether it was the shape or the proximity, or the too-frequent 'unknowns' in the reports. But something about it just wasn't right.

Matt motioned for Jared. "Hey, Jare? Something funny here…"

"Is it a joke?" asked Jared, as he walked over and looked at Matt's computer. "Because things have been way too serious here lately. I really need to hear a good joke."

"It's not a joke," Matt said. "It's this cluster in Buffalo Head. What does that look like to you?"

Jared stared at the screen for a few minutes, then shook his head. "Random plot," he said. "I don't see anything unusual. Frequency may be a bit high, but that happens with clusters. Our minds like to see patterns where there are none."

"It's not a pattern, exactly," Matt protested. "It just doesn't look quite right. Not natural."

Jared was looking at Matt's face instead of at the computer monitor. His eyes searched Matt's.

"How are you feeling lately, Matt? You getting more sleep?"

"I'm not seeing things. This is an infection map. I'm trained to read them. I'm not hallucinating about bugs. I'm looking for the source of these infections."

"Maybe it's a more virulent bacteria. Something antibiotic-resistant. Maybe there is a wooded area not marked on your map, and people's dogs are picking up fleas and ticks. Or maybe it's just coincidence. More people reporting than usual."

Matt sighed and leaned back in his chair. Maybe Jared was right. There were a lot of things they still had to investigate before designating the cluster as something more. It might be easily explained.

"You're right. Maybe I'd better go over and take a look."

"Now?"

"Why not now?" Matt challenged. "I could use some fresh air."

"I don't think you're in any shape to drive yourself right now."

Matt had been opening his mouth to protest. Then he realized he didn't have his car. He swore and gave a little laugh.

"What?" Jared asked.

"I didn't bring my car today. I was too tired to drive in."

"Oh. Well, that's good. Maybe one of us could drive you."

"No. I'll check it out tomorrow. That will give me time to put in advance notice I'll be out for field work. Wouldn't want to upset the boss with any irregularities."

"No," Jared agreed. "Better do it by the book. But what about driving tomorrow? Will you be okay?"

"I'll go later in the day," Matt explained. "She won't know the difference. I'll wait and pick a time to go when I'm not tired."

"Okay, good luck."

———

The field work turned out to be at a dead end. Matt didn't find any unmapped parks or conservation areas. He didn't see any clues to the high rate of infection in the area. He drove around for a long time and didn't find anything.

In the end, he just went back home.

In an effort to make things up to Rebecca for the way he had been neglecting her lately, he cooked dinner. Something he hadn't done in many months. He lit a couple of candles, put on some romantic music, and waited for her to come home.

———

"Matt!" The words barely registered on his senses. "Matthew Robert Malloy!" His full name had a bigger impact. The only person who had ever used his full name was his mother, and then only when he was in big trouble. In spite of the fact that Matt was in the deepest reaches of sleep, that brought him closer to the surface. Close enough that Rebecca's continued shaking eventually broke through, and he opened his eyes.

He knew immediately he had intended to be awake when she got home. He wasn't supposed to be asleep. And he saw by her wide-eyed alarm something was wrong.

"Are you trying to burn the house down?" Rebecca demanded. Her voice was hoarse with anger. Not the usual musical lilt she spoke in. Her hand was iron-hard on his arm. Her shaking was not the tentative, don't-really-want-to-wake-you-up shakes he was used to.

"What? What's wrong?" Matt asked. He sat up and looked around. He had fallen asleep on the couch. The air was acrid with smoke. "What's on fire? Is everybody okay?"

"You could have killed yourself! You would burn this place down around your ears and not even wake up before you died! How could you be so irresponsible?"

The details started to trickle into Matt's consciousness. The dinner. The candles. How could he have been so stupid? He knew his alarm clock didn't wake him up in the morning. The smoke alarm would be no different. He would sleep through it, completely oblivious. He shouldn't have turned on the oven or lit the candles. He should have ordered pizza. At least, if he didn't answer the door, the pizza delivery man wouldn't burn down the building.

"I shouldn't have fallen asleep," Matt said, straightening.

"No, you shouldn't!" Rebecca agreed, her eyes filled with furious tears.

"No… I mean… my next sleep cycle shouldn't have been until morning. Nine or ten o'clock. I shouldn't have fallen asleep in the afternoon."

"Well, guess what?"

Matt didn't have to guess.

"I'm sorry, Bec. I'll be more careful. I won't make dinner or light candles. It's just… I didn't think I was going to fall asleep. I thought I knew my schedule."

Rebecca took a deep breath and sat down on the couch next to him.

"You really scared me, Matt. You can't do this. I come home to an apartment filled with smoke… I'm surprised the fire department wasn't here ahead of me. We should check the smoke detectors." She shook her head. "You need to get help. What's going on? Have you looked up narcolepsy? People just fall asleep unpredictably…"

"It's not narcolepsy," Matt objected. "I don't know what happened today. Can you have narcolepsy *and* insomnia?"

Rebecca snorted. "Apparently *you* can."

Matt laughed weakly.

"You need to get help," Rebecca reiterated.

"I know. I'm trying. I've gone to the hospital, and I've gone to the psychologist, and I've gone to my doctor. Nobody seems to know what to do. I'm on the list for a sleep study, but… I don't know when it's going to be. It could be months away."

"Well, until then, you can't cook," she told him.

Matt nodded. "Okay. I won't. I'll do whatever you say. I'm sorry, Becca. Really, I am."

10

———

Duane groomed each of the Flopsy Bunnies carefully, combing every inch of their coats and parting the fur to examine every inch of their smooth, pink skin. When he was done, he put his specimen bottle to the side and gave them each a treat for being such good pets.

Because he had taken so long to finish with the bunnies, he was late clocking in. But he really didn't care about being late anymore. Steve glared at him, but he didn't dare fire Duane. They were already too short-staffed. New candidates were not exactly pouring in the door.

"I need to be able to rely on you," Steve told Duane. "I need you to be here when you are supposed to start, and to pick up your work orders and get started. You know the time we're going through…"

"Sorry," Duane said, without looking at Steve's face. "It was a family emergency. I got here as soon as I could."

Steve didn't say anything. He could ream Duane out or demand to know what the family emergency was, but then he would risk Duane quitting. And he already didn't have enough trucks to cover all the work there was to do.

Duane tapped his prox card until it beeped.

———

He couldn't put the rest of his plan in motion until the end of the day. There were a lot of jobs to do, and he took pride in doing a good job and helping to rid the city of pests. Bug Bee Gone was short-staffed since Brad had gone on long term disability, and then some kind of flu had taken down various of the other exterminators in turn.

After Duane had completed his call sheet, he went to Ms. Stemple's house. He hadn't forgotten Ms. Stemple and the way she had treated him. Like he was beneath her. Like he wasn't worth anything more than the bugs he eradicated.

"Who are you?" she asked when he came to the door. She looked around him and saw his truck parked by the curb. "What are you doing here? I didn't call you."

"Ma'am, when I was here before, I took a number of samples of the bugs in your yard and on your property. It's a program to help keep track of population trends in any insects reported to the CDC."

She nodded, eyes narrowed at him.

"One of the samples we sent in came back with a red flag," Duane went on. He didn't care that he sounded pompous and self-important. All that mattered was that she believed him, if only for a few minutes.

"A red flag? What does that mean?" Ms. Stemple looked around her property like there might be a quarantine notice she had missed. Or the bug Duane was referring to might come stomping down the driveway into her house.

"It's a virulent strain. Even though we have sprayed outside, it is vital I do a sweep inside the house and do a very careful inspection and dusting, to make sure that if there are any of these bugs in the house, we kill them before they can do any damage."

"Damage? What kind of bugs? What kind of damage?"

Duane searched for something that sounded official and nasty. "Umm… migrant yellow mites. You've probably heard of them. There have been several warnings in the newspaper and on social media lately."

Unwilling to admit her ignorance, she nodded as if she knew exactly what he was talking about. "Are these the ones…?" she trailed off, waiting for him to fill in the details.

"They are very dangerous," Duane reiterated. "I'm sure you've read the stories about the kind of damage they can do to homes and homeowners. Nasty little bugs. And you can have them and not even know about it until it is too late. We wouldn't know, except for the sweep we did for you before."

She was nodding again. "That's why I called you in the first place..."

Duane looked at his watch. "I'm later getting here than I had expected to be. I don't think I have the time to deal with this right now. I'll put you on the waitlist and someone will call in a week or two..."

"A week or two?" her voice rose several notches. She was not going to wait a week or two. "That is completely unacceptable. I insist you do it now. You're here. It would be silly for you to go back to the office and schedule it for someone else to do. I demand you come in here right now and do what you came to do."

Duane gave it just enough hesitation to ensure Ms. Stemple would not back out at the last minute.

"Well..." Another glance at his watch.

"Now," Ms. Stemple insisted. "It won't take long, will it?"

"I've got a paid job waiting on me. I hate to be late."

She caught on immediately. "I'll pay you. Why wouldn't I? I don't want migrant mites in my house."

"Usually, it's an included service," Duane said. "But paid jobs do take precedence..."

"How much?" Ms. Stemple was digging in her little blue purse, and in an instant, she pulled out her checkbook with a flair. "Come on," she coaxed. "What's your name? I'll make it out to you personally. The company won't know the difference. They weren't expecting to get paid for it anyway."

Duane wasn't about to get caught. He had her make it out to cash. Then he nodded and got his equipment off of the truck. "I'll need you to not be in the same room as I am working in," he warned. "I'll be wearing a mask, and you'll need to be out of the way. These chemicals can be... toxic."

"Toxic? But what about my baby?"

Duane frowned. He hadn't remembered any sign of an infant or child about the place.

"My Boofie," Ms. Stemple explained further. "My little shnoodle." At Duane's raised eyebrows, she finally clarified. "My dog!"

"Oh. I didn't know you had a dog. That makes it even more important for us to get this done right away. Dogs are very susceptible to mites."

She nodded. "We have her dusted for mites…"

"But these ones are resistant," Duane reminded her. "Just dusting won't get rid of them. You'll have to show me where Poofie's bed is so that I can take special care…"

"Boofie. I'll show you his bed. You can start there."

Duane nodded his agreement and followed her into the house. Ms. Stemple obligingly showed Duane where her dog bedded down—though by the untouched look of the bed, Boofie probably spent more time in his mistress' bed than his own—then she scurried out of sight to let Duane take care of the resistant mite infestation.

Duane sprinkled some of the contents of the specimen jar into the dog bed and watched them for a minute. Then he went through the other rooms of the house, pretending to use the sprayer while surreptitiously emptying the contents of his jar throughout the house.

Ms. Stemple was inviting in a lot more company than she was aware. Duane hoped it would make a difference to her snobby behavior.

11

It was night and as usual, Matt wasn't sleeping. He had tried. He had started off in bed, and then, as all the websites offering advice suggested, he had gotten up again after twenty minutes without sleep. Rather than bed being a place he would fail at sleep, he would simply get up and do something else until he was ready. Listen to some music, read a book, have a little bite to eat. Things to keep his body and mind quiet and calm, so he could settle back into sleep before the night was completely gone.

In the early weeks, Matt had been philosophical about his lack of sleep. It was just the aftereffects of his assault. After his brain had finished healing, it would all go back to normal again. But his brain should have healed by now. He should be able to get back to sleep like a normal person again. But instead, here he was, brain damaged. Unable to do a simple thing like sleep. Even a baby could sleep. To have suddenly 'forgotten' how to do such a natural thing was bewildering. Matt wasn't feeling so philosophical anymore. Work was becoming intolerable. Even if Mavis Booker said they were being patient and supportive, and even if his co-workers were patient and supportive, Matt was still out of step with them.

He was out of step with the entire world. Or everyone in his time zone, anyway. He couldn't keep up with his job. He couldn't spend time with his friends, who slept at vastly different hours than he did. No one understood the hell he was going through.

Matt half-wished Dr. Montgomery had just put him in the psych ward. At least there he would fit in. There would be an explanation for him being so damaged.

How was it possible a simple blow to the head could turn his life upside down so completely?

It wasn't fair. It just wasn't right.

———

"Matt?"

Matt looked up from his open, unread book. Rebecca hovered in the doorway. She had pulled on her lacy housecoat. Her corkscrew hair was delightfully tousled. He would give anything just to go to bed with her and fall asleep entwined in her arms like he used to.

"Are you okay? Are you coming back to bed?"

"No... too wide awake right now."

"I thought you were going to try to go to sleep earlier, to see if you could get your schedule turned around again."

"I did try. But there's no point in staying in bed tossing and turning. I can't sleep. I'll sleep later. Now... I would just keep you awake."

"I could sleep on the couch if you'd be more comfortable in the bed. Then you wouldn't have to worry about keeping me awake."

"No! No, I'm not going to kick you out of bed. I wouldn't sleep any better with you gone and then I'd just feel guilty about kicking you out." He shook his head. "I already feel guilty enough about not being able to get to sleep when you go to bed. Or anytime while you are in bed. I wish..." He clutched at his head, squeezing his skull from the sides. "I wish I could just reach into my head and pull out the part that's wrecked. I'm just so tired... so tired of this. So tired of being tired. So tired of being tired of being tired."

She moved noiselessly across the room and sat down next to him. "What can I do? I feel so bad you're out here all by yourself, and I can't do anything for you. Can I rub your back? Or your feet? I just want to do something."

He pulled her against himself and kissed the top of her head gently. "I know you'd help if there was anything you could do," he said. "But there's not. There's nothing anyone can do. Not me, not you, and not the doctors. It's like I fell into the black hole of medicine. No one has any idea what's going on with me or how to fix it. Hell, I'd take electroshock therapy if someone told me it would work!"

She stroked his cheek. He wished he could say it was soothing. Instead, it was like she was rubbing his face with sandpaper. He turned his cheek away. "Sorry, that just makes me anxious."

"Isn't there anything I can do?"

"No. Just go to bed, so I don't have to feel guilty for keeping you up."

Rebecca let out a long sigh. "All right. See you tomorrow... sometime."

———

"I'm still waiting for your confirmation you've cleared that last set of infection reports," Mavis told Matt. "You said you would enter them right away. Then you said you were going to do field work to follow up. I was expecting a report this morning that you've finished with it."

Matt leaned back in his chair and shook his head. "I was going to do some follow-up calls today. Phone calls to the attending doctors."

Mavis raised an eyebrow. "Do we have a problem?"

"I don't know yet. There's a cluster of infections around Buffalo Head. They don't look right. I did a field check and didn't find any obvious explanation for the cluster. But I'm not quite ready to write it off."

"Let's see."

Matt tapped a few commands into his computer to bring up the map, and Mavis came around to his side of the desk to look at the monitor. Her eyes went over the map, brows drawn down, concentrating. She picked up the glasses on a chain around her neck and slid them on, staring at the screen in silence for an uncomfortably long time.

"It's very dense," she acknowledged. "There's no wooded area or open field in the area?"

"Nothing obvious. School soccer fields. Playgrounds. Well-maintained, grass short, well-used. Trampled down. And the subjects from the cluster are not children, they are adults. Most of them without children in the home. So that doesn't seem likely. I spent quite a bit of time driving and walking around. No dogs running loose. Some squirrels. A few cats. Nothing unusual."

"It could just be an anomaly. A group of friends with similar symptoms who discussed it and decided together to call in. Rashes?"

"Some with Rocky Mountain spots. A couple even with EM rashes. There were a few positive antibody titers for RMSF. A number of negatives."

"Rocky Mountain often shows false negatives."

"Yeah. That's why I wanted to follow up with the doctors. Get some more details that didn't make it to the official reports. Make sure it was RMSF and not something else."

"Zoom in."

Matt obliged. Her eyes moved from one icon to the next on the map.

"They're not all Rocky Mountain Spotted Fever. So it's not just a more virulent strain."

"There's a mix of infections. Some Lyme-like. Tularemia. Unknowns."

"Which suggests the tick population has increased for some reason. There should be a pocket with a denser population."

Matt nodded. "But I couldn't see anything. I did a couple of drags but didn't come up with any big numbers. I gave some samples to the guys," Matt inclined his head toward Jared and Dewey. "They can test to see what strains of bacteria they are carrying."

Mavis nodded. "Okay. Make the calls to the physicians and send me an email update. Then you've got a backlog of other work you need to try to get to."

12

Jared shook his head as he handed a report to Matt. "Nothing," he apologized with a shrug. "The usual rates. No unusual bacteria. Nothing of note."

Matt's heart sank as he looked the report over, verifying what Jared had said.

"You should be happy about it," Jared said. "That means you can just pass it off. Nothing reportable. Nothing out of the ordinary. You can get on to other things."

"Yeah," Matt agreed, staring at the screen. He mouthed the words, but he didn't feel them. "No need to worry about it."

Jared gave him an encouraging smile. When Matt wasn't able to return it, Jared's smile faded. "You didn't find anything else, did you? From the doctors?"

"Most of the patients didn't remember any tick bites. They don't go hiking, haven't been out of state. Some had dogs that could have picked up ticks and brought them indoors. But no explanation for why there was such a cluster of infections."

"Then there's nothing to worry about. Different kinds of infections. No central infection source. No relationship between the patients... right?"

"Right. Not that the physicians identified. But I haven't talked to the patients. That might yield some connection between them."

Jared shook his head. "Best to just let it go. She'll throw the book at you."

Matt managed a weak smile.

"You're right. I'll let it go, try to catch up on my other work."

———

In spite of Matt's words, he didn't send the requisite email to Mavis to close off the report. He wanted to think about it. Just for the afternoon. While he worked his way through the other papers in his in basket, he tried to think of what other explanation they might have missed. He had checked all the usual factors. But he still couldn't convince himself the Buffalo Head cluster was just a random bunching of infections. He knew looking at it that there was another explanation. He couldn't justify it to Jared or Mavis Booker, but he knew it instinctively, down in his gut.

The afternoon dragged on. Matt's brain and body slowed down, telling him it was time to sleep. But he chugged coffee and kept pushing his way through the reports in his basket.

By the end of the day, he was so beat he almost forgot he was supposed to sign off on the Buffalo Head reports before he left for the day.

Almost.

———

As soon as Matt got home, he crawled into bed. He set his alarm for a couple of hours so he'd be able to get up and visit with Rebecca. But in the back of his mind, he knew it would never wake him up. When was the last time his alarm had actually woken him up when his body decided it was time to sleep? He could sleep through an air raid siren positioned right next to the bed.

But he did it anyway because he knew he and Rebecca were having problems. Like the Buffalo Head cluster, he couldn't quite put his finger on why, or how he knew. But he only knew one way to repair the rift, and that was to spend time with her. Even if it meant going without sleep when he really needed it.

He didn't even get his shoes off before falling into a deep sleep.

13

When Matt woke up around midnight, he knew he wouldn't be getting back to sleep again. He climbed carefully out of bed, so as not to disturb Rebecca and crept to the living room.

He checked his email and social media. Not a lot of people were still up, but he still got to see what was going on in their lives.

It depressed him to see how the rest of the world went on without him. He was sleeping through all the important stuff.

Matt had a series of texts from Carol, and he settled into the couch comfortably as he went through them.

MB was looking for you after you left.

Not a happy camper. Did u forget to sign off on those reports?

Do u want me to pick u up in the morning so you don't have to take bus?

Matt texted her back, though he suspected she had already gone to bed.

Trying to decide what to do with Buffalo Head. Can't sign off yet.

Thanks for ride. That would be great.

Matt turned on the TV. He just wanted to escape from reality. Find some kind of fantasy world he could just immerse in. Somewhere there weren't anomalous infection clusters, sleep disorders, or people who hit him over the head. Somewhere he could just be himself again. Where things could just be like they used to be.

His phone's vibration made him jump. He looked down and saw Carol's return message.

Okay. Pick u up at 7:30?

You really have to sign off. What else u going to do?

Matt put the phone down.

What *was* he going to do?

———

He watched the sun creep in through the window and start to work its way across the floor of the living room. Another night come and gone. Matt was ready for work, but he knew by the time noon rolled around, he'd be ready for sleep again. Or maybe it wouldn't hit until two or three, and he'd keep working his way around the clock again. He didn't know what to expect, even with the sleep logs.

Matt had a cup of coffee, showered and dressed quietly while Rebecca continued to sleep, and headed down to the street to watch for Carol. He didn't wake Rebecca up. Unlike him, she wouldn't sleep through her alarm, and if she hadn't set it, that meant she wasn't working until later in the day or she had a day off. Lucky Becca to be able to sleep whenever she wanted to.

Matt had never realized how lucky he was before the attack.

Carol pulled up and waved cheerfully. Matt opened the door and climbed in.

"Thanks again for the ride. I know it's out of your way. It's really nice of you."

"Sure, no problem. How are you feeling this morning?" Carol smothered a yawn. "I shouldn't stay up so late. But I had so much I wanted to get done. Did you sleep better?"

Matt evaded the question. "I got some sleep last night."

"Good! I worry about you. You always have bags under your eyes now."

Matt touched them. "You need to teach me how to cover them up with some foundation."

Carol laughed. "I think the point is actually to sleep, not just to cover them up."

"Well, that's just silly. That's not going to happen."

She shook her head. "I hope it gets better," she said. "You're still talking to your doctor, right? So you can get fixed up?"

"I'm doing what I can. But no one seems to know what it is, let alone how to fix it. Sorry, man, you got your brain smashed in. We can't actually do anything about it." Matt sighed. "It's too depressing to even talk about it. Let's discuss something else."

Of course, that wasn't the right choice. Because he didn't want to discuss the other matter on Carol's mind.

"You're not going to sign off on those infections? Why are you holding them up?"

"Something isn't right. I have to figure out what it is. So far… I know nobody else sees anything. But I know it's there. I just have to dig down a little deeper. I just have to keep looking until I find it."

"Or until you get fired."

"They can't fire me for doing my job. I'm supposed to identify clusters and make sure they get reported to the CDC and properly dealt with. That's what I'm there for!"

"But if all the indicators are it's just a random grouping, then isn't your job to report they're fine?"

"No." Matt didn't know what else to say to her. "No… if I think there's something wrong, it would be criminal to let it go. I can't just sweep it under the rug. Even if it's inconvenient for Mavis Booker or the department. I'm doing what I'm supposed to do."

Carol nodded slowly, staring at the road as she drove. "You're right, of course. If you passed it over, and later it turned out to be a dangerous infection, that would be really bad. If it is a new infectious agent or an outbreak, then we need to get the CDC on top of it. Make sure people are protected and treated."

"Exactly. I know Mavis doesn't see anything wrong. And Jared's report doesn't show anything unusual. I know it looks natural enough when you consider all the individual factors. But when you look at the whole picture… it's just not right. I can't say it is. Somehow… I have to figure out what is connecting those infections. Even if I have to go door-to-door."

"Is that what you're going to do?"

"No… I guess the next step is to interview the subjects."

Carol heard the anxiety in his voice and glanced over at him. "It will be okay. Nothing bad is going to happen this time. Do you want someone to go with you?"

"I'm not afraid," Matt lied. "The attack was just one of those crazy, once-in-a-lifetime things. It's not going to happen again. I know that."

"But you're scared anyway."

"I'm not scared," he snapped. Not that he would ever tell her. "I don't have a problem with conducting interviews. I can do my job."

"Okay."

Her voice was subdued, and he knew he had hurt her feelings by being so forceful about it. He should apologize. But he couldn't. That would be tantamount to admitting she was right.

And he wasn't going to admit he was afraid of interviewing the people who had gotten sick.

———

Duane waited anxiously for the door to be answered. He never visited Duncan, and for good reason. He couldn't really think of a good excuse for coming to visit Duncan now, but he hoped it would come to him. Or maybe Duncan would just be so pleased to see him he wouldn't ask why his inferior little brother had suddenly showed up on his doorstep.

That wasn't going to happen.

He rang the bell again and eventually could hear footsteps approaching the door. They stopped on the other side of the door, and Duane knew Duncan was looking through the peephole at him. Looking through the peephole and not opening the door. If their roles had been reversed, Duane knew what would have happened. Duncan would start pounding on the door, telling Duane he knew he was home and insisting he open the door.

But Duane didn't do that. He just waited. Duncan's curiosity apparently got the better of him, and he opened the door. He looked Duane over.

"Well, Duane. I didn't even think you knew my address. To what do I owe the pleasure…?"

Duane shrugged. He shifted from one foot to the other, trying to think of what to say. There was no blinding flash of inspiration. He still couldn't come up with a believable reason to be there.

"I just... I dunno. You're right, I never did thank you properly for everything you have done for me. I thought I should... I thought we should try to do better... at being a family. I don't know."

Duncan stared at him, his gaze steady and piercing. Duane knew Duncan could see right through him. He didn't believe a word of the explanation. He knew Duane didn't want to be there. Duane had no desire to be closer to Duncan.

He could see straight into Duane's soul and knew exactly why he was there.

"Come in," Duncan said finally. He opened the door the rest of the way and made a sweep of his hand, welcoming Duane in.

Duane breathed a little sigh of relief. He could still have continued with the plan if Duncan didn't invite him in. But there was a much better chance of success if he could get inside the house.

He stepped into Duncan's house for the first time ever. They had not lived under the same roof since Duncan had left home for college. Duane had never visited him. Duncan had sometimes visited Duane, but never at Duane's request. He felt a little shiver of dread on entering.

It was a relief there was no dog. He had half-feared Duncan would have another Cerberus. Another dog ready and willing to tear Duane to shreds. Duncan led him into the living room. Nothing like Duane's tiny, dark basement room with the crushed, worn carpet. Nothing like the unmatched crates and garage sale furniture Duane had. It was a palace. He felt unclean just walking into it. Duane stood awkwardly until Duncan pointed to a couch.

"Uh, have a seat. You want a coffee?"

"Yeah... that would be great."

"I'd offer you a beer," Duncan needled, "but that would be a parole violation, wouldn't it?"

"Yes," Duane agreed.

Duncan gave a sharklike smile. He disappeared into the kitchen and Duane was left to himself. If Duncan hadn't left him alone, Duane could have excused himself to the bathroom and continued to execute his plan, but the living room was better. He swiftly pulled a specimen bottle from his pocket and gently shook it over the planter, the carpet, and the big easy chair that was obviously Duncan's favored seat. He screwed the top back on and shoved it into his pocket.

Duncan returned unexpectedly. "Hey, do you eat—" He frowned, finding Duane hovering over his easy chair instead of seated where Duncan had instructed.

"That's a great-looking chair," Duane said lamely, trying to make it sound like he was excited by it. Duncan's eyes narrowed. He didn't ask Duane what game he was playing, but the question was clear in his gaze.

"Yeah, it is. Very comfortable. I'd invite you to try it, but…" he trailed off, maybe unable to think of anything; maybe intentionally making Duane feel like he was untouchable, too dirty to even be allowed to touch the furniture.

Duane felt his face turning red. He clenched his teeth to avoid losing his temper and went back to the couch to sit down.

"Do you eat cheese?" Duncan asked in a slow, deliberate voice. "I know you won't eat the flesh of any animals."

"Yeah, sure," Duane agreed with a nod.

"You do? So you're not one of *those* crazies."

"Just meat," Duane said.

He didn't point out that he reacted to meat. He hadn't chosen to be vegetarian out of his feelings toward animals. But on the same note, he felt like it would be a betrayal if he said that. He did have strong feelings about cruelty toward living things. Those feelings would just never have impelled such a big lifestyle change by themselves.

Duane was the type who had to be forced into change. He didn't embrace it.

Duncan retreated again to the kitchen. Duane let out a breath. He looked at each of the spots where he had emptied the specimen jar. No matter how carefully he looked, he could not see any sign of movement. Even in Duncan's thick white carpet, Duane could see no sign of the specimens.

Duncan returned with coffee service, and cheese and crackers. There were also ham and cold cuts to go with the crackers, a clear in-your-face gesture toward Duane after Duncan acknowledged his brother wouldn't eat such things. Duane took a cup of coffee and didn't touch the food. For all he knew, Duncan had handled both the meat and the cheese without washing his hands, and Duane didn't know how much of the residues would need to transfer to the cheese to make Duane sick. He had no desire to find out. He didn't need to be going into shock in front of his brother.

He wouldn't have accepted the cheese anyway.

14

———————

Matt returned home to an empty apartment. It felt cold, like he'd been away for a week and no one had been walking the halls to stir the air and make it feel homey. His skin crawled. He knew something was wrong. He even suspected what it was, but he was afraid to form the thought.

He went to the bedroom and rather than immediately lying down in bed, he opened the door to the closet.

He pretended to himself that he wanted a sweater to ward off the sudden chill. What he was really doing was checking to make sure Rebecca's clothes were still there.

It had been a big deal for him when he had cleared a space for her to put her clothes in the closet. He wasn't a fashion model, but he did tend to collect things and had a hard time letting them go. He had kept a lot of clothes that were worn out, out of fashion, or that he didn't even like anymore. He had had to purge his collection to make room for Rebecca's stuff.

And now his clothes hung in a half-empty closet. They looked lonely.

The shoes that had littered the floor of the closet, which he always tripped over, were gone. The purses. The racks of jewelry.

All gone.

Matt staggered to the bed and sat down. His hands were shaking. His head whirled like he'd been riding a merry go round. Tears blurred his vision.

He couldn't breathe. He was going to throw up.

She had torn the heart right out of him.

Matt cradled his face in his hands, rocking back and forth, trying to sort his world out and get control of himself.

It didn't work.

He collapsed into the pillow, holding it against his face so it would soak up his tears instead of letting them run down his face like a baby.

He sobbed and sobbed, until sleep took him.

———

When Matt awoke later, he knew he had to talk to her. He had to fix things with Becca.

She thought he wasn't interested in her anymore. That he was seeing someone behind her back. Or working too long at the office. If he could just straighten out her misperception, everything would be okay. They could still have a relationship.

She could still live there and use half his closet.

Becca had always kept her own apartment. Even though she didn't live there, she had always maintained her own residence. Like she thought that their relationship wouldn't last. It made him a little bit angry. She hadn't trusted him. She had to take some of the blame for things not working out.

She didn't answer Matt's call, letting it go to voicemail. Matt hung up and called again. It went to voicemail a second time. He called again. He would keep calling until her phone battery ran out and announced she was no longer in the service area.

"Matt." Rebecca's voice was angry. On edge.

This was her fault and she was angry with him?

"Becca. Honey. We need to talk."

"No, Matt. We've talked enough. It's over. I'm sorry things didn't work out."

"Things were working out just fine. I don't understand why you left. Explain it to me. I'll fix it. We can still make this work."

"Matt, you can't fix it. Ever since you were hurt... things haven't been the same. You used to be a fun guy. A bit of a geek, maybe, but fun to be with. Attentive. Sweet. I wish things could have kept on that way."

"I'll fix it, Becca. I can. I'll be that person again. I'm sorry. I know this sleep thing has gotten in the way. But we can work through it."

"I've tried. You've tried. But we're on two separate pages. Living two separate lives. We stopped living together as a couple a long time ago."

"Because of the… intimacy? I've just been so tired, so exhausted. But I can try. Give me another chance."

"We're out of chances. I know neither of us wanted this, but things just didn't work out. It's one of those freak things you don't have any control over. It's just… I don't know what to say, Matt. It's over. It's dead and buried."

"Please come back. I don't understand how you could just leave me, without a word, just clear out and disappear."

"I tried to talk to you. I tried to find a time to sit down with you to discuss it. To tell you I was leaving. But you were… gone. You were never there. *You* left long before I did."

"When did you try to talk to me?" Matt challenged.

"Matt…" her voice was soft. "Matt… I left three days ago. You didn't even know I was gone."

Matt felt the bottom fall out of his stomach. His head reviewed the words, but they didn't make any sense. She had left three days ago? He had tiptoed out of the dark bedroom and around the apartment, afraid of waking her up, and she wasn't even there. She wasn't sleeping in. She wasn't there at all. He thought they just kept missing each other during his waking hours, but she had left without him even knowing it.

How could he claim to care about her when he hadn't even known she was gone?

———

"Mr. Malloy, I need you in the boardroom."

Matt sighed, looking at his computer screen and at the papers covering his desk. He was swamped, and now Mavis wanted to take up more of his time with another useless meeting. He would lose another two hours of his day meeting on something that would probably have taken fifteen minutes if she just told him what she wanted.

"Yes, I'll be right there," Matt agreed politely. He didn't need to be riling her up over anything else. No attitude.

But he did roll his eyes at Carol as he set down his pen and his mouse and hauled himself to his feet. She gave him a sympathetic smile.

At least Mavis had picked the morning for the meeting. He had slept during the night, for once, and was still feeling pretty fresh. If it was late afternoon, he probably still had enough of a sleep deficit that the meeting would have had him snoring.

The collection of people in the boardroom was puzzling. Mavis Booker. A girl he thought was from HR. One of the managers. Matt looked them over uncertainly and sat down. The fact they were all there ahead of him and looked like they had already been carrying on a discussion made him uncomfortable. He didn't like being the last one to walk into the meeting.

"Thank you for coming, Mr. Malloy," Mavis acknowledged.

Matt nodded. "What's this about?"

"I note you still have not cleared the infection reports around Buffalo Head."

Matt glanced over at HR. What did this have to do with her? The mix of people in the room just did not make sense to him.

"No. As I said... I'm not comfortable clearing it yet. I've talked to a couple of the subjects on the phone, but I need to pursue in-person interviews. I believe there is a connection between the cases, but I have yet to figure out what it is."

"The infections are not all the same bacteria."

"No. There's a mix of resultant diseases."

"And you haven't been able to link them back to a specific place or activity. No common infectious environment."

"No."

"You've done sweeps and haven't found any larger than normal populations or more virulent infections within the specimens."

"No. But all that doesn't mean there *isn't* an underlying connection."

Mavis tapped the end of her pen on the boardroom table. "I believe your judgment may be impaired, Mr. Malloy."

"My judgment?" Matt glowered at her. "What do you mean?"

"It has been well-documented your health has suffered over the past few months, following a head injury sustained on the job."

"Yes, but that doesn't mean there's anything wrong with my thought processes. I'm having problems sleeping, not thinking."

"Dr. Montgomery believes you are suffering from PTSD following the attack."

"Dr. Montgomery would think a scrambled egg was suffering from PTSD. I told him I'm fine."

"But in this case, he is the professional, not you. And he believes you are suffering Post Traumatic Stress Disorder. That is where your sleep disorder stems from."

"I do not have PTSD. I have... a sleep problem. That's all. And I've signed up for a sleep study. I'll get a proper diagnosis and they'll be able to sort it out. You'll see."

"You have been having problems completing your work, or even keeping track of it."

Matt opened his mouth to argue and she held up her hand.

"That has been documented." Mavis looked significantly at the HR girl, who nodded confirmation.

"I made a few mistakes. That has nothing to do with the Buffalo Head cluster."

"I don't want you to focus on the Buffalo Head cluster. That is not what this meeting is about."

"You're the one who led with it," Matt growled.

"You have had hallucinations on the job."

Matt wondered who had squealed on him. He couldn't imagine it had been Carol or Jared. Dewey?

"That was minor. And only one time. I went to the hospital. I was treated for sleep deprivation. You know I got a doctor's note and took several days off to catch back up on my sleep. It hasn't happened again."

"But it could, couldn't it? Because you still don't have the issue under control."

"It's a health issue," Matt pointed out. "Not a choice!"

"I know," Mavis agreed in a soft voice. And for a moment she looked human and concerned about him, before she continued on with the litany. "Nevertheless, the work we do here is important. Mistakes you make could put the public at risk. Until you can get this health issue under control..."

"You're going to suspend me from work because I won't clear the

Buffalo Head cluster?" Matt demanded, hardly able to believe what he was hearing.

"I said this is not about the Buffalo Head cluster. That is just one of many examples of the degradation of your work. I believe if you were well, you would not be second-guessing yourself and would be able to quickly evaluate and clear that infection cluster."

"But you are suspending me."

There were looks exchanged around the table.

"We are putting you on *leave*," the manager explained.

"How is that any different from a suspension?"

"It will be classified as short-term disability. We will be monitoring your progress and if we have evidence you have been able to lick this thing…"

"What would constitute evidence?"

"We will require notes from medical doctors and from Dr. Montgomery. We would need a signed statement from you indicating you are able to properly address your work once more."

"And while I'm gone, who is going to take over my job and clear these reports?"

"We will be getting a qualified temporary worker. He will investigate the infection reports and clear them where appropriate."

"And then I can come back."

"When we have confirmation you have recovered," Mavis insisted.

"Right." Matt looked around at the three of them. "When does this leave begin?"

"Immediately."

"I have a few things I'll need to clear off my desk—"

"That will not be possible."

Matt looked at them, his stomach a tight, hard knot. "Immediately?" he echoed.

Mavis nodded.

Matt stood up.

"There are some papers you will need to sign," the woman from HR advised, standing up and circling the table to stand beside him and lay them in front of him.

Matt was in a daze as she pointed out each signature line to him and he signed his name. There was a buzzing in his ears and he didn't know where it was coming from. The manager gave him a false, tight, smile and offered to walk him back to his desk to pick up his personal items. Like a sleepwalker, Matt walked back to his desk. Was he supposed to clear everything out? As if he was fired and never coming back? Or was he just supposed to remove his lunch and anything that might go bad while he was gone?

The lab was silent as he moved toward his desk. There was already an empty box placed in the middle of it. More than just his lunch, then. His coworkers gave no pretense of work as Matt started to go through his desktop and drawers, removing all personal items.

He sat down at the computer.

"I have to log out of my personal accounts," he said to no one in particular.

The manager nodded.

As Matt finished filling the box, his fingers numb, Carol approached.

"I'll drive you home, Matt."

"No, it's okay." His voice was choked. "I'll just…" He couldn't think of what else he might do. Walk? Take the bus? With his box?

"We will provide Mr. Malloy with a taxi home," the manager said. "There's no need for you to miss work."

Carol stood there, not liking it. "A cab? Matt needs a friend."

"No, it's okay," Matt told her. "I'll be fine. We'll talk later."

"Are you sure? I'll take the rest of the day off unpaid. It doesn't matter. I don't want you to be alone."

"I'll be fine. I'm just going to go to sleep."

"You're sure?"

He nodded.

"Will you call me when you get up? Even if it's late?"

Matt nodded again. "Sure. I'll call you."

15

———

Duane was out on a job when the call came through. The caller ID was for the County Hospital. He answered it more because he was curious than anything else. It was likely a wrong number. There was no reason for the hospital to be calling him.

"Is this Mr. Duane Grant?" a woman's voice demanded briskly, without so much as a hello or inquiry after his health.

Duane was surprised. His heart sped a little. It *had* said the County Hospital, not some other agency that would be more likely to inquire after him by name.

"What's this about?" he asked cautiously.

"Are you the next of kin of Duncan Grant?"

"Oh." Duane blew out his breath in surprise. His heart sped even faster now. Next of kin? Did that mean Duncan was dead? Maybe he'd been in a car accident. Or someone had finally gotten sick of his officious attitude and shot him in the face. Duane could think of half a dozen scenarios that would warm his heart. "He's my brother. So, I suppose I am. What happened?"

"Your brother is in critical condition at the County Hospital. We need you to come in. Can you do that?"

"I'm at work… can it wait a few hours?"

"I'm afraid not. It's his heart."

Duane blinked thoughtfully. So Duncan's rich diet and sedentary life-style had finally caught up with him. He should have taken better care of himself, knowing he had heart problems.

"I'll try to get there as soon as I can. Where do I go when I get there?"

She gave him the unit number and told him to check in with the nursing station as soon as he got there. Duane ended the call. He called Steve to inform him of the emergency and headed straight to the hospital in his bugmobile, in spite of the fact he wasn't allowed to drive it anywhere but to official jobs.

———

At the cardiac unit, the nurses gave him strained smiles and asked him to wait for the doctor. He didn't ask to go in and see Duncan but sat in a chair in a small grouping at the end of the hallway. There were well-thumbed magazines on the table and a sad, dingy little silk flower arrangement. There was a window with an uninspiring view of the city; overcast and gloomy. Duane flipped through one of the magazines without any real interest. In a few minutes, a dark-haired doctor who looked impossibly young approached him.

"Mr. Grant?"

Duane stood up to shake the doctor's extended hand. "Duane. Yeah."

"I'm sorry to have to meet you under these circumstances."

"Yeah. What happened? He had a heart attack?"

"Have a seat." The two of them sat on chairs facing each other. The doctor looked grave. "It looks like a combination of an allergic reaction and rejection of his transplanted heart valves." His brows drew down, and he shook his head. "It's a very unusual case. We're still trying to sort it out."

"He got those new valves years ago," Duane pointed out. "I thought he was safe as long as he was on anti-rejection drugs."

"It's unusual to suddenly reject a transplant so many years later," the young doctor agreed. "I think it may be connected to the allergy attack."

"How?"

"You know the valves he got were not human…?"

Duane shook his head. "No… what were they, then?"

"We commonly use pig heart valves. Human heart valves are in short supply, but we can harvest pigs' quite easily."

"Pigs."

"There is one documented case where a patient died from a failed valve transplant because he was allergic to pork."

"But Duncan's transplant was years ago. He isn't allergic to pork." Then he remembered the doctor's comment about Duncan's allergic reaction. "You think he suddenly became allergic to pork?"

"It's been known to happen."

Duane knew what was coming.

"There's something called mammalian meat allergy, where the person suddenly becomes allergic to a sugar in red meat called alpha-gal."

Duane nodded.

"Current studies are linking it to the bite of a particular species of tick."

Duane nodded again, unable to think of any verbal response.

"Do you know if your brother had recently had a tick bite? Has he been hiking?"

"No. He doesn't do that. He didn't mention any bite to me."

The doctor nodded. "Sometimes people are bitten without realizing it. The little bit of research I have done today says the kind of tick that causes it doesn't live in Colorado. But since we get cases of alpha-gal in Colorado, there must be some other species of tick or another insect that carries it that they haven't identified yet. Maybe something as simple as a mosquito bite. Who knows?" His shoulders lifted and fell in a tired shrug. "Your brother does have a compromised immune system due to the anti-rejection drugs he was on. Maybe that made him more susceptible."

Duane waited. Now he knew why Duncan was in hospital. But what did that mean? He couldn't have the valves replaced a second time with pig valves. He would need human valves now. Duane couldn't give him any.

"So... are you doing another transplant? Why am I here?"

The doctor rubbed the back of his head. "We can't do another transplant, Mr. Grant. If things had happened differently and we'd had a larger window, then maybe we could have swapped in an artificial valve. But as it happened..."

Duane looked at him expectantly.

"Your brother died on the table. The allergic reaction was devastating and destroyed all hope of repairing the heart."

Duane nodded.

Duncan was dead.

Never again would Duane have to put up with his bullying, officious ways. He was finally free of his brother.

"We put him on a heart bypass machine while we were trying to save him," the doctor went on. "He is still on that machine now, and on a respirator to keep him breathing. But for all intents and purposes, he is dead. We need your permission…"

"To pull the plug?" Duane was a little too quick with the question. He saw it in the doctor's eyes. Trying to compensate, Duane covered his eyes and face as if overwhelmed with grief.

The doctor put his hand on Duane's back comfortingly. "Your brother's life was once saved by a transplant. And now… he could save others. Maybe it would give his death some meaning… if you agreed to donate his organs."

Duane took a long, shuddering breath. He spoke hoarsely through his hands. "Yes. Yes, of course."

The doctor rubbed Duane's back, making his flesh crawl.

"Thank you. I know this is a terrible decision to have to make, at an impossibly difficult time. But time is of the essence. I will get the forms for you to sign and then we'll get the transplant team started. He can't remain on the bypass machine for too long before the organs start to degrade."

Duane nodded. The doctor left him alone, and Duane hurried to find a restroom. He splashed water on his face, rubbed his eyes vigorously, and returned to his chair, where he sat dabbing at his nose with a tissue.

16

Matt didn't know how Rebecca was going to respond to him showing up, but he couldn't just leave things as they were without some attempt to mend the rift between them.

Rebecca opened the door and stood there looking at him with her big brown eyes.

"Matt," she said without inflection. He didn't know whether she was irritated or glad to see him. He handed her the irises—she had a thing about roses—and didn't say anything. He didn't know what to say. Actions would speak louder than words. She accepted the flowers and looked down at them for a few minutes, a crease between her eyebrows. "Come in, then."

She withdrew from the doorway, and Matt entered the apartment.

It was a long time since he had been there. It was Rebecca's place, her retreat. He had been there a few times early in their relationship, but they had quickly settled on his apartment after going out on dates, and eventually she had moved in. It was bright and homey. Lots of feminine touches. Little clutter. It reflected her personality.

Without speaking, they agreed on the living room and sat down, Rebecca on the couch and Matt in the chair. Not side-by-side. Not touching. It was a discussion, not a date.

"I miss you," Matt said.

"I miss you too. I've missed you for months, ever since you got hurt."

"I'm not… it's not my choice… not to be well. I am trying. But I know I've neglected you. Neglected our relationship. That's not fair to you."

"I don't see how anything is going to change. Like you said, it wasn't your choice to get hurt. To have these problems. You can't choose not to be… sick."

Matt wiped his damp hands on his pants.

"I'm taking leave from work. So I won't be trying to sleep around my work schedule. I won't be tired all the time."

She didn't answer right away. Her soft brown eyes were thoughtful.

"You're taking leave?"

Matt nodded. "Short term disability. Until I can get a handle on this thing."

She bit her lip. "I'm not going to say *no*," she hedged. "But things have to change. I'm not going to be invisible."

"I'll do better. I promise."

She gave no indication whether she believed he could change. "Do you want to stay for supper?"

"That would be really nice."

"Are you going to eat?"

Matt paused to consider his body's signals. It wasn't just his sleep schedule that was messed up, but his appetite as well. Even when he knew it was time to eat, he just couldn't sometimes. "Yeah, I think I can eat."

"Good. Why don't you start making a salad and I'll thaw something out?"

———

Matt had planned just to sleep as his body dictated while he was on leave, and hopefully, he would find his natural sleep cycle. Then he would work it forward until he was on a normal schedule, as he had the first time.

But Rebecca complicated things. While she enjoyed partying late on weekends or days off, she followed a pretty strict schedule during the work week. She expected Matt to follow it closely as well. It wasn't that she minded an hour or two deviation one direction or the other, but sleeping the shift opposite to her was a problem. Even if he tried to get his sleep in while she was at work. She expected him to be able to meet her for lunch, to chat with him on the phone when she was on a break, and to be ready to spend time with her in the evening when she got home. And so far, he was striking out on all counts.

At the drug store, Matt spent two hours reading through the information on every single sleep or alertness aid in the place. Herbs, caffeine, melatonin, everything he could find. Something was bound to work. He finally left the store with a bag full of enough remedies to put an elephant to sleep. And that was just from reading the packages.

Drugs to take before bed so he would sleep. Drugs to take when he woke up to increase alertness and keep him awake until the next night. Somehow, he was going to lick the disorder.

At home, he lined the bottles up on the counter in two groups. When ten o'clock rolled around, he wasn't tired yet, but he took one of each of the sleep aids. Then he sat in front of the shopping channel on TV and waited for them to take effect.

———

By two o'clock in the morning, Matt knew he wasn't going to get to sleep. That meant he would be all the more tired the next night. He would force himself to stay awake all day, taking whatever caffeine and stimulating herbs he needed to. Then when night rolled around again, he would be able to sleep.

Not only was he not feeling tired, but he was feeling a little hyper and loopy like a little kid kept up too late at night. On the off-chance he really was tired, and just didn't know it, he retired to his dark bedroom and lay on the bed for fifteen minutes. When he didn't feel drowsy or fall asleep, he got back up again. That was what all the insomnia advice websites said. Don't stay there trying to fall asleep. Get up and do something else.

So, pretending it was the middle of the day instead of the middle of the night, Matt booted up his computer and read through his email. And his newsfeed. And the discussion boards he sometimes followed. Eventually, he went back to his email.

The manager who had supervised Matt packing up his personal items was, Matt presumed, supposed to ensure he did not take any files home with him. But he hadn't been watching when Matt said he was logging out of his personal email and social networks, so he hadn't seen Matt mail the folder of infection reports and research he had done on the Buffalo Head cluster to himself. Maybe the man wouldn't even have realized what Matt was doing if he had been watching. Some of the senior staff were Luddites where computers were concerned. But the manager wasn't that old. He probably would have figured it out.

If he'd been watching.

But he hadn't been.

Matt hadn't touched the research the first few days. He had tried to do what he was supposed to. He tried just to sleep and get his body back under control, something that seemed so natural for the rest of the world. Every time he had puzzled over the Buffalo Head cluster, he had deliberately put it out of his mind and focused on other things. Researching insomnia cures. Going over his sleep graph. Thinking about what to do about Rebecca.

But now he was bored, and he was tired of thinking about all those other things. He went back to his email, downloaded the attachment, and uncompressed the folder. He started to read through the infection reports. Just the bare facts. What the patients and doctors had reported in dry, clinical terms. Like reading a cookbook or encyclopedia one entry at a time. It was different than looking at all the data compiled and collated on the screen. Rather than seeing points on a map, or graphs showing the data split up in different ways, he read a story.

Behind the reports, he sensed a guiding hand. Something was happening that was beyond their experience. He had said over and over again this was not a natural cluster. And if it wasn't a natural cluster, someone had interfered. Someone had caused this change. Maybe it was accidental and maybe it was intentional.

Something had caused a change in the environment and pushed the cluster of infections out of the normal bounds.

———

Matt woke up with his head on the keyboard. His skin stuck to the keys as he lifted his face and looked at the screen again. If he looked in the mirror, he would have the imprint of the keys on his forehead.

He had pressed random keys when he fell asleep, so he had to sort through the various screens to delete any garbled text and make sure he hadn't damaged any files.

The nap had caught him unaware. He hadn't even known he was getting tired. None of the usual signs had been present. One minute he was reading the infection reports and the next he was prying himself off of the keyboard.

Matt rubbed his eyes and wiped small tears from the corners. Although he rarely dreamed anymore, he *had* been dreaming. Not just low-level, normal nightly dreams, but wildly vivid, emotion-filled dreams. Maybe one of the sleep aids had caused a change in his brain waves. More slow waves. More REM sleep. That was good. Matt figured it was, anyway. Any change had to be good.

In his dream, he had seen a man behind the infections. Not a blundering fool. Not someone who had accidentally caused the situation. But a calculating, malevolent force.

Matt shook his head to disperse the thoughts. It was a dream. Vector-borne bacteria could not be weaponized. They could not be aerosolized. They could not be distilled into a liquid or dried into a powder. They had to go through the vector to be infectious. A tick-borne disease had to be carried by a tick. You could not take the tick out of the cycle.

17

———————

Duane could not have planned things better if he had tried. Work was going better with Brad gone and Steve short-staffed so he couldn't bully Duane. Rich Adams was no longer tormenting Duane, but instead was his fast friend. He was always asking questions about recipes and products and delighted whenever Duane brought him a new dish to try or tested a new barbecue sauce for his grilled veggie burgers.

And now, Duncan was gone.

Gone from Duane's life. Gone from the earth.

Duane had no more surviving family and that suited him just fine. It was freeing. He could be himself, his own person, and not worry about what his mother or brother would think. How they would react to him or what they would do. And while Duncan had always said he was going to leave all his money to charity when he died, jumping from heart research to rehabbing criminals and addicts to golf for disabled kids, he had actually died intestate.

No will could be found. Not even a letter setting out his wishes. Since he had no children and no parents, Duane was Duncan's sole heir. The big house had a fair-sized mortgage on it, but enough equity to give Duane a nice little nest egg. And there were stocks and bonds, Duncan's fancy muscle car, and some man jewelry. Other bits and pieces kept popping up as Duane went through his possessions and papers. Sometimes Duane laughed aloud when he made a new discovery.

He had never liked his brother much.

Until now.

Now, he loved Duncan.

———

Matt was a trained investigator. Not a private eye, but trained in digging up the hidden details that affected infectious outbreaks. It wasn't like following someone's wife around with a camera to see if she was being unfaithful. More like putting together a puzzle. Or taking one apart to see how it was constructed.

He couldn't leave the Buffalo Head cluster alone. He knew that another investigator had been assigned to work on it and had probably signed off on the reports by now. There would be no further investigation by the DOH. No alert sent to the CDC. Just a routine, random cluster. No need to panic the public. No need to cause anyone a headache.

So he started his own investigation. A private investigation. He didn't have a paying client, but maybe when he solved the mystery, he would be rewarded in some way. He'd get his job back. He'd get a promotion. Recognition. They couldn't just ignore someone who made an important discovery. Who recognized a dangerous threat when no one else saw it. There had to be some good karma associated with it.

Stuffing down his anxiety over face-to-face interviews, he talked to the first couple of people in the stack of reports. A man with a serious Lyme-like infection keeping him on the disabled list and a woman whose nasal, upper-crust affectation drove Matt up the wall.

The man, Brad Berkley, had been cooperative enough. He sat in an easy chair in front of his TV, not budging when Matt entered and not bothering to mute the game show and other daytime television programming that came on while Matt was there. He had, in spite of his general bad manners, been eager for someone to talk to. He enjoyed expounding his symptoms and giving Matt a play-by-play on the progress of his disease.

"You want to know the ironic thing?" he asked, after giving Matt a lengthy report. "I'm an exterminator! I kill the damn things all day long, and somehow one of them gets to me and near enough kills me! Like he was a kamikaze or something."

Matt could see the irony, but he was also disappointed. The fact that Brad was an exterminator explained how he had been infected. He had managed to pick up a tick bite on the job. Plenty of exterminators and infectious agent investigators got bites in the course of the job. No matter how careful you were, sometimes a questing tick was so aggressive there was just no escaping it. Matt was always very careful. He knew to check for ticks after every field job, checking his scalp, armpits, and anywhere else the hair was dense and might hide a gorging tick. Removing them immediately greatly reduced the risk of infection. Somehow Brad had missed one, not checking himself for ticks at the end of the day or being too casual about it.

"Had you been around ticks in the days before you came down with your illness?"

Brad's attention was on *The Price is Right*, and he yelled his answers at the contestants as if they could hear him. Matt was already tightly enough wound without the shouting, which put him even more on edge. Looking away from the TV, Berkley asked Matt to repeat his question.

"Around them? Hell, yeah. Plenty. We did lots of spraying. Dragged for counts. Collected samples for the CDC to test. We make reports to help the CDC identify problems before they become an issue."

"That's great. We sure appreciate all your company does. Can you tell me the areas you might have sprayed or done other work in, during the days before you got sick?"

His eyes on the TV screen, Brad listed off a few neighborhoods. His voice was distant. He wasn't really paying much attention to Matt or the answers he was giving. There was no telling how much he might be leaving out.

"Is there anything else you can tell me? Anything unusual that happened before you got sick? Anything that stands out in your mind, whether it has anything to do with ticks or not?"

"No, nothing. Just routine stuff at work. The usual around here."

"And you haven't been hiking? You don't have a dog?"

"Filthy animals. No. I'd never have one after seeing some of them crawling with fleas and ticks." Brad made a face. "There's no way I'd let one bring vermin into my house."

He glanced around with the air of the master of the house. Matt threw a quick glance around the living room. It was nothing special. Bachelor decorating. Unwashed dishes on the side tables. Matt didn't believe the beer cans on the floor didn't attract ants or other insect life. The place was probably crawling with pests.

"Yeah, I know what you mean," he agreed. "Has anyone else at your company been sick lately? Before or after you?"

"Nah." Brad gave a shrug. "Just the usual. Hangovers after the weekend. Colds and flu. Just the usual stuff that goes through offices."

"Sometimes tick-borne diseases can look like the flu. Aches and pains. Fevers that come and go. Malaise. There isn't always a rash…"

"I haven't heard of anything. But even if I did… what's the difference? I didn't pick this up at the office; I picked it up in the field. Dealing with the critters. Any of the other exterminators could have done the same thing. But we all work different plots. Different yards in different neighborhoods. We don't go to the same job together."

"Right." Matt closed his notebook and nodded. "Well, Mr. Berkley. I want to thank you very much for letting me come and talk to you. I'll be putting the final touches on this report, and you shouldn't be bothered by it again." Matt took out one of his business cards and wrote his cell phone number on it, crossing out the office number. "If you have any questions, or if you think of anything you wanted to mention to me, please feel free to give me a call. That's the best number to reach me at. Leave a message if I don't answer. I might be out on an interview, but I will get back to you as soon as I can."

Brad held the business card between his index and middle finger and nodded. "Sure, of course." He flicked it onto the side table, where he would likely never look at it again, except to sweep it into the garbage. "Thanks for coming by." He looked back at the TV, lost again in the onscreen drama. "You can show yourself out. I'd get up, but my joints… it's best if I just stay put."

"Thanks. Take care of yourself."

Matt let himself out of the stale house.

———

The woman was at the other end of the social spectrum. Rather than a small house in a middle-class neighborhood, she had an estate house on an acreage with plenty of landscaping. Her furnishings were obviously picked and arranged by a professional decorator. There were few personal touches. No pictures of family or friends. No ratty bathrobe thrown over the arm of the couch. It was a home kept in pristine order, not a pin out of place. It couldn't be less like a prison, but Matt still found himself anxious, glancing over his shoulder to make sure he was safe.

The potential sources of infection were obvious. The large yard meant she didn't have to go off hiking in the woods to chance an encounter with a questing tick. There were plenty of trees and shrubs on the property that could harbor them. Even without any long grass or weeds for them to breed in, they could hitchhike on a songbird and reach any part of the big yard.

And Matt had only been there five minutes when he met Boofie. The little dog had the run of the house, and Matt assumed the run of the property as well.

As with Brad, Matt felt a little let down. This was not the work of a malevolent terrorist. This was a natural occurrence. The little dog could easily pick up a tick outside. And Ms. Shirley Stemple probably let the dog sleep in bed with her. Certainly she picked it up and patted and cuddled with it. And while Matt watched, she plopped the dog into an oversized handbag and carried him around the house like a prized possession. Again, no mystery where she had picked up an infection.

He spent less time talking to her than he had to Brad. He was glad to put her and her stuck-up nose behind him.

———

Matt had been up for three days straight. It didn't seem to matter which herbs and sleep aids he took at ten o'clock; there was no way to force his body to be tired enough for sleep. He suspected one of the herbs might be making him stay awake instead of making him tired. At least, before he had started taking them, he had been able to sleep some of the time. Now it was like he'd forgotten how, except for those stolen moments when he nodded off suddenly at the most inconvenient times.

He had even done it in Dr. Montgomery's office the other day. Montgomery had taken it as a sign Matt was feeling more comfortable with him, but also believed Matt was holding back vital information. Matt's unconscious mind was obviously working against his conscious mind. Unconsciously, he trusted Montgomery and knew he was there to help, while consciously, he fought against opening up to him about the stress and trauma.

Matt cut out all the bedtime sleep aids. Since he couldn't isolate which one was causing him problems. He would take the stimulants during the day, but at night, he would take nothing, falling asleep naturally as the caffeine and other pep pills tapered off.

But it still wasn't working. He was sitting up through yet another night, with his brain wound up like the flywheel in a toy, spinning crazily every time he tried to rein it back in again. Matt went to the fridge and got himself a cold beer. He needed something to take the edge off and calm his thoughts.

After finishing the first can, he was feeling a little calmer. A little sleepier. He went to the fridge and pulled out the rest of the six-pack. Matt had never been much of a drinker. He rarely had more than two drinks in a night. But his nights had never been so long.

He told himself it wasn't a problem. He was drinking slowly enough his body could process the alcohol between one drink and the next. He wasn't going out anywhere, so he didn't need to worry about driving. He wasn't cooking or doing anything else that might cause him to hurt himself. He was just watching TV and puttering around on the computer, pretending to ignore the Buffalo Head cluster. Pretending it didn't really matter to him and that he had put it out of his mind.

It was the first time he had slept in four days, and if a six-pack was all it took, who was he to argue?

18

—————

Four days without sleep meant Matt's body wasn't going to be satisfied with a mere eight hours once he fell asleep. But he didn't have to go to work, so that didn't matter. Matt had plans to do more interviews around Buffalo Head, but they could wait another day or two.

When he awoke, his mouth was as dry as cotton and his clothes were sweaty and wrinkled. He could smell his own sour breath and body and was glad there was no one else around to comment on how he had let himself go to seed. It was hard to explain to someone who had never suffered from a real lack of sleep what it was like. How hard it was to do anything in the way of self-care.

But having wakened, Matt staggered to his feet to use the john and to rinse his mouth and get a drink of water. While he wasn't hungry, he knew he had better eat as well.

It was only ten o'clock in the morning, and initially, Matt was proud of himself for being able to get up so early the morning after his first sleep in days. But when he looked at the date on his computer calendar, he saw it wasn't the next day, but a full twenty-four hours later than he had thought.

In the kitchen, Matt found a note from Rebecca weighted down with a coffee cup. His heart sank as he read it and realized he had not only slept for over twenty-four hours, but he had slept through their planned date.

He put a pod in the machine and the coffee mug under the spigot as he read through the note, eyes blurring. What was he going to say to Becca now? He had promised to do better, not to ignore her, and now he had missed their date. Slept right through it.

He leaned on the counter as he waited for the coffee, crumpling the note in his hand. His eyes traveled to the living room couch where he had sat watching TV and waiting for sleep to come. The room was a mess. Empty beer cans had been kicked around when he had gotten up from the couch to move to the bedroom.

He saw it through Rebecca's eyes. Her boyfriend drinking himself into a stupor. An alcoholic waiting to happen. And a messy one at that. She wouldn't want to spend her life, or any significant part of it picking up the trail of empties he left behind. It was amazing she had even bothered to leave him a note after finding him in that condition.

———

Matt threw himself into his work to distract himself. He would talk to Rebecca later when he had figured out what to say. It didn't matter that he didn't have any legitimate work to throw himself into. He had the Buffalo Head cluster. He would finish interviewing subjects.

And then what? He had already analyzed all the data. It was inconclusive. If he didn't find anything significant from the rest of the infected subjects, what would he do?

If he was right and there was a face behind the cluster of infections, how was Matt going to find it? The infections were going to continue, but he wouldn't be getting any more of the DOH reports. They would land on his desk at the DOH, but he wouldn't be there. They would be entered into the computer, but he didn't have any way to access it remotely.

He needed to find a way to get more information.

———

"It's over, Matt." Rebecca's big brown eyes were dark and deep. "I'm sorry, I love you, but I'm not going to do this. I can't be in a relationship where my needs don't matter."

"It isn't that you don't matter," Matt protested. "You know I just sleep right through the alarm and anything else, once I get to sleep. I hadn't slept for four days, so I just conked out."

"You said you were going to be able to get it under control now that you're out of work. This isn't under control. And the drinking..."

"*You* drink! I didn't have much!"

"I'm not going to argue it, Matt. I'm not comfortable with the way you're dealing with this. And I expect to be a bigger part of your life if we're in a relationship. That just can't happen right now. You're too..." She made a hopeless shrug. "You're too caught up in this sleep thing to care."

Matt couldn't let go. He couldn't just accept she wasn't going to be a part of his life anymore.

"I'm not 'caught up in this sleep thing'! I do care! Don't you understand I can't control it? I can't just decide when to sleep and when not to sleep. I can't just decide to be normal and think about other things and other people."

She held his gaze. "That's exactly what I mean," she agreed. "You can't think about anyone else. I can't change that, and you can't change that. And I can't be in a relationship like that." She shook her head. "I need someone who can put me first."

———

Looking back later, Matt would realize he wasn't thinking straight. The combination of his pain and distress over the breakup with Rebecca and the chronic lack of sufficient REM sleep left him in a manic state. That night as he stared out his dark window and considered what to do about his investigation of the Buffalo Head cluster, he was hit by the impulse just to go into the office and look up any new reports on his computer. He still had his security swipe card. Chances were, no one had bothered to change the login on his computer or disable his user account. No one would be in the building so late

It made logical sense to his sleep-deprived brain, so he just acted on the impulse, grabbing his keys and wallet and heading out the door.

There were no cars in the parking lot. There would be a security guard doing rounds periodically, but Matt had a parking pass on his rearview mirror and his security card and proof of identity. The guard would have no way of knowing Matt was supposed to be on leave.

Matt swiped his card at the door. The security pad beeped and the green light turned on. Letting out his breath, Matt turned the handle and entered. The building was mostly dark, with only the security lights on. Matt had never been there at night before. He couldn't decide whether it seemed peaceful or creepy.

In the lab, Matt stopped at the door to turn the lights on. They were bright and garish, and he wished he hadn't. But he needed to be able to see what he was doing. If he immediately turned them off again, the flashing just increased the risk of someone paying attention.

He went to his desk and sat down. The chair was cold and was adjusted too low for his long legs. Everything was strangely familiar and foreign at the same time.

He might have thought it was a dream. But he knew he couldn't be dreaming because he couldn't sleep.

Matt turned on the computer and waited for it to boot up, looking around the strangely still and quiet lab. He'd never been there before when there weren't other people working. He heard the fans for the air conditioning turning on and off, far away along the ducts.

A beep brought his attention back to the computer. Matt typed his username and password into the login screen and waited, holding his breath. It beeped again and continued to log into the operating system. Matt blew out his breath in a long, slow whistle. In a few minutes, he was into the system, tapping away furiously to locate any new infection reports that might tie into the Buffalo Head cluster. There were new reports. More than he had expected. Matt quickly emailed them to himself, then put them up on the map to visualize them. There was still no epicenter. No denser clustering that would red flag the infection source.

He brought up the reports one at a time, skimming them quickly for any patterns. Street names. Professions. What outdoor activities they had reported taking part in. Children, pets, nearby yards or parks with bushes or long grass.

Still unable to find any pattern, Matt looked through the symptoms and diagnostic testing. Rocky Mountain Spotted Fever. Lyme-like disease. Tularemia. Positive culture for Ehrlichiosis. He looked back at Tularemia.

It was considered a rare infection. Rabbit fever. It was generally spread through mammals, not birds, so that helped to narrow the focus a little bit. It could still be squirrels; they could roam over a range of ten acres or more.

Matt closed his eyes and considered, rubbing the bridge of his nose. He didn't have a hangover, exactly. He had headaches frequently since the attack. He wasn't sure if this one was because of the head injury itself or the lack of sleep or food.

Perhaps a combination of all three, with a beer chaser.

19

W hat are you doing here?"

Matt jolted upright, the voice cutting through him. He knew, even unconscious, he wasn't supposed to have fallen asleep.

He'd been wide awake when he arrived at the DOH. He couldn't understand why he had drifted off. He looked at Carol wildly.

"You can't be here," Carol said, looking around. She was apparently the first one there. "I don't know what you're doing here, but we have to get you out. Come on. Get up."

She jostled him, encouraging him to get to his feet. Her head turned to look at the computer screen, cocked to the side like a curious bird. There was no time to close all the documents and log out of the system, so she did the only thing she could, reaching over and powering the machine off.

"Come on," she told him again. "Get out of here."

Matt pulled out of her grasp as they walked toward the door. He blinked his eyes and cleared his throat, trying to come up with some explanation.

"If anyone stops us," Carol said, "you came here to return a casserole dish. It's in your car." She glanced sideways at him. "You do have your car here, right?"

Matt nodded. "Yeah. Thanks."

"Were you sleepwalking or something? What were you doing back here?"

It was as good an explanation as he could have come up with.

"Uh… yeah. Sleepwalking, I guess. So used to coming here… I suppose it was just automatic."

She didn't ask him if he'd been sleepwalking when he turned on the computer, logged into the system, and started reading the latest infection reports.

"It's a good thing I got in early," Carol whispered. "We're getting behind, and I wanted to see if I could catch up on a few things. I don't know what Mavis would do if she saw you there!"

"I wasn't fired," Matt said with a shrug. "I'm just on short term disability. Because I'm sick. You don't blow a gasket over someone stopping in when they're on sick leave."

"Mmm." She shook her head. "Mavis Booker might."

They walked down a few hallways and were almost to the door.

"Who did they get to cover for me?" Matt asked.

Carol lifted her hands in a helpless shrug. "A college grad. Like, he graduated last week or something. No experience. No real idea what he's doing. All of us are trying to train him and cover for him."

"Why would they get someone like that?"

"Because there aren't a whole heck of a lot of vector-borne infectious disease experts kicking around looking for jobs. I wish there were." She paused, with her hand on the door. "And the other reason I think they picked him is because he'll do what he's told. If Mavis or one of the administration tells him he needs to clear a report, he'll clear the report. Just like that."

"No field work?"

"He's still cutting his teeth. He has no idea how to go about field work. We're teaching him all we can, but we all have our jobs to do too. And you're the expert on vectors."

"Yeah." Matt nodded. "Yeah, I am. I'm the expert."

She pushed through the door into the parking lot, and Matt followed her. She led the way to his car and stood beside it to talk for another minute longer.

"How are you doing?"

"Not the best. I thought once I could just get onto my own schedule, everything would smooth out. I'd just let my body sleep and wake when it wanted to…"

"But it's not working out?"

"It's crazier than ever. I was trying to keep to a schedule for Becca…" his voice cracked.

"How is Becca?" Her eyes searched his face. She touched his arm as if she already knew the answer.

"She broke it off. I either keep her awake, or I sleep when she wants to do something. And apparently I'm paying too much attention to my own problems and ignoring her."

"She can't expect you to be the same or give her the same level of attention as you used to. You can't just stop worrying about your health because she wants to go out partying."

"I guess she expects me to. I don't know what to do. I've tried to be there for her… but I fall asleep when we're supposed to be out on a date. I don't call her. We don't spend time together. I just… can't."

"No," Carol agreed, shaking her head. "Of course not. Oh, Matt… hang in there. The stress can't be helping you. Maybe it's best she's broken it off for now. You can stop worrying about her and just focus on your own health. You don't need to be pulled two different directions."

"Yeah." Matt put his key in the car door and opened it. "Maybe you're right."

"Are you okay to drive? I woke you up; are you still tired?"

"No. I'll be fine to get home. I'm not sure why I fell asleep last night, I was wide awake when I got here."

Her lips pressed together, and Matt remembered belatedly he was supposed to have sleepwalked to the office. Or sleep-driven. He shrugged and got into the car.

"Thanks, Carol. I'll talk to you later."

"Take care of yourself, Matt. I mean it. You just worry about *you* for a while."

She patted him on the shoulder, then withdrew and closed the door.

———

Duane arrived early at Bug Bee Gone to clock out. Steve was working busily at the computer. He looked up, startled when Duane walked in.

"Duane? What's up? Something wrong with your truck?"

"No." Duane raised his eyebrows. "No, I just have some family issues I need to take care of."

"You need to finish the jobs on your work list."

"You'll need to reschedule the last two. Tell them there was an emergency."

"But there isn't an emergency. You need to finish."

"I need to go see the lawyer," Duane said. "My brother's lawyer. About his estate. Lots to be done."

"Oh." Steve cast about for something to say.

The previous week Duane had taken time off for the funeral. Even though Duane had just had Duncan cremated and there was actually no service. Duane had taken great delight in telling everyone who contacted him to express their condolences that there would be no service. People had sent flowers or cards. Duane just threw them straight out. But Steve didn't know any of that. As far as he knew, Duane and Duncan had been best buddies. Duane could have been devastated by Duncan's death. Steve had no way of knowing.

"So, you'll have to let these people know we'll get back to them," Duane said, tapping the unfinished work orders.

"Couldn't you have let me know about this lawyer's appointment a few days ago? So I didn't overbook you?"

"I don't always know. Sometimes he just calls me, and I need to drop everything and get in. My brother had a lot of assets, you know. There are a lot of papers to be signed and things to be sold."

"Okay... well... try to let me know ahead of time, if you can."

Duane shrugged and didn't say he would. He suspected he would probably have a few more emergency appointments before the excuse was worn out. He swiped his card a few times until the light turned green.

"Any specimens?" Steve asked.

"No, not today."

"Don't forget we need to send samples on to the CDC regularly, so they can keep track of population and infection rates."

"I've had my mind on other things. I haven't seen anything out of the ordinary."

"Okay... tomorrow, maybe, bring me some in."

Duane hung up his keys and went to the locker room to change out of his Bug Bee Gone coveralls. It was nice having the locker room to himself. Nice not to have to worry about sharing the space. He threw his coveralls and kit in the locker and departed.

It was time to check on the Flopsy Bunnies and decide what to make for supper that Adams might like.

———

One thing about not sleeping at night or working during the day; it was a lot easier to get out to bars or night clubs. Alcohol was the best sleep aid he had tried so far and Matt was lonely for some human contact. He decided to go to the club instead of just to the liquor store. He would go to the liquor store to update his stocks in a day or two. He didn't have a schedule to follow. He needed the human contact at the club for his own mental health.

He was familiar with the Eagles Nest. He and Rebecca used to go there quite a bit before Matt had been injured. But they hadn't been there much since then. And Matt had rarely been there alone. At first, he felt awkward walking in the door without her. Without any woman on his arm. Just a bachelor, out on his own for the night. But the bartender, a dark man who looked like he had an East Indian background, nodded at him and smiled.

"Nice to see you again, sir. It's been a while. What can I get you?"

Matt wasn't a cocktail man. Usually, he just went for whatever was on tap. But he didn't want to wait that long for a buzz this time. He was there to drink, enjoy himself a little, and go home pleasantly pickled to be able to fall into his bed and sleep. That was how he envisioned the evening. That would be success.

"Scotch, rocks."

"Yes, sir. Coming up."

Matt looked around. A booth? Something near the dance floor? Eventually, he just picked a stool along the bar. He wasn't feeling adventurous enough to head to the dance floor. He would just chat with the barman and not worry about female company. Just some human interaction where he didn't have anything to prove to anyone. He didn't have to entertain anyone or even be attentive.

The bartender placed a napkin in front of him and placed the tumbler on top of it. The name stitched into his apron was 'Nick'.

"Long day?" Nick suggested when Matt didn't pick up the drink or look away immediately.

Matt rubbed at the bags under his eyes, feeling suddenly self-conscious.

"Long few months."

Nick nodded. "That why we haven't seen you here much? Or the lady?"

"Yeah. The lady and I… are no longer together."

"I'm sorry to hear that, sir. You made a nice couple. Seemed to have fun together."

"Yeah, we did, didn't we? Haven't had much fun with anyone lately."

Nick wiped the counter and moved down to refill someone else's glass before returning.

"Just been too busy?" he asked. "Is that it?"

"No. I actually…" Matt hesitated. Nick looked down, not pressuring him to finish. "I actually was attacked at work." His hand went to the back of his head. To the ridge along his skull. "Skull fracture, brain injury…"

Nick's eyes widened, and his constantly busy hands stopped moving for a long minute while he considered this. "Wow. But you're okay now?"

"Well… mostly. The fracture is healed, and most of the neurological stuff has gone away… but…"

After waiting a decent interval of time, Nick completed the thought. "But not completely. You still have some aftereffects."

"Right."

Nick shook his head and continued to work. He refreshed several drinks, marking them on a tally sheet behind the bar so he wouldn't lose count.

"That's really horrible, sir. I'm sorry to hear it. I'm glad you're feeling better and healing, but…"

Matt nodded. "Yeah. Thanks." He picked up his drink, almost forgotten, and took a few swallows. It wouldn't take him long to get buzzed with the scotch.

"How did it happen?" Nick asked. "Do you mind me asking? You don't have a dangerous job, do you? I always tagged you for an accountant. Some desk job."

"It's not supposed to be dangerous. I'm an infectious disease expert for the Department of Public Health and Environment."

Nick blinked at the explanation.

"I track infection rates, watch for outbreaks," Matt explained.

"Like flu epidemics."

"Like that. Except my specialty is vector-borne disease."

"Vector…"

"Diseases carried by other species. Diseases that need to go through a cycle of hosts."

"Like the plague?" Nick's eyes got a little wider.

"Like the plague. Though I haven't seen any outbreaks of that lately."

Nick wiped the counter. "Good thing." He considered the explanation. "But who would attack you for that? Was it terrorism?"

"No. No, nothing like that. It was somebody… who was sick. He had a fever, hallucinations, and thought I was a threat. So he attacked me before I realized what was happening."

"That's horrible."

"Yeah, it really was," Matt agreed.

He sipped at his drink and thought about it for a while. Ever since he had been attacked, he had been minimizing it. He told himself it was only a bump. He told himself he would heal quickly. He thought when the bone had knit, he would be all better. He had minimized his sleep disorder, calling it 'this sleep thing,' promising people he would be healthy and sleeping properly again soon. Looking up insomnia tips like he was a restless college student who just needed to implement some better sleep hygiene and everything would be fine.

He didn't tell anyone, even Dr. Montgomery, how terrifying it had been. The attack. Being rushed to the hospital in a cervical collar, strapped to a backboard. Learning about the fracture and about the swelling in his brain. All the neurological symptoms, which the doctors and nurses assured him were 'minimal' and 'normal,' but to him were baffling and alarming. He had worried he would never recover. And when he had mostly healed, and sleep continued to be a problem, he began to fear life would never be normal again. Never again would he be able to lie down at a regular hour and just go to sleep like anyone else.

He had lost his health, his girlfriend, and his job; and he was still pretending to himself that next week things would be different. Next week he'd get a handle on it. Next week he would start sleeping again. Even if it were at the wrong time of day, at least he would find the pattern again.

It was time to stop pretending.

"It *was* horrible," he agreed. "And things aren't getting better anytime soon."

Nick looked sympathetic. He didn't offer any platitudes. He didn't tell Matt that he would be okay, or he was overdramatizing. The bartender was a skilled listener.

When Matt finished the first glass, Nick raised an eyebrow at him, checking whether he wanted another. Matt gestured toward it.

"You want to be careful," Nick warned. "Too many of those will go straight to your head."

"That's what I'm counting on."

"You won't be able to drive."

"I didn't drive here. I'll walk home."

Nick nodded and refilled Matt's glass. "Just take it slow. You're not usually a heavy drinker."

———

As the night progressed, Matt found himself more and more talkative, expounding at length on his sleep disorder and associated problems to anyone who sat down close to him. Most people had some kind of advice for him. Some simply moved further away.

"I'll tell you what you do," one man told Matt.

Matt waited for the suggestion to go to bed at the same time every night. Or to move his bedtime by fifteen minutes each night until he was going to sleep at the proper hour.

"You pop one of these," the pale, round-faced man told Matt, laying a light blue pill on the bar beside Matt's glass. "And you lie down, and you go to sleep. Just like that. Like magic."

Matt eyed the pill. "What is it? I've tried lots of sleep remedies."

"This one will work every time," the stranger promised. "Guaranteed."

Matt picked up the pill and examined it. "Prescription?"

His advisor shrugged. "You don't need a prescription to get them from me," he hedged.

"What's in them?"

"This is my own little proprietary formula. I compound them myself."

"And they will make me sleep?"

"Like a baby. Nothing to it."

Matt shifted. He looked up and down the bar. "I can have this one? To try?"

"Of course, my friend."

"And if it works…?"

"It will."

"And if it does?"

"You and I can work out an arrangement. To make sure you always have a stock."

Matt slid it into his pocket. "Imagine being able to sleep," he muttered.

"Every night," the man promised again. "Every night, the moment you choose."

"What's your name?"

"Why don't you call me… the Sandman?"

Matt frowned. "You live around here? How can I get a hold of you?"

"Not so fast. First you try the goods. When you are convinced as to their efficacy, then you and I can talk."

"Efficacy." Matt tried the word. He wasn't slurring, but the soft F and the sibilant S sounds pleased him. They were soft, crisp sounds.

The Sandman nodded and smiled. "Go home," he suggested. "Try it out. Then you and I will talk."

———

When Matt got home, he was afraid to try the pill. On one hand, he was desperate just to be able to lie down and go to sleep. But on the other hand, he was terrified it would fail. He couldn't bear one more failed sleep aid. It was like the whole world knew how to sleep except for Matt. The herbal pills might as well be grass clippings and the pharmaceuticals sugar pills. They did nothing but get his hopes up, only to dash them down again.

If the Sandman's pill failed too, what was he going to do?

Sandman had sounded so sure of himself. So confident. Surely he wouldn't have guaranteed success if he'd even thought it might not work.

But what did he have to lose? If Matt tried it and it worked, he had a new client. If Matt tried it and it failed, he was just out one more sugar pill.

It was Matt who had everything to lose.

Except he had already lost everything.

Eventually, he filled a glass with water, and standing over the sink, washed the tablet down without thinking any more about it. He didn't want to think of consequences or complications. He just wanted the magical sleep the Sandman had promised.

He walked to his bed and sat down, waiting for the pill to take effect. He automatically looked at the clock. He would only stay in bed for fifteen minutes and then if he wasn't asleep he would get up and do something else.

20

———

When Matt awoke, he lay in bed just thinking for a while. He knew something had happened but was too disoriented to be sure what. If he continued to lay there, it would all come back to him.

He felt hung over. Not just mildly nauseated, but completely wrecked, like he had been when he had binged as a teenager. His mouth was full of cotton and tasted like something had crawled into his mouth and died there. He was nauseated and his head hurt worse than it had after fracturing his skull. His stomach roiled with acid. Matt wasn't even sure if he could make it to the bathroom if he moved.

He had drunk the night before. That much was obvious. On further reflection, he remembered going to the club. The bartender had warned him about over-drinking, but Matt hadn't paid any attention.

At length, he remembered the Sandman and the little blue pill. He remembered sitting down on the bed and looking at the clock. He did not remember his head hitting the pillow.

It was like nothing he had ever taken before. And it worked. Matt didn't care if it was prescription or black market. It worked. That magical little pill held the answer to all his problems. Only next time, he wouldn't mix it with scotch.

———

Adams had obviously been watching for Duane to get home. As soon as Duane pulled his car into the carport—he actually ranked a parking space now—and started to unload the groceries, Rich was there, offering to help carry them in.

Duane was in a good mood. A very good mood. He had just finished depositing a check from the estate into his bank account. Never before had there been so many digits in Duane's account balance. He felt like he was walking on air.

"Get anything good?" Rich asked, poking his nose into one of the bags he was carrying.

"How would you like to taste the best chili recipe in the world?" Duane asked.

"Bean chili?"

"Uh-huh."

"Is it spicy?"

Duane nodded. "Sure."

Rich grinned. "I always did love a good spicy chili."

"Good. I'll show you how to make it. Easy as pie."

When they reached the house, instead of opening the door for Duane, Rich stopped, leaning his shoulder against the side of the house and breathing heavily. Duane juggled his grocery bags to open the door himself.

"Are you okay?"

Rich followed him in.

"Just not feeling so hot. Actually… I am feeling *really* hot." Rich put down his bags on the kitchen table and used the back of his arm to wipe his glistening forehead.

"You have a fever?" Duane asked, eying him for a moment before he started putting the groceries away.

"Yeah, I guess so. I just can't seem to kick this flu. The fever goes away, and I start feeling better and then a week later, the fever is back. My boss is getting irritated with all the sick time I've been taking." Rich shook his head. "I feel as weak as a girl. I gotta sit down."

He sat himself down on one of the kitchen chairs and breathed out heavily.

"Maybe chili isn't the best idea," Duane said. "Maybe I should make a clear soup."

"Oh, no." Rich waved this suggestion aside. "Really. Chili would be great. I know I shouldn't be imposing on you. Seems like I'm always down here sniffing around. But you can't know how much I have appreciated you making me stuff and showing me how to cook new things. I don't know what I would have done without you to lean on as a resource."

Duane nodded and continued to unpack.

"I used to think you were just a little wuss," Rich confessed. "I know there's no excuse for the way I acted. You're a good guy. I just thought... I dunno. I guess I grew up treating the smaller boys like they were... you know... feminine... I don't know where I learned that kind of thing. My dad. Other kids at school. You push the other boys around, establish your place, or you get eaten alive. I didn't want to be the one on the receiving end."

"No," Duane agreed. "Neither did I."

Rich's eyes were downcast. "No, I guess not. Who would? I know my behavior was inexcusable. We're not schoolboys anymore. We're men." He looked at Duane. "We're equals. I know I'm not any better than you."

Duane turned away to put the milk in the fridge and hide his smile. He knew he and Rich weren't equals. Duane was superior to Rich in all the ways that counted. Intellect. Wealth. Physical health. Rich's physical prowess was gone. Wiped out like he had never been a football player in school or lifted heavy at the gym.

A tiny tick, almost too small to be seen, and Rich's health and strength had been wiped out. And he would probably never have any clue how. Only Duane knew what he had done. And while with the right diagnosis, Rich might get some of his health back, he would never be the same again.

———

Matt paged through the new infection reports he had emailed to himself, able to take his time and study them now. Like with the previous reports, he tried to build a picture in his mind of what had happened. Each report was a story, and he attempted to fill in the blanks.

There were several cases that included alpha-gal allergy. Alpha-gal allergy had only recently come to the attention of investigators like Matt. Being allergic to a sugar instead of a protein was previously unheard of.

Wiping out nearly a whole food group had a huge impact on people's lives. They had to figure out a whole new diet.

Matt began to smile as he thought about the impact of this. The DOH would never be able to track down all the people with flulike symptoms, fever, rash, or joint pain. Many of the cases of tick-borne diseases would simply never be diagnosed or reported. Which made finding the root cause of this new outbreak much harder. But finding the people who were suddenly allergic to meat was more promising. There were places he could go to find them.

———

"We have a special guest tonight," Cara Honeybee announced.

People were eying Matt curiously, and he saw a couple turn aside to make comments to one another. It was a small class, but he hoped he would find a new subject or two there anyway.

"This is Matt from the Department of Public Health and Environment."

"Uh-oh," someone intoned. There were giggles around the room.

"Not to worry! He isn't here to investigate me! Matt has a particular reason to be interested in new vegetarians. I'll let him explain it to you. Since we don't want to lose any time during this discussion, I'm going to ask you to work on chopping the vegetables at your stations while he is speaking." She indicated the vegetables lined up at her own workstation. "Carrots, potatoes, etcetera. Small dice, please. Everyone work on that for the next few minutes."

She gestured to Matt. He stepped forward to the front of the room, behind her cooking station.

"Uh, hi. Good to see you all." Matt was not an accomplished public speaker, and he was nervous standing in front of the class, but he plowed on through his prepared speech. "Like Cara said, my name is Matt, and I'm from the DOH. A few weeks ago when you had your first class, Cara talked about reasons for choosing to be a vegetarian. There are a lot of reasons for making this lifestyle choice."

Cara nodded at him and gave him a smile.

"But one of the reasons you might not have talked about, a reason that's not so much a personal choice, is that you have developed a sudden allergy to red meat."

The class responded immediately with looks around at each other and whispered comments. Matt hoped it was a good sign.

"What you may be experiencing is alpha-gal allergy. A lot of doctors have not heard about it, so they may not have explained it to you. Alpha-gal is a sugar found in mammalian meats, and you can develop a sudden allergy to it after being bitten by a tick."

There were widening eyes and more whispered comments. The students continued to chop their vegetables.

"I would really like to talk to you if you've suddenly become allergic to red meat. You may not even know you were bitten by a tick. But we're seeing an increase in alpha-gal allergy. I'm hoping by talking to you, we can pinpoint the source of the vector."

"I thought you said it was from ticks," one of the men in the back blurted.

"Yes, it is from ticks, as far as we know. There could be other vectors as well, but ticks are the one we are aware of. With the increase in numbers of alpha-gal allergies, it is possible there has been an increase in the tick population in some small pocket of the city or a more resistant bacterial population in the ticks. That's what we're trying to find out."

There were nods from most of the students.

"Has anyone here experienced hives, vomiting, or anaphylaxis several hours after eating meat…?"

Three hesitant hands went up. Matt let out a slow, pent-up breath of relief. He noted their locations in the classroom and studied their faces.

"That's great. I'd like to arrange to talk to each of you. It would be extremely helpful."

———

Duane answered the knock at his door. It was Rich, of course, and he had a plastic bowl.

"Is it too late?" he asked. "Are you headed to bed?"

"No, come on in." Duane stepped back to allow him to enter. "You went to your class tonight?"

"We made curry." Rich offered, holding the bowl out to him. "You want to try it?"

"Yeah, sure," Duane agreed. He had learned not to eat too much the evening of Rich's 'Introduction to Plant-based Cooking' class, leaving room to sample whatever Rich cooked.

They went into the kitchen, and Duane put the bowl into the microwave for a minute. It was still lukewarm from the class.

"I hope it's not too spicy," Rich warned with a mischievous smile.

Without a word, Duane went to the sink and filled his pitcher with water. He got out a small bowl and a fork.

"Do you want any?"

"No, I've already had enough."

When the microwave beeped, Duane pulled the bowl out, and they both sat down at the table.

"We had a special guest at the class tonight," Rich offered.

"Yeah?" Duane put a mouthful of curry in his mouth and let the complex combination of spices flow over his tongue. He closed his eyes and savored it.

"Good?" Rich asked, as eager as a child to please.

"Mmm. Very good." After chewing and swallowing, Duane downed half a glass of water. "Very spicy, but very good."

Rich laughed, looking pleased with himself.

"So who was your guest?" Duane wondered if it was a local vegetarian celebrity or chef he would know.

"An investigator from the DOH."

"DOH?" Duane took another mouthful of curry. "Is that a cooking school?"

"No! An investigator. Like a scientist. From the Department of Health."

"Oh." Duane frowned. "Is there a problem with the class? Some kind of health violation?"

"No." Rich leaned forward eagerly. "He knows something about this meat allergy thing! I forget what he called it. He said you get it from tick bites!"

Duane struggled to keep his face impassive. He shoveled another spoonful of curry into his mouth, even though it was already burning up.

He started to sweat. He grunted, unsure what to say in the face of this revelation.

"He wants to interview me."

Duane choked. A hot piece of curry lodged in his windpipe, and he coughed, trying to get it out. Rich's eyes widened in alarm. He refilled Duane's glass.

"Do you want a drink? Are you okay?"

Duane coughed uncontrollably. He couldn't stop for long enough to take a drink. He inhaled more of the curry sauce, and it burned in his lungs. It was several minutes before he could dislodge the chunk of vegetable in his windpipe and calm the coughing. Even then, his lungs and windpipe still burned. He pushed the curry bowl away from him slightly. Wiping his teary eyes, he looked at Rich.

"You okay?" Rich asked again.

Duane nodded. He breathed slowly but shallowly, trying to avoid any more coughing.

"I'm really sorry," Rich said. "I wasn't trying to kill you!"

Duane nodded again. He cleared his throat. "So did you agree to meet with this guy?"

"Who? Oh! The DOH guy! Yeah, he wants to talk with everyone who has developed this allergy lately. See if he can figure out how they got it."

"But you were never bitten by a tick," Duane told him.

"Not that I know of," Rich admitted, scratching the back of his neck. "But he said you can be bitten and never realize it. Some of them are really tiny and you never even know they were attached to you. I guess maybe when I was hunting…"

Duane shook his head. "Seems like a scam to me," he said. "What does this guy want from you? I wouldn't give him any personal information."

A crease appeared between Rich's eyebrows. "You think so? I can't think of what he would get out of interviewing me."

"In my experience, government monitoring is never quite as innocent as it sounds…"

"Huh. I never thought anything of it… I already set up an appointment."

"You could cancel it."

"But don't you think… that would look suspicious? What reason would I give?"

Duane rubbed his throat. He coughed a little, trying to work the rest of the burning liquid out of his lungs.

"I don't know. Just say something came up. Put him off."

"He'll just want to reschedule."

"Tell him you're too busy. You'll call him when your schedule calms down."

Rich got up and got a glass and poured himself a drink of water from the pitcher. He was looking tired and drawn. Duane knew Rich still didn't have much energy following his infection. He really should be getting ready for bed.

"You really think I should blow it off? I was kind of looking forward to figuring out how I picked it up. Wouldn't it be good to find out where I got it and prevent other people from getting it?"

Duane shrugged. "Wouldn't the world be a better place with more vegetarians? Maybe it's the next step in human evolution. It's better for our health. For the environment." He eyed Rich. "Less violence and aggression."

The bigger man flushed a little. "So we just let everyone get bitten? I don't think forced vegetarianism is the answer to society's ills."

Duane pushed himself back from the table and started to clear the dishes.

"Maybe not. But I don't think it would hurt."

21

After Rich had gone up to his own room to sleep, armed with a few aspirin for his fever and aches, Duane found the DOH investigator's business card on the floor near where Rich had been sitting. He looked at it for a minute, held between two fingers, and then stepped toward the garbage can to toss it out. Rich couldn't very well follow up if he didn't have the investigator's contact information. Then Duane would be safe.

But he stopped with his hand over the garbage can. His eyes fastened on the name.

Matt Malloy.

The name was so familiar he froze, racking his brain to try to figure out where he had heard it before.

Matt Malloy.

Duane had remembered the investigator who came to discuss his own case as being from the CDC, but was that wrong? Was he from the DOH? Or had he moved from the CDC to the DOH? Surely people moved occasionally between the two organizations. How many places were there for a trained infectious diseases expert to work?

Duane closed his eyes. He pictured himself in the infirmary bed. He had been terribly sick. All his joints ached deep down inside. His head pounded. Even breathing had been difficult. And even worse was his mental state. He was sure he was losing his mind, and yet he knew what was happening to him. He experienced wild, frightening hallucinations. Even though he knew he was hallucinating, he still reacted to the visions as if they were real. He felt removed from himself, too distant to control himself. To stop himself from believing what he was seeing.

He envisioned the investigator being shown to his bedside by the doctor.

"Mr. Grant? My name is..." Duane strained to remember. He could put the words in the investigator's mouth now, but was he remembering correctly? Was his brain just happy to accept whatever information he provided to fill the holes? "My name is Matt Malloy. I'm an investigator with..." Duane could swear he had said the CDC. But at the time, he was weak. He was off his head. Was that just a detail he had filled in because it made sense to him after he had recovered?

"My name is Matt Malloy. I'm an investigator with the DOH. If you're up to it, I need to ask you a few questions."

Duane hadn't really been up to it at the time, but for weeks, he had been trying to tell his story to the officials. He had been trying to explain something was wrong with him. He was sick. They had made him sick. But they had refused to listen. Until both he and his roommate had been too sick to function.

Once given the opportunity, Duane had taken it, spilling out all the details, airing his grievances. The investigator had listened. He'd listened attentively to every word. He'd asked questions of his own, digging deeper.

Duane had been so glad to have someone finally listen to him. It didn't matter how sick he was, he felt better after being given the chance to tell his story.

———

"I'm sorry," the woman said pleasantly, "this is not a public building. If you want the DOH public building, you need to go over to—"

"I'm looking for an employee," Duane interrupted, thrusting the card toward her. "I need to talk to him urgently."

She looked down at the card and stopped protesting. "Matt. Did he make an appointment with you?"

Duane sensed she already knew he had done no such thing. "No, not exactly. Not now. I can't meet at the time we arranged, and it's urgent—"

"What do you mean, at the time you arranged? You *do* have an appointment to see him?"

"I do, but it isn't now. I tried to reach his phone, but I don't think it was connecting properly. I just kept getting silence when it should have been voicemail. Something misconfigured or glitched, I guess. But it's urgent I talk to him, so I thought I would come by here…"

"Matt isn't in."

"Oh… I guess he's out on another interview."

She looked like she wanted to answer him, but wasn't sure what she was allowed to say. "He's…" She looked around, frowning. "He's on leave. *When* did he make this appointment with you?"

What was an employee on leave doing making appointments with Rich and the other new vegetarians?

Duane was reluctant to answer. Something strange was going on.

"What's he on leave for?" Duane asked, taking a step back from her.

"Would you wait here for a minute?" she said, "I'll get someone who will talk to you."

Duane didn't answer. She backed away from him for a step or two, and then turned around and retreated down the long hall she had come down. Duane watched her turn down a corner out of sight. He knew instinctively she was going to get a security guard. She didn't believe Matt Malloy had made an appointment with Duane. She thought he was some kind of threat.

He fled before she could make any trouble for him.

———

Duane waited at a stop light, scowling to himself and trying to figure out what was going on. Why would that woman say Matt Malloy was on leave? It obviously wasn't true, because Malloy was out making contact with new vegetarians, looking for more people with alpha-gal allergy. The only other explanation was that Malloy was already onto Duane, and something Duane had done had tipped the woman off. Somehow, Duane had made her suspicious, and she had known who he was.

He had to stop Malloy. Things were going too well for Duane. Malloy could ruin everything. If he figured out what Duane was doing, Duane would be behind bars again. There would be no money, no respect, no good life.

Duane obviously wasn't going to be able to get a hold of Malloy through his office. They were too savvy. Malloy was already closing in. Duane was still holding the business card. He tossed it onto the car's dash, disgusted. The light turned green, and Duane moved his foot as he scanned to make sure the intersection was clear.

He stomped on the brake again, his eyes catching on the scribble on the back of the business card. He hadn't noticed there was anything on the back. He reached and grabbed it as the car behind him blew its horn.

Malloy had written his mobile number on the back of the card.

Duane released the brake and gently pressed down the gas, easing through the intersection at a snail's pace, driving the car behind him wild. The man hammered on his horn and followed Duane about two inches behind his bumper. Once they were across the intersection, the car pulled out into the other lane and pulled past Duane, tires screeching.

Duane could meet Malloy away from his office. Away from any security guards. As long as Malloy thought Duane was Rich, the man he had set up the appointment with, there would be no reason for him to be suspicious. As long as he didn't see Duane or recognize him as the man he was looking for. Duane would put an end to his investigation and preserve himself.

He wasn't going to go back to prison.

———

Matt glanced around the cafe but didn't see the man from the vegetarian cooking class. He breathed evenly, trying to keep his anxiety at bay.

"May I help you?" a girl who didn't look old enough to be out of junior high asked him with a perky smile. She had a stud through her lip, which Matt thought spoiled her fresh-faced schoolgirl image.

"A table for two," Matt told her. "I'm meeting a friend; it doesn't look like he's here yet."

Her eyes flicked over him, and she nodded, her tongue flicking out to lick her lips.

"Sure. This way." She led him across to the outside patio and selected a table in the shade. "How's this?"

"Great, thanks." Matt sat down. "Could I get a pitcher of lemonade?"

It was a hot day, and the pitchers he could see on some of the other tables looked perfect.

"Yeah, you bet," she agreed. She played with the stud in her lip. "How about some cookies? Our special today is a chocolate chocolate chip and pecan soft cookie."

Matt glanced nervously over his shoulder. "Uh… sure. Why don't you give me two?"

Hopefully, Rich Adams liked lemonade and chocolate chip cookies. Who didn't like chocolate chip cookies? Matt didn't bother asking if they were vegan. He had a feeling Rich wasn't vegan, since he'd only been forced into vegetarianism by his recently acquired alpha-gal allergy.

The girl left to get his order.

———

Duane watched Matt Malloy sit down. He had been afraid he wouldn't recognize the investigator he had only seen once while sick and hallucinating months earlier. But he knew Malloy as soon as he walked in. He heard the man's voice in his head much more clearly now. *My name is Matt Malloy. I'm an investigator with the DOH. If you're up to it, I need to ask you a few questions.*

Even across the patio, Duane could see the investigator didn't look well. He had aged several years. He had dark, puffy bags under his bloodshot eyes. He had lost weight. Had he come down with an infectious disease himself? Maybe his job had put him in contact with some pathogen, much as Duane's had. That would explain why the DOH woman had said Malloy was on leave. But not why he was investigating Duane. Duane felt a twinge of guilt over his plan. This was a man who had once tried to help him. Who was dedicated to his job despite being ill himself. He didn't deserve to be sick.

He waited while Malloy got settled. A couple of minutes later, the waitress brought him a pitcher of lemonade and cookies. Duane's mouth watered at the sight. Malloy wasn't a bad guy. He'd even ordered cookies for his meeting with Rich. If Rich had actually been coming, he would have been delighted by the treat. But Duane had to put all these thoughts aside. It didn't matter whether Malloy was a good guy, was already sick, or had a sweet tooth. Duane had a plan, and he needed to put it into action to protect himself.

Malloy looked behind him, then slowly scanned the patio. Duane turned his face quickly away. He had donned an amateur disguise, but he was afraid Malloy would still recognize him. He waited a few seconds, then cast another glance back at Malloy. He was no longer looking around. Duane got up and made his way across the patio. As he walked, he pressed the 'send' button on his text message.

On cue, Malloy pulled out his phone and looked down at it. It was almost too easy. As Malloy read the text message and composed a reply with his thumbs, Duane walked past him, surreptitiously shaking the opened specimen tube over Malloy's hair and neck. Malloy absently slapped at the back of his neck, but Duane knew the majority of the contents had ended up in Malloy's hair.

Now Duane only had to let nature take its course.

22

———

Matt looked at the clock and tried to decide whether to take one of the Sandman's magic pills. They were so powerful; it scared him a little. At least they had been when mixed with alcohol. Maybe if he didn't drink, they wouldn't be quite so strong. But then, maybe they wouldn't work. That possibility scared him too.

One benefit of being wide awake was he could go back to the DOH to download any new infection reports. He'd be more careful this time to just get in and get out, without allowing himself any time to fall asleep. No one would even know he had been there. He felt he was getting closer to an answer. And the more information he had, the likelier he was to solve the riddle soon.

The new vegetarians were a boon. Even though it caused him anxiety, he was excited about the opportunity to interview subjects previously missed. Only one of those he had found so far had been properly diagnosed and informed by her physician. The rest had all been dismissed or brushed off by their doctors and had no clue why they had suddenly developed an allergy to meat. They didn't have any idea they could still eat fish and poultry without developing a reaction to it. They just couldn't eat meats containing alpha-gal.

The one woman who had been properly diagnosed with alpha-gal allergy had not shown up on Matt's list, which meant her doctor hadn't bothered to report it to the CDC or DOH. It wasn't on the list of infectious diseases doctors were required to report, so most didn't, unless it showed up co-morbid with Rocky Mountain or another infection.

The phone rang, making Matt jump. He looked at the time before the caller ID, wondering who would be calling him so late. Not that it mattered when anyone called him; he was just as likely to be awake in the middle of the night as midday. Maybe more so.

It was Sharon. It had been some time since they had managed to connect. A few exchanged emails or texts, but nothing more personal. He tapped his phone.

"Hi, sis!"

"Hey, big brother. I gather I didn't wake you."

Her voice was good-humored. Not an emergency call like he'd feared.

"No, I was just trying to decide whether to take something."

"Oh… well, if you want to go to sleep, I'll let you."

"No, that's okay. I hadn't made a decision yet. I don't have to go to bed at any particular time. I don't have to be up in the morning."

"I guess since you're on leave…"

"Yeah. I'm trying to keep to a schedule, but I'm not sure it really makes any difference to my brain. It's supposed to, but…" he trailed off.

"Well, I hope you can figure it out soon. It really sucks, the way it's messed up your life."

Matt tried to swallow the lump that swelled up in his throat. After all the assumptions he was just lazy or slacking, it was a nice change to have someone just be understanding. He cleared his throat.

"Yeah. It does. So, you called because…"

Sharon laughed. "I couldn't sleep. So I thought: 'I know who to call!'"

Matt chuckled at this. "Yes, I can empathize."

"I was getting so frustrated, tossing and turning, so I got up. I'm too wound up to read or watch TV. Wanted to talk to someone. So I figured you might still be up."

"I'm glad you called." Matt pushed the bottle of pills across the table, away from him. He leaned on the table, getting comfortable, and listened to Sharon's voice as she rambled on about her day. It was nice to have someone to talk to. When his sleep schedule was off from the rest of the world, he felt so isolated.

———

After the call with Sharon, Matt was feeling buoyed up. He wanted to get on with the investigation. To do something productive. He decided he would make another trip to the office. He'd be more careful this time so he wouldn't get caught. He needed to keep a finger on the pulse of what was happening with the Buffalo Head cluster.

He could sleep when he got back. But he couldn't go to the office during the day. He had to do that while the building was empty.

There was little traffic on the roads, and Matt was sailing along, still cheered by Sharon's call, when red and blue lights sparkled in his rearview mirror and the whoop of a siren sounded.

Matt swore and pulled over to the side, hoping the police car would just continue past him, busy pursuing another car. Instead, the cruiser pulled in behind him. Matt banged his head down on the steering wheel. Brilliant.

When the officer tapped on his window, Matt took a deep breath and lifted his head. He rolled down the window, giving himself a mental lecture. It was just a speeding ticket. Not the end of the world. A few minutes and he would be on his way. He would pay the ticket online as soon as he got home and wouldn't have to think about it again. It was nothing.

"License and registration, sir," the police officer said in a flat tone.

Matt tried to get the requested documents out without fumbling. He knew the officer would be watching him for signs he was impaired and didn't want to do anything to make him suspicious. The cop shone his flashlight on Matt's hands and flicked up to his face, making him squint.

"I'm sorry, I didn't realize how fast I was going."

The officer took the license and registration and attached them to his clipboard.

"Have you been drinking tonight, sir?"

"No. I haven't had anything to drink."

"A beer or two?" he pressed.

"No, not anything. I'll blow if you want me to. I haven't had anything to drink tonight."

"You were going pretty fast."

He was filling in Matt's information at the top of the ticket, his printing slow and deliberate. He looked up at Matt every few letters.

"I'm sorry. It was a clear night, and I just got carried away. I didn't realize."

"You made some erratic turns and lane changes. Failed to signal."

Matt wrinkled his brow. "Did I? I… didn't realize."

"Where are you going so late?"

"I was actually going to stop in at my office for a few minutes. Just to pick up some things. For a meeting tomorrow."

"You were going to the office." The officer's name bar said 'Wilkins.' Officer Wilkins stared at Matt and shone the flashlight in his eyes again. "Do you have any idea what time it is? When is your meeting tomorrow?"

"Uh—um—" Matt couldn't come up with anything. If he said it was too early, Wilkins would know he didn't have time to get enough sleep before then. If he said it was too late, then why wouldn't he pick up his papers in the morning, instead of going out at a crazy hour at night to get them. "What time is it?" Matt asked, looking down at his dash clock. His eyes were still dazzled by the flashlight, and he couldn't make it out.

"It's two-thirty," Wilkins advised.

"Two-thirty. That is late, isn't it?"

"You still going to tell me you were going to the office?"

"I… was planning to… but that probably wasn't such a good idea."

"Have you taken any medications tonight? Any illegal drugs? Over-the-counter pills?"

"No. Nothing tonight."

Wilkins' lips pressed together. Matt swallowed. He wasn't handling the interview very well. He was starting to sweat, his forehead beading up and the back of his shirt sticking to him.

"Would you get out of the car, please. We're going to try a field sobriety test."

Wilkins opened the door for Matt. Matt got out and waited for instructions. The cop walked him through the field sobriety test. He frowned at Matt, brows drawn down.

"Would you please put your hands on the car… walk your legs back… hold there, please."

Matt was baffled as the officer frisked him. He didn't know what Wilkins was looking for. He should have known from the field sobriety test that Matt wasn't drunk. He hadn't asked Matt to take a breathalyzer test.

What was going on?

Wilkins methodically emptied each of Matt's pockets. His wallet. The bottle of pills from the Sandman. Matt's heart pounded hard as he realized those pills were going to be a problem. Wilkins made no comment on them, simply putting them on top of the car. He continued to work his way down, patting Matt for any concealed weapons or other illegal substances. He pulled one of Matt's hands down from the car and back behind him. He pulled the other hand around and clipped his handcuffs over Matt's wrists.

"Just come over to the curb here and sit down, sir. I'm going to perform a search of your car."

"My car? What for? Can you do that without a warrant?"

"You have unidentified pills on your person. You have bloodshot eyes and appear to be impaired. I have cause to search your vehicle."

He walked Matt around to the curb and sat him down. Cars were slowing as they passed, people staring out the windows at the spectacle. No one that Matt knew, but he was embarrassed all the same. He bowed his head so they couldn't see his face and waited while Wilkins went through the car.

Matt kept a pretty clean vehicle, so the search did not take long. Wilkins didn't seem to have discovered anything else suspicious.

"You want to tell me what the pills are?" he asked.

Matt swallowed and stared at Wilkins' shoes. "I don't actually know what's in them. They're to help me sleep."

"Where did you get them?"

"Um… from a friend."

"You can get sleep aids over the counter or from your doctor. These could be anything. How do you know how they're going to affect you?"

"I tried one… it helped me to sleep."

"So you'll take it even though you have no idea what's in it or whether it's an illegal substance."

Matt shrugged.

"Mr. Malloy, I'm taking you in for impaired driving. Please stand up and I'll read you your rights."

"I'm not impaired! I haven't had anything to drink, and I haven't had any of those pills. You didn't give me a breath test."

"I don't think you've been drinking. Maybe you had some of these pills, and maybe you've had something else. But you did not do well on the field test, and your eyes are bloodshot."

"I'm just tired."

"Tired can qualify as impaired. Lots of horrific traffic accidents happen because people were too tired to drive. We may run a blood test and we may not. Either way, the field test shows you are impaired."

He helped Matt to his feet and walked him over to the police cruiser. Matt looked at his car. "What are you going to do with my vehicle?"

"It will be impounded."

"Can't I call someone to pick it up?"

"No, it will be impounded. It will be searched more thoroughly. Maybe with a narcotics dog."

Wilkins opened the door of his police car and pushed Matt's head down as he got in.

———

If Matt could sleep, he might have thought he was having a nightmare. Everything seemed strangely removed and distant. The police station was quiet, but there were other arrestees being escorted in and out. Matt was searched again, changed into a uniform, booked and fingerprinted. He wondered if his bloodshot eyes would show up in his mugshots. He probably looked pretty dissolute, with the bags under his eyes and the heavy fatigue he carried with him.

He had expected them to put him directly into a jail cell. Or maybe they would take blood and *then* they would put him in a jail cell. But instead, he was put into one of the tiny conference rooms. There were three tubular metal chairs, a small round table more like a side table than a meeting room table, and nothing else. The walls were painted white. Numerous coats, from the looks of it, the surface marred by various dings, smears, and scratches.

It felt like hours passed, but there was no clock, and he had no watch or phone to check the time. All he could do was sit and stare at the walls, waiting for reprieve. Would he have to go to court? Would they allow him out on bail? Who would bail him out, if they did?

He should have just stayed home and taken one of the magic pills. Then he wouldn't have been pulled over and arrested. He wouldn't be sitting there by himself, with no sleep and no pills. He swore to himself aloud, because he needed to hear something other than the oppressive silence around him.

Finally, Officer Wilkins returned. He had a bigger clipboard now, not just the little ticket clipboard. There were a number of forms clipped to it, which he referred to as he sat down across from Matt as if he had to refresh his memory of what had happened that evening. Another man came in with him. A tall, gray-haired man in a suit rather than a uniform.

"Sorry to keep you waiting, Mr. Malloy," Wilkins apologized without any perceptible emotion.

Matt shrugged. What was there to say? It's okay?

"I'm surprised you didn't fall asleep while waiting. If you're so tired it's affecting your driving…"

"I can't sleep when I want to. That's the problem."

Wilkins nodded. "You said you didn't know what was in the pills you had."

"Right. They make me sleep. That's all I know."

"Oh, they'll make you sleep, all right. If you're lucky, they won't put you to sleep forever."

Matt looked at Wilkins' face, surprised. "Oh?"

"These are some very potent drugs. Usually, when we see something like this, it's in the bloodstream of a girl who was drugged and assaulted. What is called a DFSA."

Matt held up his hands in protest. Blood rushed to his face, hot, making him break out in a sweat even though the room was cold. "I wouldn't do anything like that. They were just to help me to sleep."

Wilkins stared into Matt's face for a long minute, then finally dropped his eyes back down to his papers.

"You've heard of GHB?"

Everyone had heard of GHB. It was synonymous with date rape. Matt nodded numbly.

"How about Etizolam?"

"No."

Wilkins' eyes were piercing. "Etties?"

"No. Never."

"Benzodiazepine?"

"Yeah. Something they use at hospitals. To calm patients down."

Matt thought fleetingly of the attack. The psychotic patient who had attacked him had been given some kind of benzodiazepine. Apparently some people reacted the wrong way, and it made them more agitated.

Wilkins sucked in his cheeks and nodded. He glanced over at the other man, still unintroduced, and then back to Matt. "Yes, they can be given to patients who are experiencing anxiety or who are violent. They are a tranquilizer."

"So they help you sleep, like I said."

"Yeah, they do. Etizolam is a fast-acting benzodiazepine. It acts quickly. Mixing that with GHB, which is also a nervous system depressant, is a very dangerous proposition. Especially with someone who has been drinking."

Matt thought back to the amount he had drunk the night he had taken the first of the Sandman's pills. He wouldn't do that again. No more mixing alcohol with sleeping pills.

"Your pills were mostly a combination of those two drugs. While either can be used to treat insomnia, no doctor would ever prescribe the two of them together. These pills were intended to knock someone out, pure and simple. Take too much or mix them with alcohol, and the girl— or you, if you're taking them for yourself—might never wake up again."

"I never used them on anyone else. I would never do that. They were just to put me to sleep."

"If you need something to help you sleep, you see a doctor," the gray-haired man said. "You don't take street drugs. These are prohibited substances. You've been charged with possession, but I think we could probably make all the charges go away and just leave you with the traffic violations, if you would give us some information on the guy who sold you these pills."

Matt shifted uncomfortably. "I... I don't think I can do that."

"You don't think you can? What kind of crap is that? You know who sold them to you. And you know the reason he's selling them is to facilitate sexual assault. Help us to put this creep behind bars."

Matt didn't know why the Sandman had made the pills. But he knew why the man had sold them to Matt. The Sandman had never suggested Matt use them for anything other than a sleep aid for himself. He had never suggested Matt use them on anyone else or for any other purpose. Maybe he did sell them to other people for that, but he hadn't seemed like that sort of person. Matt couldn't turn the Sandman in for just being helpful. Those pills were a lifesaver and Matt fully intended to replenish his supply once he was able. Now that he knew not to take them with alcohol, they would be safer.

"They are sleeping pills," Matt asserted.

"They are illegal."

Matt held his hands up in a shrug. "I can't turn him in. He didn't do anything wrong. It wasn't about hurting anyone. Just about getting some sleep."

———

Eventually, they had decided Matt wasn't going to give them any information about his supplier and put him in a cell for the night.

Matt was anxious about facing possibly dangerous cellmates, especially considering the attack that had caused all his problems to begin with. Who knew what another head injury would do to him. But when he got there, he found he had a cell to himself. There were others within talking distance, and the cells were tiny and cramped, but Matt was okay with that. He was safe from attack.

The immediate problem, once Matt sat down and calmed his panicked breathing, was boredom. There was no entertainment available. No books, no TV, nothing. Most of the other inmates were sleeping. Not all of them. Some of them paced or cried or yelled at the guards. But most of them were sleeping. Matt was pretty sure it was morning, late enough for the normals to be up, but still most of the cell block slept.

Eventually, Matt would be able to sleep. He wasn't sure what time his natural sleep cycle was going to hit, but without anything to stimulate his brain, surely he would be able to sleep, even to catch up on sleep, once the time came.

———

The arrival of breakfast confirmed the sun was up in the world outside the jail. The prisoners were all roused, and breakfast trays slid in through the delivery slot of each cell. Matt looked down at the rectangular divided plastic tray. There was a single frozen waffle with no syrup or toppings, some scrambled eggs he strongly suspected were reconstituted, and some coin-sized chips he supposed were hash browns. No ketchup, salt, or pepper.

Matt wasn't hungry, and the breakfast was far from appetizing, but he figured he'd better have something to eat. Maybe a boost to his blood sugar levels would encourage sleep. If nothing else, breakfast was the most interesting thing likely to happen for the next few hours.

"Hey," he called out, before the guard who was delivering the breakfasts could get too far away. "I didn't get a fork."

The guard looked back. He laughed. "Prisoners don't get forks."

Prisoners don't get forks? Matt looked down at his meal with new eyes. He was expected to eat scrambled eggs without a fork?

"But…"

"Just use your fingers," the guard advised.

Never mind there was no way to wash up in the cell. There was a toilet, yes, but no sink, fountain, or faucet.

"How am I supposed to…?"

"Eat it or don't eat it, I don't care," the guard growled. He walked on, ignoring any further attempts at reason.

"You know what I like to do?" the man in the cell next to Matt asked.

Matt looked over at him. He was a big man, bald head covered with ink. A biker maybe. Or just your run-of-the-mill murderer.

"Uh… what?"

"I like to make a sandwich with the waffle and eggs." Matt watched as he broke his waffle in half, and used the half waffle and his fingers to scoop scrambled eggs on top of the other half. He topped it with the first half of the waffle and showed the assembled 'waffle sandwich' to Matt with a smile. He was missing several teeth.

"You don't get your fingers so greasy, see?"

"Yeah… ingenious…" Matt agreed.

———

As the day wore on, rather than getting tired, Matt was starting to feel ill. At first, he attributed the rockiness in his stomach to the stellar jail food. No surprise the greasy, processed food would make him feel a little ill. He ignored it at first and focused his attention on the other prisoners. Since there was no TV, he had to find his entertainment elsewhere.

Throughout the day, the majority of the other prisoners slept. Matt thought back with nostalgia on the days he could lie down and have a brief nap in the middle of the day, on cue and without sleeping the entire day away.

There were other inmates who were more entertaining. People were brought in and taken out, sometimes in full shackles and chains. Sometimes yelling and fighting or weeping brokenly. Some of the prisoners in their cells did calisthenics or other exercises. Some conversed or read books.

Matt found himself sweating, though he was sure the temperature in the cell block couldn't have changed. When he moved around, he got giddy and more nauseated. Sweat started to drip down his back. He realized he was truly getting sick. Not just a little sick from the poor food, but some kind of virus was really starting to bother him.

The next time the guard went walking by on his rounds, Matt called out to him.

"Sir? Sir, could I get an aspirin and something for my stomach? I'm not feeling well…"

The guard stopped and looked him over. He looked unsympathetic. "You look all right to me."

"I'm coming down with something. I have a fever, nausea, joint pain. Don't you have something for flu you could give me?"

The guard shrugged. "We don't concern ourselves with little things like that. Lay down and sleep it off. You're here for a while."

"Here for a while?" Matt repeated. "Don't I have a hearing?"

"Court's backed up. A few days, I imagine. Why? You got somewhere to go?" The guard laughed at his own wit.

Matt couldn't claim he did. Even though he had an investigation he wanted to pursue and interviews he wanted to complete, including setting up a new appointment with Rich Adams, it wasn't like he had a job he needed to be at or a family to care for.

"What about a lawyer?"

"Have you *called* a lawyer?"

"Well… no."

"Do you *have* a lawyer?"

"No."

"Then don't waste my time," the guard growled. He walked on.

After a while, Matt did lie down and close his eyes, hoping he would be able to sleep it off. His body's immune system was probably shot because of his chronic lack of sleep. His head swam. The cell spun around him. The voices of the other prisoners and the guards came in and out of focus, seeming far away one minute, and like they were talking right in his ear the next.

He missed his supper. Matt didn't know whether they delivered it and he just missed the fact, or whether it wasn't brought to him at all. Not that it mattered, he wasn't going to be eating anytime soon.

The lights were not dimmed at night, or else his sense of time was completely off, and it was still day when he thought it was night. The voices around him quietened, except when a new prisoner was brought in from time to time.

He did sleep, but not soundly. Not REM sleep, but the feverish, disturbed sleep that went with being sick. He woke up once and vomited the remains of his breakfast, still sitting like a lump in his stomach, into the toilet. At least with the cramped space of the cell, he didn't actually have to get off of the bed to reach the toilet. He hunched over, waiting for the heaves to settle down. There were catcalls from some of the other prisoners, but the buzzing in his head blocked them out to a large extent.

In a more lucid period, Matt checked his body for a rash. Had he been bitten by a tick during his investigation? If it was Rocky Mountain Spotted Fever, it was too early for the rash to show up yet. It couldn't be Lyme. If it was tularemia, there wasn't likely to be any rash. But tularemia was rare. RMSF was far more likely.

He tried to turn his mind away from vector-borne diseases. Of course, that was what he thought of to begin with, but what were the chances he had contracted one? He always checked his skin, hair, and clothing after any field studies. He didn't go hiking for sport. He'd been isolated lately, rarely out of his apartment and not in any wooded areas. More likely it was just some kind of gastritis. It would work its way out in a day or two, and he'd be feeling better once he got out of jail.

Despite repeatedly assuring himself he didn't have a vector-borne disease, he kept dreaming he did, and his mind kept wandering back and considering the possibilities.

If it was a bacteria he'd picked up from a tick bite, he needed to get the proper antibiotics right away. The sooner it was treated, the less damage there would be. He didn't want to end up like the patients in the infirmary, their infections so advanced they were off their heads. Paranoid, delusional, having hallucinations while talking to him. And attacking him, seeing as a threat the one person who was able to help them.

23

Matt had no idea how much time had passed in the midst of the fevered nightmares. The only cues as to time passing were the meals slid into his cell and removed an hour or two later.

He awoke to hands on him. Someone in his cell. It was such a shock to have someone touching him he pulled away violently, crying out in surprise.

"He was complaining about being sick a while ago," a voice said. "He hasn't been eating his meals. He was scheduled for a hearing, but I couldn't wake him up and get him on his feet."

"I'm sick," Matt protested. "Leave me alone, I'm sick. Infectious diseases. I have an infectious disease."

"There, there, son. Calm down. Looks like you've got a touch of the flu. Just stay calm."

"Tick-borne diseases need treatment," Matt insisted. "Antibiotics. Stat. The longer you leave them, the more dangerous they are. People can die. Damaged forever."

"You sound like quite the expert on it." The doctor's voice, if he was a doctor, projected amusement.

"I am. Infectious disease expert."

"Then you probably know tick-borne diseases are quite rare. And you're not likely to contract one in jail, now, are you? There are no ticks here."

"Not in jail." Matt's mind went back to the men at the prison. Of course a person could contract tick-borne diseases in jail. Those men had been crawling with bugs. "Before. Incubation period could be weeks."

There was an electronic thermometer pressed into his ear. It beeped almost immediately.

"Well, you've got a real nice fever going there, don't you? Has this man had anything to drink?" There was a firm press on Matt's arm, then the pressure was released. "Look at that. He's very dehydrated. We've got to get some fluids in him right away."

"He's not eating or drinking," the guard said. "I don't know how you're going to force him."

"Not me. Let's get him transported to the hospital. They can put him on an IV."

"Antibiotics," Matt pressed. "IV antibiotics to treat the infection. Streptomycin or a tetracycline. Doxy. Doxy is the preferred course of treatment."

The doctor laughed.

"Antibiotics won't do a thing for the flu, my boy. But let's get you rehydrated and see if we can't do something about the fever. That will make you feel a lot better."

"Antibiotics for vector-borne diseases," Matt repeated. "Tests can show a false negative. If the hallmarks are there, treat anyway. Report to DOH. Try to identify the origin of the infection."

"Yes, I'm sure."

"The Buffalo Head cluster is exploding. They have to pay attention sooner or later. They can't keep sweeping it under the rug. What is the origin of the infection?"

Matt blinked and tried to get a clear look at the doctor and guard crammed into the cell with him. His eyesight was blurry but he could make out the guard's concerned look and the doctor's increasing consternation.

"Who is this man?" the doctor asked in a low voice.

"Matt Malloy," Matt told him. "Department of Public Health and Environment. Infectious diseases expert. Vector-borne disease division." He proceeded to give his phone number, address, and email coordinates.

There was only silence from the doctor and guard. Matt held his hands up in front of his face. "Any rash?" he asked, blinking and squinting at them, trying to will his eyes to see clearly. "Starts with a flat pink rash. Petechial spots don't show up until six days after fever…"

The doctor took one of his hands, and looked carefully at the palm, wrist, and forearm. "I don't see anything, do you?" He spoke to the guard, turning Matt's arm toward him.

"No. He's got a fever. He's off his head. It's just the flu, like you said."

"He does have a *high* fever."

"Exactly."

"I mean, with the flu, I don't know if it would be that high. A low to moderate fever, but…"

"Are you telling me you believe this nonsense?"

"He's an infectious diseases expert."

The guard shook his head in annoyance. "Look, do you really want to transfer him to the hospital? Because the paperwork is a bear."

"Yes. We can't rehydrate him here when he's not taking any oral fluids. And if it *is* one of these diseases he's talking about… he will need antibiotics. It won't just run its course like the flu. Not likely, anyway, with how ill he is already."

"Fine. I'll get started on the forms. You deal with transport and the hospital so they know to expect him." The guard started to leave the cell, then looked back over his shoulder. "Infectious diseases… that doesn't mean we can catch it from him, can we? I mean… do we need some kind of mask and gloves, or something?"

"No, zoonoses can't be transmitted from person to person," the doctor said confidently. "They need a tick bite to be transmitted."

"Tularemia," Matt interposed. "Tularemia doesn't require an intermediate host."

The guard and doctor exchanged looks. Shaking his head, the doctor took a pair of gloves out of his pocket and pulled them on.

———

Matt didn't remember getting to the hospital. He didn't remember anything until a day or two later.

When he awoke, he recognized the sights and sounds. He wasn't in jail anymore. That was obvious. He turned his head and found Sharon beside his bed, reading a paperback.

"Hey, Shar."

She lowered the book and looked at him. "Well, sleeping beauty. How are you feeling?"

Matt tested his body, moving as much as he could. But his wrists were in bed restraints.

"Uh, okay, I think. Fever's broken. Joints feel a lot better."

"Good."

"I guess you heard..." Matt looked down at the wrist restraints. "About the arrest."

"That's not why you're restrained," she informed him. "Your hearing was held in absentia, and I bailed you out. You're free. Those are because you insisted on getting up to talk to and treat all the other patients. You had the entire ward worried they had rabbit fever."

Matt laughed. "Oops. I was convinced I did. I remember that. I'll have to apologize to the nurses for causing a ruckus."

"Well, as it turns out, you did test positive. They've had you on antibiotics for a couple of days."

"I did have it? I do?"

"Yeah. And they've done all the reporting, which means some of your coworkers have been by to check on you and to demand to know where you picked it up."

"Oh. Well. That's awkward."

"Why?"

"Because... I don't know. I'm always careful. I shouldn't have gotten it, even if I was in an area with infected ticks..."

"I guess you didn't know you got bitten."

"Yeah. Who came by?"

"Carol. And someone a little awkward with a weird name. I can't remember..."

"Dewey?"

"That was it!" Sharon laughed.

"I'm surprised Dewey came. I guess I'll give Carol a call, if she doesn't come back."

"She's waiting for your call."

Matt was no longer in restraints when Carol arrived to interview him.

It was weird being on the other side of the clipboard. Matt couldn't count the number of interviews he had conducted, but he had never had to report an infection himself. He knew other investigators who had ended up with infections. He had always scoffed at them for not following the proper procedures that would protect them from tick bites. He knew investigators who didn't care about bites and didn't believe they would ever pick up an infection because they had hardy immune systems. He'd never been that bold, but he had always thought he could avoid infection by being careful.

"How are you doing, Matt?" Carol asked, sitting beside him and meeting his eyes.

"Well, all things considered… I guess I'm feeling all right."

"You were smart to figure out it was a tick-borne infection so quickly. You got treated fast. How did you know?"

Matt shook his head, bemused. "I don't really know. I had a high fever. I kept thinking it was Rocky Mountain or something, even though my symptoms could have just been the flu. I just… I don't know whether my brain knew what my body had on a subconscious level or whether I was just hallucinating and spouting random facts."

Carol laughed. "Well, whichever it was, it certainly worked in your favor, didn't it?"

"It did."

"I'm sure you must have been thinking this through, ever since you found out you tested positive for tularemia… can you tell me how you acquired it?"

The smile left Matt's face. "No. I've been thinking about everything I have done the last few weeks and I just can't put my finger on it. Any field work I did, I always wore long sleeves and pants and a hat. I always checked my skin and hair for ticks after. I suppose it's possible I missed a tiny nymph in my hair… but I did everything right. I can't figure it out."

"Have you been around any rabbits lately? Live or dead? Have you eaten rabbit?"

"No, no. Nothing like that. And even a squirrel or some other small mammal… there hasn't been anything. I didn't test any bodies. I didn't eat any wild meat." He wrinkled his nose at the thought.

"If you haven't been around any sick or dead animals, then it must be from a tick."

"It must be… but I still can't think of how or when."

Carol sighed. She filled in some of the boxes on her form, a small crease between her eyebrows. "Matt… there was somebody by the DOH the other day looking for you."

"Looking for me? Do you mean someone from head office or something?"

"No. I mean a civilian. Showed up asking for you by name. He had your business card."

Matt swallowed. He had been indiscriminately handing out his business card, writing his cell number on them, on the assumption a recipient would always call the handwritten number as the first point of contact. It never occurred to him someone would show up at the office.

"Well, that's kind of weird, isn't it?" he asked lightly, as if completely unconcerned. "Did he give his name?"

"No. I said I was going to go get someone to help and when I got back he was gone. It just all seemed very… unusual."

"I don't know who it was. Who knows how long he's had my card sitting around."

"He said he had an appointment with you. He had to reschedule and he couldn't get you on the phone, so he had stopped by."

It had to be Rich Adams. He was the only one who had missed his appointment. But he had texted Matt when he was at the restaurant. There wouldn't be any reason for Adams to show up at the DOH office looking for Matt.

"Huh." He didn't know what to say to Carol. He couldn't think of any excuse he would have for setting up appointments with subjects while he was on leave. She hadn't said she knew he set it up while on leave. He could have set it up weeks ago.

"Matt…" Carol couldn't seem to decide whether to look at Matt's face or at the clipboard. "You're coming back to the office to use your computer in the middle of the night. You're giving people your business card and making appointments to interview them. You *do* know you're on leave, right? You're not supposed to be working."

"I know. And… I guess maybe I'm at the point where I should just give up. But… I'm convinced this isn't just a natural, random cluster. It's an outbreak. And more than that…" He squirmed a little and looked away from her intense gaze, trying to figure out what to say. "I think… someone has intentionally altered the infection model."

Carol wound a strand of hair around her finger.

"What does that mean, *intentionally altered the infection model?*"

Matt didn't answer. Carol continued to wrap and unwrap the lock of hair around her finger, gazing at him.

"You think a person is intentionally spreading the infections," she said.

Matt nodded, and looked down at where his toes poked the hospital bedsheets up like two little peaked mountains. He waited for her argument, the laughter, the mockery. What he was suggesting was ridiculous. It wasn't easy to intentionally infect someone with a vector-borne disease. Even if a person tried, he was unlikely to be very effective. There was no way someone could infect enough people for it to even show up as a blip on the DOH's radar.

"That's… that's not possible, is it? You think somebody has weaponized the bacteria? It's theoretically possible for tularemia, but even then… and there's no way to weaponize Rocky Mountain or a lyme-like bacteria. You have to have the vector. How many cases of tularemia were reported?"

"Two. Plus mine, so three now. It's supposed to be extremely rare. Other than where more than one person has handled an infected corpse, you shouldn't find two cases so close together."

"And there may be cases that have been missed. Most doctors wouldn't ever suspect tularemia, much less test for it."

"Yeah."

"I know the cluster around Buffalo Head appears to be getting more dense. But is it? Or are we just paying more attention to it, so we're finding more cases?"

"How about the alpha-gal?" Matt said.

"What about it? It's not a reportable disease."

"But it is tick-borne. And there's been a big jump in cases."

"Again, you're looking for it. So you're going to find it. We don't have proper stats, because there's no tracking."

Matt nodded. He swallowed. "Yeah. I don't know, Carol… I'm tired. I know I should stop, and just leave it alone."

"Yes," she said gently. "You should."

"No one is going to listen to anything I have to say. And I can't get the data while I'm on leave."

"Do you have any reports that need to be filed because of your independent investigation?"

Matt considered. "No. Just new cases of alpha-gal."

"I really think you should just leave it alone. Let us take care of it while you're on leave. Just focus on getting yourself better."

"Uh-huh."

She smiled. "At least you've had some sleep, the last couple of days," she observed brightly.

"And all it took was a little tularemia and being tied to a bed."

———

Sharon had finished reading her book and she and Matt had exhausted all the usual topics of conversation. She moved around restlessly, looking for something else to talk about.

"Do you have deja vu," she asked, "being in hospital again?"

"It's kind of weird," Matt admitted. "I'm tired and still a bit rocky, but I'm not hurt. Last time… there was a lot of pain. And confusion. With my head injury… I didn't really understand what was going on a lot of the time. And I couldn't tell anyone what I wanted."

She nodded. "I remember. It was frustrating not knowing what you wanted."

"For me too."

"I would guess so."

She stared at the window for a few minutes.

"You've never talked about what happened."

Matt waved a hand. "You know what happened."

"No. Not really. Other than knowing you were hurt in the course of your investigation… and that you were at the prison infirmary… I don't know anything."

Matt chewed the inside of his cheek.

"Do you remember it?" Sharon asked. "I know they say with car accidents or big traumas, a lot of times the person can't remember what happened."

"I remember."

She leaned back in her chair, cocking her head to the side. "Do you mind talking about it? I'd like to know what happened. Besides being bored."

"You don't need to stay here. I'm fine. You probably have things to do…"

"I don't want to leave."

Matt considered. Finally, he shrugged. "Sure. Why not?"

He remembered checking in at the prison. He'd never been there before, so it was exciting and anxiety-producing all at the same time. He had to turn in all his personal items. Be x-rayed and searched for weapons. Then he was escorted to the infirmary.

It was just a small place, five beds or so. Any big emergencies were sent to the hospital. The infirmary was for minor injuries and illnesses. Run-of-the-mill stuff like the flu, fist fights, cuts and bruises.

"There are two cases," the warden informed him. "No one had any reason to believe it was anything other than the flu or some other virus. Or just plain goldbricking. We have an active service program, providing prisoner labor for the state. Prisoners are always deciding they're too 'sick' to be on work detail. We give 'em an aspirin and send 'em back out. Usually, they're fine."

"But these two cases were more serious."

"Grant, he's spiked a fever and has a rash. The other one, Menendez, his fever comes and goes. He's fine for a week, then gets it back again. I'd think he was faking, except the doctor has one of those in-the-ear electronic thermometers. You can't fool that."

"And there's no connection between the two men? They both came down with these illnesses without contact with each other?"

The warden stopped and looked at Matt. "They're roommates," he said, scowling. "You think one of them gave it to the other? Should we be isolating them?"

"If it's a vector-borne disease, then they didn't give it to each other. Though they might have picked it up the same place."

"What the hell is a vector?"

"An animal that carries a disease for part of its transmission cycle."

"An animal. You mean like rats? We don't have any rats in this building."

"More likely ticks, fleas, mosquitos…"

"Bugs. Why didn't you just say insect-borne diseases?" he grouched.

Matt bit his lip, refraining from pointing out ticks were not insects. The warden would not understand or care about the difference.

"Have both men been on the same work details? And attending all the same activities inside and outside the building?"

"Pretty much, yeah. Since they're roommates, they have all the same activity blocks. They may choose different activities during their free time, but otherwise they'll always be in the same place, doing the same thing."

Matt nodded. "And what was it that made you think this might be a vector-borne—an insect-borne—disease? You contacted the DOH, so something must have made you think about the possibility it was transmitted by insects, rather than just being the flu."

They walked on. The warden scratched at his short-cropped mustache.

"It was Grant, I guess. He's the one who kept complaining about bug bites. Then when he got the fever and rash… to be honest, he's been paranoid, ranting we infected him with Lyme disease or West Nile. He's a complainer. Couldn't get him to shut up about it, so we finally decided to just… get someone in to rule it out."

"He was complaining about bug bites. When?"

"For weeks. Everybody on work detail gets bug bites. The guards get bug bites. He's just a sissy about them. No one else was complaining."

"What kind of bites was he complaining about? Mosquitos?"

"Everything. Mosquitos. Flies. He said we had bed bugs. Something in the bedding. Ticks. I don't know what else."

"Did he have any confirmed tick bites?"

The warden shook his head in irritation. "Like I said, everyone on work detail gets bites. If they have ticks attached, we send them to the infirmary to get them removed. The doc knows how to do it properly. Done in five minutes and they can go back to work."

"Does he send the samples in for testing?"

"What samples? Testing for what?"

"The ticks he removes. They're subject to mandatory testing. Does he send them in to the CDC and make the proper infection reports?"

The warden frowned at him. "I don't know what the doctor does. That sounds like a lot of extra work to me."

"It may be work," Matt said. "But it's necessary. That's how we keep track of any outbreaks and keep the public safe."

"These boys aren't the public," the warden growled. "They're out here for a reason and they're not infecting anyone else. If they pick up a virus from a mosquito, you think anyone cares?"

"It's mandatory reporting," Matt said firmly. There was no point arguing reasons with the warden. Mandatory reporting was mandatory reporting. Matt didn't have to justify it.

In a few minutes, they had reached the infirmary. The warden let him in through the series of locked doors and introduced him to Doctor Sikes, the physician on duty. The warden then excused himself and made his escape.

"So, you think your patients might have a tick- or insect-borne disease?" Matt suggested to him.

"Me? No, I don't think so. It's the prisoners who are making all the racket. The warden figured the only way to shut them up was to get an investigator in here to prove them wrong."

"Okay. Symptoms?"

"Grant, he's got a high fever and a rash. A virus of some sort, probably."

"The warden said he was showing signs of paranoia? Any other mental health symptoms? Or sore joints?"

"That one *came* with mental health issues. We've got more than enough to go around. Yeah, plenty of complaints about sore hips and knees especially. Stiff neck. Backache. Everything he can think of."

"And he thought he got sick after a bug bite?"

"Ever since the first day he was on work detail, he was complaining about bug bites. He's one of them that seems to smell sweet to bugs. They're attracted to him. We get some men who work outside all day and don't get a single bite. Then you've got babies like Grant who come back, their tender skin covered with bites." Sikes shrugged. "Mostly mosquito. Certainly nothing he's going to die from."

"Did he have any tick bites?"

Sikes appeared to be considering it. "Yeah, he probably has. They've had the boys clearing a wooded lot we're going to put some additional buildings up on. The place is full of ticks."

Matt jotted a few notes on his form. "How are they dressed on work detail? Are they in long sleeves and pants? Hats? Pants tucked into their socks?"

"They have long sleeves and pants. Most of 'em will tie the arms around their waist to stay cool. It's up to them. No hats. Socks… a lot of them don't wear socks. Just bare feet in tennis shoes. It's cooler. They're not provided with steel-toed boots."

Matt shuddered at the thought of all the prisoners being sent into a tick-infested bush with bare arms, heads, and feet. And they probably rolled up their pant legs to keep cooler. All that bare flesh calling to the ticks and blood-sucking insects.

"We're going to need blood samples and throat swabs of both men. If it is a tick-borne bacteria, which it sounds like, they're going to need antibiotics immediately. I'll give you the protocol. You should start treatment immediately; don't wait for the tests to come back."

The doctor rolled his eyes, but he nodded. "All right."

"Great. Okay. I'll talk to the patients, now."

"Start you with Menendez," Sikes said. "He's the one who's got a recurring fever. Not a lot of other symptoms, but this fever knocks him out every week or two. I'd think he was loafing if it wasn't for the thermometer."

Sikes took him to the bedside of a tall, slim Mexican. The man's eyes were bright with fever. Sweat beaded his forehead. He had an IV drip.

"Mr. Menendez. My name is Matt Malloy. I'm an investigator from the Department of Public Health and Environment."

He hesitated. This was where he usually shook hands, but he didn't particularly want to shake Menendez's hand and he wasn't sure it would be allowed. The man just nodded his head.

"I understand you have a recurring fever."

"Yeah, that's right," Menendez agreed.

Matt was surprised he could hear no trace of a Mexican accent in Menendez's speech.

"Where are you from?"

"New York."

"Oh." That explained the lack of accent. "When did this fever first start? Can you identify the first time?"

"More than a year ago. What's it to you?"

Matt ignored the animosity in Menendez's voice. A lot of people were suspicious of government investigators, no matter what branch of the government they were from. It wasn't unusual for subjects to be a little anxious about being interviewed.

"I'm looking into where and when you might have picked up this illness," he explained. "If I can identify it, we can get you the proper treatment, so you start to feel better."

"Ain't nothin' wrong with me," Menendez asserted.

"So, other than the fever, you're feeling fine?"

"I am fine."

In watching him, though, Matt was already picking up on other signs. Menendez's facial expressions were asymmetrical. Like he might be experiencing Bell's Palsy. And he kept turning his head and rubbing the back of his neck.

"Do you have a headache?" he asked.

Menendez continued to rub his neck and the base of his head. His eyes were dilated. "It's killing me," he said. "Feels like my damn head is ready to split open."

"Do you mind if I make a brief physical examination?"

Menendez shrugged, but as soon as Matt got started on the examination, his attitude changed. He shoved Matt back, bellowing an objection.

"You can't touch me! Nobody can touch me!" he insisted.

Sikes had been tending to other patients and moved closer to Matt. "Best not to get too close," he warned. "This one tends to get violent. I'll give him a sedative if he gets too worked up. I wouldn't touch him if he objects to it."

"Have you noticed any other symptoms? Neurological? He doesn't have a rash?"

"No, all I've seen is the fever. And being damn hard to get along with."

"Mr. Menendez," Matt tried again. "Have you had any tick bites while you've been here?"

"Course I've had tick bites. But I know how to take them out. Got plenty hiking around New England before I came here."

"When you were in New England, did you ever... get tested for Lyme disease or any tick-borne diseases?"

"Do I look like a weakling milksop like *that* one?" Menendez demanded, jerking his head to indicate the man in the next bed. "I don't get sick."

"How long have you been here?"

"Moved to Colorado 'bout nine months ago. Been here in lockup... I dunno. Six months?" He looked at the doctor as if expecting him to provide the information.

The doctor shrugged. "Maybe," he said unhelpfully.

Taking the doctor's advice not to press Menendez too much, Matt went to the man in the next bed. Grant. He was a small, skinny man. So pale he was almost grey. He turned his gaze as Matt approached.

"Mr. Grant? My name is Matt Malloy. I'm an investigator with the DOH. If you're up to it, I need to ask you a few questions."

"Questions?" His voice was weak. "What kind of questions?"

"About your health." Matt stood at the side of the bed, not too close to Grant, having learned his lesson from Menendez. "The warden said you had some complaints. About tick and insect bites."

Grant lifted his head slightly to look at Matt, then settled back again. "They make us work outside," he whined. "We come back covered with bites and ticks. All over." He turned his head to look toward Menendez. "We have to check each other. Remove any we find. But if you miss just one... they can be tiny, look like a freckle... and then they make you sick."

"Not all ticks carry infectious disease," Matt said. "Only a few of them will actually carry a bacteria that makes you sick. Most won't have any effect."

"Does this look like no effect?" Grant indicated himself. He obviously knew how bad he looked. "And all that stuff..." he waved his hands to indicate the rest of the room. "Does this look normal?"

"Does... *what* look normal?"

"The ghosts? The weird noises? Everything keeps appearing and disappearing. Changing. Even you. I don't know if you're real or if I'm dreaming you again."

Matt studied Grant. He could be shamming. He could be trying to make Matt and the doctor think he was worse off than he was.

Grant's eyes did not stay on Matt, but flickered frequently around the room.

"How long have you been hallucinating?" Matt asked.

"I don't know. Before they put me in here. I kept telling them I was sick. They just kept giving me aspirin and telling me to work." Matt nodded, encouraging him to continue. Grant seemed happy to have someone listen to him. "They kept sending me on work detail. I was almost too weak to stand. Fainted, and they just threw water over me and told me to get back to work."

"Can you describe your other symptoms?" Matt didn't want to feed them to him. He had a feeling Grant would admit to having any symptom Matt suggested.

"So sick… thought I had the flu at first. Aching all over, but especially my joints. Fever. Weird rashes that came and went. Head hurt so bad."

Matt made notes on his interview form. "Anything else?"

"The food makes me sick. Someone is poisoning it. I eat and then I get hives. My throat starts to swell. I throw it all up."

Matt pursed his lips. "Right away or is there a delay?"

"A few hours. But it's the food. It's always after I eat."

"The doctor, does he think it's an allergy?"

"He gives me antihistamines and the hives go away. He says if my throat was swelling, I wouldn't be able to breathe. It's the meat. The meat is bad."

Matt noted 'alpha-gal' with a question mark.

"What kind of rashes have you had, other than the hives?"

"It's from the bugs. I know it's the bugs. He—" Grant jerked his head toward Menendez again. His eyes were wide. "He put bugs in my ears while I was sleeping. I could feel them crawling around in there. I'd wake up and be covered with bites…"

Matt moved closer to him.

"What lies are you telling now?" Menendez shouted. "I'm gonna come over there and—"

"Behave yourself," Dr. Sikes growled from the other side of the bed.

Matt glanced over his shoulder. Sikes stepped closer to Menendez and injected a syringe into the man's IV port, staying carefully out of reach.

"We'll see how you like that stuff," Sikes sneered. He watched Menendez for a minute. As Menendez's eyes shut, he gave Matt a nod.

"He shouldn't bother you." With that, he disappeared through another locked door. Matt was alone with the patients, other than a guard at the far end of the room. Matt took a quick look at the other beds, but didn't see any threat.

"What kind of bites did you get?" Matt asked. "The warden said you thought there were bedbugs."

Grant scratched his arms. "The place is crawling with bugs," he insisted. "Just look at the sheets!"

Matt only glanced casually at the sheets at first, but Grant was insistent, plucking at them.

"Look! See for yourself!"

Matt bent closer, squinting at the dingy bedsheets. As he looked, he saw what he had originally taken for dirt and grit on the greying sheets was moving of its own accord. His stomach twisted in revulsion as he reached out a finger and watched the infinitesimal fleas and ticks jump and scuttle away.

"It's crawling with them!"

That was when the first blow fell. A crushing blow to the back of Matt's head. It didn't knock him down, but left him paralyzed with shock, unable to protect himself from the repeated blows. The guard shouted out a warning and called for help. Menendez was yelling, ranting paranoid delusions. Before the guard could get close enough to help, more blows had fallen, and Matt was headed for the floor, bouncing off of the infirmary furniture on the way.

There was chaos around him. Menendez shouting, Grant shrieking for help from the bed, the noise of other guards and of Sikes running back into the infirmary. Matt lay on the floor, unable to move or process any of it. His head throbbed and he couldn't speak or get himself up off of the floor.

Sikes knelt beside him, initially trying to pull him to his feet. Then, realizing the severity of Matt's injuries, he immobilized Matt's head and ordered the guards to get an ambulance.

Matt hadn't realized Menendez, not sedated but with a paradoxical reaction to the tranquilizer the doctor had given him, had gotten out of bed and approached him from behind. While Grant was the one they had identified as being paranoid and psychotic, Menendez was the violent one. He had decided he didn't like Matt poking around asking questions.

"But why did he hit you?" Sharon asked Matt.

Matt shook his head. "They both had Lyme disease which had not been treated, possibly for months. It affects the brain, something like syphilis. Who knows what he thought, why he thought he should attack me?"

"Isn't Lyme disease the one you told me doesn't exist in Colorado?"

Matt nodded. "These cases will skew the stats. Menendez must have picked it up hiking in New England. And he transmitted it to Grant."

"But you can't transfer Lyme from person to person. Isn't that right?"

"It hasn't been proven to be transmissible from person to person. There is speculation about intimate contact..." Matt shrugged uncomfortably. "They *were* roommates. But that prison was crawling with ticks and fleas and other possible carriers. It's possible a tick bit Menendez, was infected with the Lyme bacteria from him and then weeks or months later, fed on Grant and passed it onto him. Lyme still isn't in the Colorado wild, but it was in that one closed environment."

———

Matt's visitors were gone, and he would have been bored to death if Sharon hadn't brought him his laptop. The hospital had good wifi, so he was able to access his email and keep busy and occupied.

Now that he was no longer investigating the Buffalo Head cluster, he decided to get caught up on recent research. There was nothing wrong with him reviewing scientific papers while he was on leave. He wasn't interfering with the DOH, just keeping himself current.

He logged into his aggregator and started to read through the abstracts of the papers. Research, speculations on transmission, trial drugs to be used as vaccines or treatments against vector-borne diseases. Research in the field was really taking off.

Matt read the abstract about a fascinating case of alpha-gal allergy. He brought up the full text of the document and read through all the information the doctor had reported. Looking up at the header of the report, he realized the doctor was in Denver. Matt glanced over at his phone. Calling the doctor to discuss new implications of alpha-gal allergy would be a good distraction. And it was professional development. Information his department should have.

It was evening, and he expected to have to leave a message. He talked to the hospital switchboard, and they put Matt through to the doctor's office phone.

"Hello?"

Matt was so startled to hear a live voice when he was mentally preparing his voicemail message that he just about dropped the phone.

"Hello?" the voice repeated sharply.

"Uh, hello. Is this Dr. Burk?"

"Yes."

"I didn't expect to get you. Uh, my name is Matt Malloy, and I'm an investigator with the DOH."

"DOH? What do you want?"

"I'm calling about a paper you published on a patient with alpha-gal allergy."

"Alpha-gal is non-reportable."

"Yes, of course. I'm not calling about failure to file reports. I'm just interested in the case."

"Oh. Well." The doctor's voice became less strained. "It *is* an interesting case."

"I wonder if you would mind just running through the details with me. I've read your paper, but there's always things you can't include."

"Certainly. I think all the relevant details made it into the paper. Grant was brought in by ambulance in full anaphylaxis—"

"Grant?" Matt repeated, his stomach feeling both hollow and heavy at the same time.

"The patient," Dr. Burk said impatiently. "Grant."

"Sorry. His name wasn't in the paper, and it just took me off-guard. I also had a subject with alpha-gal allergy named Grant."

"Well, he wasn't the same Grant, or he would have been dead."

"Sure. Of course. There are lots of people in the world named Grant. It just threw me."

"The patient's name was Duncan Grant," Dr. Burk announced, irritation clear in his voice.

Matt struggled to remember the name of the man he had talked to in the prison infirmary. Duncan was close, but not quite. He closed his eyes.

"Okay, yeah. Mine was..." Matt sighed in frustration. "It started with a

D as well." He flipped through boy's names starting with D in his mind. Then it came to him. "Duane. I think it was Duane Grant."

There was silence from the doctor.

"I'm sorry, doctor. Please continue, I won't interrupt again."

"Duane Grant? My patient's next of kin was Duane Grant."

24

Jared had come to visit Matt, and at Matt's request, had dragged Dewey along. His voice had taken on a curious tone when Matt asked for Dewey, but he was too polite to ask why Matt wanted Dewey to come. None of them were really friendly outside of the office, and of the group, Dewey was the nerdiest and least social.

"Hey, thanks for coming!" Matt greeted.

"How's it going?" Jared offered Matt a fist-bump and Matt obliged. Dewey just stood there.

"Hi, Dewey."

Dewey nodded.

"So, what's up?" Jared asked. "I got the feeling you were working on something. You're not still on this Buffalo Head cluster, are you? Carol said you were going to leave it alone."

Matt didn't answer directly. "What do you guys know about alpha-gal allergy?"

They exchanged glances.

"You didn't get alpha-gal too, did you?" Jared asked. "I know you got tularemia, but Carol didn't say anything about alpha-gal."

"No, no."

"It's an IgE-mediated allergy to alpha-galactose," Dewey offered.

"Mechanics still unknown, but believed to be spread by the saliva of ticks."

"Right," Matt nodded. "What would you say if I told you I had a case of two brothers with alpha-gal allergy?"

"First I've heard of. But it's not out of the realm of possibility. Two kids playing in the same wood would both pick it up. They could even be playing a game that encouraged infection, like… I don't know, sword-fighting each other with infested sticks or making crowns out of leaves or grass."

"Adult brothers," Matt filled in. "Not living in the same household. They both acquired alpha-gal allergy a year apart."

Dewey started pacing, scratching the back of his neck with his ear pushed against his elbow. He grimaced, making pained-looking faces as he thought it through.

"There could be a genetic component. Recessive, probably. A predisposition to developing the allergy if exposed to the trigger." He paced back the other direction. "We know there is a genetic component to food allergies. Children start with a twenty percent risk. With one parent with food allergies, it doubles, and with both parents with food allergies, it's all the way up to sixty or seventy percent." He paced back again. "Let's say you or I get bitten by the right kind of tick. Say we have a twenty percent risk of becoming allergic. You get a half dozen bites, and the odds start to stack up, but not until then. But your subjects, they have a genetic predisposition from mom or dad or both. And then all it takes is one or two bites."

He stopped and looked at Matt.

"I see why you needed Dewey," Jared laughed. "But here's the thing. I thought alpha-gal was only caused by the Lone Star tick. And we don't get Lone Star here."

"Lone Star tick has been identified as one carrier," Dewey said. "But the phenomenon extends to areas outside the Lone Star's range. Alpha-gal must also be carried by another species of tick or another vector altogether. Any vampiric species could conceivably cause it, since we don't know the mechanics yet."

"Do you think it is caused by a bacteria?" Matt asked. "Or some other component in the saliva?"

"Borrelia miyamotoi has been implicated, but that's a long way from proof. It could be something other than bacteria. Antibodies the tick develops when it feeds on mammal blood. Anticoagulant. Who knows."

"What other effect does miyamotoi have?"

"Lyme-like disease. EM rash, relapsing fever."

"Like Menendez," Matt mused.

"What?" Jared looked at him.

"No, nothing. Just trying to figure this out…"

"Your brothers don't know where they got it?" Dewey asked.

"One of them apparently got it in prison, either on work detail or from an indoor infestation. The other is a blank. We don't know."

"Have you interviewed him?"

"Dewey…" Jared warned.

"What?"

"I told you on the way here not to ask anything that could get Matt in trouble."

"Oh." Dewey looked at Matt and then away again. "I didn't know it could."

"It's okay." Matt gave Dewey a reassuring smile. "As it turns out, I did not interview him. He's dead."

"What?" Jared demanded.

"He had a porcine heart valve."

"And he became allergic and rejected it," Dewey deduced immediately. "What a way to go. I'd like to read the report."

"I'll email it to you. So do you think that's all it is? A genetic predisposition and then being unlucky enough to be bitten?"

"What else would it be?"

"Well… I actually wonder if the surviving brother, the one who got it in prison, if he intentionally or unintentionally infected the one who died."

"How?" Dewey demanded. "Alpha-gal is not spread by person-to-person contact."

"He'd have to have a carrier tick," Matt mused.

"How would he get one? And how would he know it was infected? Once he had an infected tick, how would he pass it on to his brother? And why?"

"I don't know," Matt said. He shook his head. "I'm trying not to get involved in it, but it's such an intriguing situation…"

"How would you weaponize ticks?" Dewey asked. Behind the lenses of his glasses, his eyes were far away. He too found the case fascinating.

"Well, if you're trying not to get involved, then what are we doing here?" Jared asked. "Come on, let's talk about something else."

———

Laying the case to rest was the last thing Matt was going to do. He didn't know whether Duane Grant had anything to do with the Buffalo Head cluster. It was unlikely; he wasn't exactly the sharpest knife in the drawer. But Matt strongly suspected Duane Grant had something to do with his brother's death. The odds Duncan Grant would just happen to contract alpha-gal allergy with no obvious source of infection were so astronomical, Matt couldn't accept it as a coincidence.

Matt was released from the hospital. When he got home and got his computer plugged in, he immediately started to run background on Duane Grant and his brother Duncan.

Matt looked for an obituary first. He wanted to confirm Duncan Grant and Duane Grant were brothers, and the names weren't just a bizarre coincidence. Matt could have remembered his name wrong. The doctor might have remembered the next of kin's name wrong. It might be nothing at all.

He got hits on a search of Duncan's name. A dead artist in Britain. An elderly twin in Toronto. A man in Pennsylvania. But nothing that matched up with the dead Grant brother in Colorado. Matt tried other search terms, but could find nothing on Duncan Grant's death. Eventually, he just looked for any background information on Duncan. He was a chess champion. He was a CMA. There was no mention of him being married, which matched what the doctor had said. There had been no spouse or children or even parents, just a brother. Just Duane Grant.

There wasn't much on Duncan's social networks. Matt found a couple of five-year-old pictures, but nothing recent. Nothing that showed any current relationships. Maybe a girlfriend or a coworker. He seemed to live a solitary life, doing nothing but working or playing chess when he wasn't in front of the TV or sleeping at home.

After some more fruitless searching, Matt went to his email and searched for Duane Grant's name. He tried alternate spellings in case

Duane was Dwayne, or he had remembered Grant when it was really Brandt. But it turned out there was nothing in his email with Grant's name on it. He couldn't remember how to access his work email remotely, and he had never mentioned Duane's name to anyone in his personal email. Why would he? Duane was just a guy, an interview suspect. A convict. Matt hadn't wanted to humanize him. He didn't want to feel sorry for the guy, being bullied or abused on work detail. Forced to spend all his spare time with Menendez. Getting sicker and sicker because nobody would believe he had truly contracted a disease from the rampant vermin on the prison grounds and in his bed.

The only way to be sure of Duane's name was through the DOH office. Matt considered what would be the quickest, easiest way to get confirmation of the name. Eventually, he called Carol. Late in the day, when the administration was leaving for home and Carol was still working a few extra minutes to try to stay caught up on the work accumulating in Matt's absence.

"Hi, Carol."

"Matt!" She paused for a moment. "You're at home. Are you feeling pretty good? They didn't send you home too early, did they?"

"No, I feel fine. Just about back to normal. As normal as I'll get, I mean."

"Yeah," her voice was soft. "As normal as you can be."

Matt laughed as if he was fine.

"So what can I do for you?" Carol asked. "I can take a short break to talk, but I have some reports I have to clean up and get filed."

"I need you to look up a name on a report for me."

"Matt… you know I can't do that."

"No; no, you can. It's information I have access to or had access to already. I just want confirmation I remember right."

Carol didn't say anything, and Matt could picture her look of distrust.

"I promise, Carol. All I want is the name of the patient I was interviewing at the prison before I got attacked. I think it was Duane Grant."

"Mmm." He could hear Carol's keyboard clicking and waited to see what she would find. There was silence for a few minutes and he didn't push her. He just waited.

"Your recollection is correct," she said finally.

"Great, that's a big help. Thank you. You don't have any personal information on him, do you? Next of kin? Where he would go when he was released? I don't even know what he was in for or how long."

"Why would you need to know any of those things?"

"Just curious. Dr. Montgomery says I have PTSD as a result of the attack, you know. Maybe if I found out some more information on what happened to those two prisoners, it would help me to sleep better."

He hoped he didn't sound as full of crap to her as he did to himself. She would know it didn't have anything to do with PTSD, which he didn't have.

"We don't have anything like that," Carol said with a sigh. "You'd have to go back to the prison or some government agency. And chances are, they wouldn't tell you a thing. Privacy laws and all that."

"You're probably right," Matt agreed. "Thanks. I just wondered."

———

There were a lot of sites offering to do background checks or criminal conviction checks for free. But each one Matt went to still required an account and credit card number. He was loathe to leave any that footprints he'd been searching for information on Grant. He did find a DOC website that allowed him to search for whether Duane Grant was still in custody of any correctional facility. In ten seconds he had confirmed Duane was no longer incarcerated.

Playing around with some other searches, he found a couple of sites that offered matching records with the subject's age, recent residences, possible relations, and current zip code. Matt couldn't get any further information without giving them his credit card, but he noted down the information he found. There was a Duane Grant in Colorado with a possible relation named Duncan Grant. That wasn't really any more information than he already had, but at least it was confirmation.

Plugging the zip code into Google maps showed him the boundaries of the area. It was huge, encompassing eighty or more city blocks. But it did confirm one thing—Duane Grant lived in Buffalo Head.

25

Matt had worked the computer to squeeze out as many details as he possibly could, spending hours chasing down rabbit trails before pulling himself back and refocusing on the information he needed to find. He worked until he could barely keep his eyes open. He knew if he kept it up, he was going to do a face-plant on his keyboard, and he didn't intend to have to clean drool out of a short-circuited keyboard.

So after many hours of research, he pushed himself back from the computer and stretched out on the couch to close his eyes for a few minutes of rest.

Of course, it wasn't a few minutes.

Even after getting caught up on his sleep during his hospital stay, Matt's sleep problems had not simply disappeared. He half-wakened a few times but wasn't able to make himself get up. That was better than usual, when the time just passed without him having any awareness of it. But functionally, it wasn't any better.

Once he managed to really wake up, he dragged himself off of the couch to walk around and make a cup of coffee, which hopefully would help him to wake up the rest of the way and to stay alert. As he stood by the counter, his mind was whirling with the details he had discovered about Duane Grant.

He knew Duane's age, zip code, and that Duncan Grant was likely his brother. He knew Duane had been in prison and was now out. What he didn't have was proof or even the barest evidence that Duane had somehow infected Duncan with the alpha-gal allergy, resulting in his death. Or that he was involved in any way with the Buffalo Head cluster. Matt knew there was no way anyone would investigate or grant a warrant for Duane Grant on a couple of coincidences.

Matt blew on his coffee and took a sip. He saw the indicator light flashing on his phone and picked it up, touching the voicemail button to see who had been calling him. He had tried to get Sharon and the friends who occasionally called him to only leave one voicemail at a time, even if they couldn't reach him for several hours or days. Otherwise, his voicemail was full before he could pick them up, and no one else could leave a message.

This time, there were only a few messages. People were learning. Matt noticed one of them was from the Sleep Disorder Clinic and swiped on it first.

An irritated female voice informed him he had missed his appointment for a diagnostic sleep study. Matt gripped the phone more tightly, his fingers going white. She informed him he would still be charged for it, even though he hadn't been there, because it had not been canceled twenty-four hours ahead of time. He would have to call back to rebook the study.

Matt slapped his head with a loud smack, furious with himself. He had only been vaguely aware of the upcoming appointment, and his arrest and his stay at the hospital had completely thrown off any sense of what day it was. And once he was asleep, there was no waking up again for any measly little phone alarm. Maybe a gong and an electrical shock. But not a phone alert.

He would have to rebook the sleep study. He wasn't about to tell the nurse receptionist he had slept through it.

———

He returned a call that Carol had made while he was asleep.

"Matt, I found something!"

Matt jolted upright at the intensity of Carol's announcement. It was like an electrical shock and sent a bolt of lightning right up his spine.

"Found something? About the Buffalo Head cluster?"

There was only silence for a reply. Matt looked at his screen to make sure the call hadn't disconnected.

"Carol? Sorry, I wasn't thinking. What did you find?"

"I found… something for you. Can I come over and see you?"

"Sure of course. Right now?"

"Is it… not a good time?"

"No, no. It is a good time. Later on… you know, I might… fall asleep before you get here. Then it would be a wasted trip, because the doorbell wouldn't wake me up."

"Okay. I'm going to come straight over then, okay?" Her voice was high and excited. Matt had no idea what she had found, but she was certainly enthused about it. Matt knew it wasn't about the Buffalo Head cluster, and that disappointed him just a little. He could have used a break on tracking Grant down and figuring out what was going on.

It took Carol about twenty minutes to get there. If she was coming from the office, she must have had her foot on the gas the whole way there. Matt let her in and invited her to sit on the couch, getting them each a cup of coffee.

He sat down, handing one cup to Carol.

"You're here," he said. "Do we need to do the small talk thing for ten minutes, or will you just jump straight in?"

"Normally I'm a big believer in small talk," Carol said with a smile. "It puts people at ease and sets things up for a successful social interaction. But today… I have to just tell you."

"Okay, what?"

"N24."

Matt raised his eyebrows. "Are we playing Bingo?"

"No. It's a sleep disorder, and its full name is Non-24-Hour Sleep-Wake Disorder."

Matt worked his way through the name. "So it means… you stay awake for twenty-four hours?"

"No," Carol shook her head. "You remember your experiment? Following Dewey's advice about his aunt? You put your bedtime an hour later every night, until it was at the right time of day, when the rest of the world was going to sleep?"

"Yeah. But it didn't work. It didn't stay there."

"That's right." She looked smug. "Because you went from DSPS to Non-24. Instead of just going to sleep at the wrong time, you converted to a twenty-five hour circadian rhythm."

"Non-24. Sleeping on a schedule that's not a twenty-four-hour schedule."

"Right."

Matt nodded slowly. "I couldn't stop going to sleep an hour later each day, because it was a twenty-five-hour cycle instead of a twenty-four-hour cycle."

"Exactly."

"What's the other one you just said? DS…"

"DSPS. Delayed Sleep Phase Syndrome. You were on a twenty-four-hour cycle, or pretty close to one, but it was set for the wrong time."

"Afternoon instead of night."

Carol nodded. She sipped at her coffee and sat there looking pleased with herself.

"It could be," Matt mused. He reached over to the side table and opened the drawer, pulling out a sheaf of sleep record charts he had printed. He tapped them into a neat handful and showed Carol the first sheet or two. "See; this is my sleep schedule. Ignore all the noise," he gestured to the random blue clumps scattered throughout the chart. "And look at this diagonal here." He traced a roughly diagonal blue line down the page. "And here, because I chart two twenty-four hour periods to one page." He traced the other diagonal.

"It's not the *best* trend line," Carol said, "but I can see it."

"Even though my schedule is really messed up right now, not clear like it was after I tried Dewey's aunt's trick, you can still see the trend. Still getting a little bit later every day."

She studied the charts. "You're still not sleeping a lot of days. Going two or three days without sleeping at all."

"Yeah." Matt shrugged. "I try not to go to sleep when it's the wrong time, but then when it's the right time, my body won't cooperate. We sort of have this war for two or three days, and then I crash. Sometimes I sleep for eight to twelve hours…" He pointed to the blocks of sleep. "And sometimes it's worse, and I sleep for forty-eight hours straight without meaning to. When I got put on leave, I tried to find my natural sleep cycle, but I couldn't." He looked down at the charts. "Maybe because it was later every day."

Carol nodded.

"So," Matt said, "if that's what it is, then how is it treated? How do I get back on a regular schedule?"

"Light therapy in the morning. Make sure you're getting sunshine during the day and don't just stay in your apartment. High doses of melatonin at night. Cutting out computer and screen time before bed…"

Matt put the papers back away, turning his face away from Carol so she wouldn't see his disappointment.

"I've already tried those things. You can get those suggestions off of any insomnia website."

Carol grimaced. "Well, first let's get you properly diagnosed. The doctors should be able to tell you what to do once it's confirmed. And you can get in contact with other people with N24 to see what they are doing…"

"Sure," Matt sighed. "I'm sure it will all work out."

———

It wasn't as easy as all that. Matt knew it wouldn't be. If it were that simple to get diagnosed and get useful advice, he would have had it straightened out months ago. The doctor at the sleep clinic was uninterested in seeing Matt before his rescheduled sleep study, but Matt finally talked his way in to see him.

Dr. Fish glanced over his charts.

"I'm not seeing any obvious trends," he said. "I think you see what you want to. I don't know if you're aware of this, but N24 is something blind people get. You're not blind."

Matt had discovered this after Carol left and he turned on his computer to do research of his own.

"It's *usually* blind people who get it. But sometimes sighted people do. And my sleep problems started after a brain injury. N24 can be triggered by physical trauma."

"Those cases are very rare." Fish handed the charts back to Matt. "I want you to reschedule your sleep study, Mr. Malloy. Then we'll see whether you have sleep apnea or something else we can treat. N24 is not something we can help you with."

"But there are strategies for people who have it…"

"And you're welcome to pursue them and see if they help. In the meantime, please reschedule your sleep study. And have a friend lined up who will make sure you get there this time."

26

Matt went back over the interviews he had done and started calling people back to see if he could find any connections with Duane Grant. With the first half dozen, he had no luck. Then out of the blue, a hit.

Matt remembered the man. Brad Berkley. The one who had sat watching TV for the whole interview.

"I thought you were finished your investigation," he complained.

"I thought I had gathered everything I needed," Matt soothed. "But there have been a few more things come up. I just have a few more questions; it will only take a minute."

Brad sighed heavily.

"I'm a busy man. Seriously. It better be quick, or I'm going to be calling your superiors."

"I'll be as quick as I can. I'm wondering if you know or have any connection with a man named Duane Grant?"

"Little Duane?" Brad's voice was mocking. "Prissy little milksop Duane? Sure I know him."

"You do! How do you know him?"

"From work. Duh. He's an exterminator."

A chill ran through Matt. For a minute, he didn't know what to say. The words wouldn't come.

"He works at Bug Bee Gone," Matt said stupidly.

"Yeah. Sure. He's a newbie. Hasn't been there for very long. Or I assume he's still there. I didn't think he would last."

"How long before you got sick did he start working there?"

"I dunno. Few weeks, couple of months. You'd have to call the office."

What Matt wanted to ask was if there was any possibility Grant could have intentionally infected Brad. But he couldn't figure out a way to put it into words. He didn't want to be accused of slander once Grant found out about the investigation. And he didn't want to take the chance Brad might go back to Grant and warn him off before Matt had a chance to gather the evidence he needed.

So he didn't ask. He just finished the call with a few more polite phrases and hung up the phone.

Then he put his phone down on the desk and stared at it.

Duane Grant was an exterminator. That put him in contact with potentially infected ticks every day. Was he accidentally acting as a host, carrying them from one job to another, in contact with his coworkers, spreading them from one environment to another? Could the Buffalo Head cluster be explained simply as an accident?

Matt had met people who attracted insects. Who could wear Deep Woods Off or DEET and still be the only one in a group of friends who came in from an outdoor activity covered with bites. Pheromones or vitamins or something else in their system actually attracted insects. Could it be something as simple as Duane having sweeter-smelling blood than anyone else? Ticks were attracted to him? At the prison, the warden suggested he had attracted more attention from the ticks and insects than others.

Was that why he had gotten so sick when others had been fine?

———

Matt vacillated between calling Bug Bee Gone and going to the office in person. Eventually, he decided he was far more likely to be able to get information face-to-face than if he just placed a phone call. It was too easy to just say no to someone on the phone. He would have to wait until office hours, which meant a long wait through the night.

Remembering what Carol said about screen time, Matt reluctantly shut off his computer. He moved automatically to the couch and reached for the TV remote. He realized what he was doing before pressing the power button and laid it back down again. How was he going to entertain himself until morning? After considering the options, Matt finally got up and looked through his sparse library. He had more books on his phone, but if he were trying to stay away from screens emitting the sleep-killing blue light, he couldn't use that either. He'd have to get a book reader with e-ink and the option of no backlight if he wanted to read the books he had downloaded over the past couple of years. He always intended to get to them but never really made a dent in his reading list.

Sighing, Matt sat down with a paperback and started to read.

———

When Matt arrived at Bug Bee Gone in the morning, it was obvious he had caught them at their busiest time. Most of the bug trucks were still in the parking lot. There was a bustle of people going in and out, talking with the young-looking man at the reception desk, and tapping their prox cards to clock in. Matt stood back, not wanting to be in the way. But he was obviously an outsider and the man at the desk demanded to know what he wanted.

"My name is Matt Malloy. I'm with the Department of Public Health and Environment. I was hoping to be able to talk to the person in charge."

"You're looking at him."

Matt glanced at the brass nameplate on the front of the desk. Steve Bolt.

"I'm sorry I picked such a busy time to come by. Would it be better if I came back in a few hours, when things are quieter?"

Steve shrugged. "Doesn't make any difference whether you ask your questions now or later. What is this about? We file all our documentation. Do plenty of voluntary reporting too. Because we're concerned about the environment and the world we live in."

"That's great, and we sure appreciate it. I'm actually here about one of your employees." Matt glanced around, but so far he had not seen Grant come in.

"Which one?" Steve asked briskly.

"Duane Grant."

The man snorted. "He won't be in today. Already called in to say he has to deal with lawyers on his brother's estate. With the number of days he's taken off for that, he should have been finished long ago. Exactly how big could the guy's estate be?"

"That would be Duncan Grant's estate?"

"How would I know? I don't know his name."

Matt nodded. "Okay. It's probably best he's not in today anyway. And I'd appreciate it if you could keep this investigation under your hat for now..."

Steve raised one eyebrow curiously. "Yeah, sure," he agreed. "So what's this about?"

"First off... I'm wondering how many of your employees have been sick since Grant started."

"Sick? I assume you're talking about Brad Berkley. Grant didn't have anything to do with that. Berkley got one of those tick diseases. Obviously didn't follow our safety protocols to avoid getting infected. Decided to work without a hat or in flip-flops. Our outdoor gear is designed to deter any access by ticks or spiders."

"I'm not doubting your safety procedures. I'm aware of Berkley's illness. Has anyone else contracted a tick-borne disease?"

"No," Steve shook his head confidently. "Definitely not."

"Have you had any more employee illness than usual? A flu outbreak?"

"There's been a lot of flu," Steve admitted. "But some years are like that. Everybody just keeps passing it around."

"And Berkley's the only one on medical leave? No arthritis? Fibromyalgia? Migraines?"

"Fibro-whatsit. One of the workers is trying to get disability for that. But a lot of doctors say it's just a sham; it doesn't exist. I'm hoping she doesn't get leave. Between Berkley getting Lyme or whatever and Grant taking off all the time because of his brother's death, I can't keep this place staffed. But I can't afford to hire anyone else, either."

"That's really a problem," Matt sympathized. He waited while a couple of employees tapped their cards, eying him curiously. They left, toting their kits out to their bug trucks. "How did Duane get his job here? Was he experienced?"

"No. We did a big client a favor. I think the brother was involved somehow. Grant trained up okay, but it sure wasn't his calling, and he's no expert." Steve punched a few keys on his computer emphatically. "At least *he* didn't get himself infected."

"Does he get along with the other employees?"

"No. I never told anyone he's a convict, but people have instincts. They knew there was something about him that didn't fit. He doesn't have any friends. Takes a bit of heat from the others. You know, like anyone who's kind of... a geek. Awkward. Socially."

"Yes... I don't expect Berkley gave him much of a break."

"You don't want harassment charges, but you can't jump in every time there's a little friction between employees, either. They have to try to work it out."

"Did Grant ever make threats about harassment charges?"

"No. You just know... I know the kind of guy who will pull that sort of thing."

Matt nodded. He wrote some notes. Not because he was afraid he would forget any of it, but because he wasn't sure how to get all the information he needed from Steve. The man was talkative now, but as soon as he sensed his company might have some liability in the Buffalo Head cluster and within his own doors, he would clam up.

"Is he in trouble?" Steve asked, stretching his neck a little to try to catch a glimpse of what Matt was writing. "Because I gotta say... I wouldn't be sad to be quit of the guy. And once he was off the books, I could hire a replacement."

"I can't really tell you anything at this time," Matt said. "I wonder if I could get his address from you, though."

"You don't have it?" Steve asked, his eyes narrowing. "Doesn't the government have all that stuff in a database?"

"His last known address isn't correct," Matt bluffed. "He didn't leave a forwarding address."

"The address we have is the one on his Driver's License," Steve said sharply. "I know, I checked. You'll have to check with the DMV. I can't give you his private information."

"This is a government investigation..."

"Then check the DMV or get me a warrant."

Matt rolled his eyes. "Fine. I will. Now, if I could get the name of the employee with fibromyalgia..."

"I can't give you her information either. If you hang around here at closing, you'll see her. I probably shouldn't have told you about her claim, either…"

"I won't mention that to her," Matt promised. "That's just between you and me."

Steve nodded stiffly. "I'd appreciate that." He hesitated for a moment. "Marg is the only woman exterminator I've got right now. You'll see her if you're here at six."

"That's great. I appreciate it. The other thing I need is… a list of the jobs Grant has done since he got here. The names and addresses of the places he's done work."

Steve stared at him. "You want our client list?" He made a noise of disbelief. "There's no way! If you want information like that, you need a warrant. And you don't have one."

———

Matt still had the Buffalo Head infection reports he had emailed himself, so the next step was to see how many more of them were connected in some way to Duane Grant. He tried to arrange them chronologically and then started placing calls.

A lot of people were unreachable. Maybe they were at work or maybe they just didn't like answering the phone when they didn't recognize the name or number of the caller. It was easier when Matt was calling from the office. When people saw "Department of Health" on their caller ID, they were always worried about the possibility they had been exposed to some horrible pathogen, and they picked up to find out what they were dying of.

A woman answered the phone, and Duane immediately recognized the horrible nasal voice of the woman he remembered had a big yard and a little dog.

"Mrs. Stemple, this is Matt Malloy of the DOH. You and I talked some time back about your infectious diseases report. For your…" he scanned the report. "Rocky Mountain Spotted Fever."

"Yes? What is this about?"

Her voice cut right through him. Matt winced and tried to go on. "I just had a couple more questions for you. Did you have any extermination work done before you got ill?"

"Yes, of course. All those mosquitos and other bugs that breed in the pond. You have to spray for them, or they are impossible. And insecticide on the roses and the other flowers. They get so yellow and awful if you don't spray to keep the bugs off."

"Do you remember the name of the company that sprayed for you?"

"No. One of my friends recommended them. I haven't a clue."

"Would you happen to have the invoice still?"

"Certainly not. They sent that awful little man and he was late. I can't abide it when workers are late!"

"That's understandable," Matt agreed. "Very frustrating."

"Yes. Oh… I know!"

Matt's heart lifted. "Yes?"

"The one with the trucks. Horrible tacky things with the dead bug on top. I told my friend, I don't want a truck with a dead bug on it parked in front of my house! It's hideous!"

"Bug Bee Gone," Matt suggested. "The bug is a cockroach? Upside down?"

"Yes. Yes, that's the one!"

"That's very helpful, ma'am. Thank you so much."

———

Finding the exterminator connection was a big plus. A number of the subjects recalled having extermination work done before they came down with their illnesses. The horribly tacky bug trucks made it easy to identify whether the work had been done by Bug Bee Gone, even if they couldn't recall the name of the company.

Not all of them had exterminator connections or recognized Grant's name from some other part of their life. Matt imagined the random connections they might have with Grant. Waitress at a restaurant. Tax collector. Utilities salesman. Had the infections been intentional? Or was Grant simply a vehicle for the ticks, unknowingly spreading disease to everyone he had close contact with?

Accidental infection seemed just as unlikely as intentional harm. Ticks didn't transfer from one person to another in a handshake. A tick that had its fill dropped off and found a crack to lay eggs in, or a nymph grew to the next stage of its development before it needed another blood meal. It didn't suck one person's blood for half a meal and then transfer to another for dessert.

Matt finished all the phone calls he could manage and put the papers aside to have a bite to eat and a bit of a break. He wasn't hungry, but he knew it was time for a meal. As he waited for his single-serving pasta to heat up, he pulled out his phone and texted Rich Adams.

This is Matt Malloy, DOH. Could we get together to meet?

There was no response for a long time. Matt sat down and chewed his way through the pasta not even tasting it, his mind miles away. As he finished, his phone chimed, and he looked at the text.

Changed my mind, don't want to meet u.

Matt frowned. That was not the response he had expected. He considered it.

What's up? Can we talk on the phone?

No. Not interested.

Matt was rapidly running out of options. He was going to lose Rich altogether, and he was desperate for an answer.

Do you know Duane Grant?

There was no reply. Matt waited. Did that mean yes? Was Duane a friend, and Matt had pushed it too far? Or was he irritated by something completely different and it was just one too many questions?

The minutes ticked by. Matt tried to go back to the infection reports and his notes, but he couldn't stop looking at the phone, waiting for a reply. He knew after the first couple of minutes Rich was not going to reply. He wasn't just driving or busy with something else. He was gone, beyond Matt's reach.

Matt swore and banged the table with his fist. He had worked so hard to find these people and to make the connections between them. He had to gather every bit of evidence he could. Every piece counted. Together, they would add up to a case the CDC or the police could pursue.

He needed to find as many connections as he could.

He had to find out whether the infections were intentional or accidental.

27

———————

Duane put down his phone, his head whirling. It was proof positive that Malloy was onto him. It wasn't just a coincidence. He was looking for Duane, and he knew there was a connection between Duane and Rich's alpha-gal allergy.

Infecting Malloy hadn't worked. Maybe Malloy had had one of those vaccine shots they were working on to prevent tick-borne diseases. They said they weren't effective and ready for market yet, but it wouldn't be the first time the establishment lied and was only concerned about protecting themselves. If they had a viable vaccine, it would make sense to test it on their own employees first. Give them the protection. That way they could walk into environments like the prison or out in the wild and not risk infection.

Duane wasn't a violent man. Using the ticks, there was no guarantee his target would actually be infected. There was an element of fate involved. Duane didn't decide whether the person got sick or not. It was up to the universe. If the person were destined to be sick, then it would work. If not, then they wouldn't. And in many cases, Duane would never see them again. He wouldn't know whether the universe had decided to make the person sick or not.

In Duncan's case, fate had agreed with Duane that Duncan didn't deserve to live. He was too cruel, too evil. Eventually, karma had to catch up to him, cutting him down in his pride. Duane had never realized Duncan could die from one of the infected ticks. But the universe knew and had made Duane its instrument to remove Duncan from the earth. To take him out of the equation completely.

But Malloy… Duane's thoughts returned to him.

Malloy hadn't been fated to get sick or die. Malloy *had* come to the prison to help Duane. Malloy had ensured Duane was properly diagnosed and treated. Did that mean Duane shouldn't or couldn't hurt him?

But he couldn't just ignore Malloy's continued interference. Duane had to try again. Maybe this time, fate would be on his side.

———

Matt looked at his watch again. The time was creeping by. He had thought with rush hour traffic it would take him an hour to get back to Bug Bee Gone. Instead, he had sailed through and gotten there far too early to catch the returning employees.

He tuned the radio to find a better station and closed his eyes for a minute, dazzled by the lowering sun.

It couldn't have been more than five minutes later, someone had a hold of his arm and was shaking it hard. He opened his eyes to look into the broad, red face of a rather plain woman.

"You can't sleep here," she told him. "This is private property. We don't want drugged-up freaks sleeping in cars here. Get on your way!"

Matt rubbed his eyes and looked around, taking a minute to remember where he was and why he was there.

"Are you Marg?"

She blinked and let go of his arm. "Well, who are you, then? I don't owe a soul money, not even taxes."

Matt straightened up. "That's fine, because I'm not a tax collector. I was hoping you and I could talk. My name is Matt Malloy, and I'm an investigator with the Department of Public Health and Environment."

"Oh… I see." Clearly, she didn't have any idea what he was there about. "Did I miss dotting an I or crossing a T on a form? No one has ever complained about them before."

"No. It's nothing like that. Do you want to check out," Matt motioned to the administrative office, "and then we could go somewhere for coffee?"

Her heavy black eyebrows lowered as she studied him with suspicion. Matt waited, not offering any further explanation. Finally, she nodded.

"All right then. I will. It will take me twenty minutes to half an hour." She glared at him. "Don't fall asleep again."

He wasn't sure why she cared whether he fell asleep or not. She stepped back from the car and shut the door. Matt made a mental note: next time he was going to fall asleep in his car, he should lock the door. She could just as easily have grabbed his phone and his wallet; he wouldn't have budged. He stretched his legs and rolled his shoulder, working out the kinks the best he could while still in the car. He should probably get out and walk around if he wanted to ensure he didn't nod off again. But he didn't, he just waited.

He was starting to get dozy again by the time Marg got back. He shook it off and sat up when she opened his car door.

"Do you want me to ride with you or follow in my car?" she asked.

"Whichever you want." He thought it a little odd she hadn't asked him for any form of identification and was willing to get into the car with a perfect stranger. But maybe Steve had said something to her, putting her mind at ease.

Marg considered for a moment. "I'll follow in mine," she decided. "Then you don't have to drive me back after."

"Sure."

"Where are we going?"

"Anywhere around with decent coffee?"

"Fair Grounds, over on Seventh. You know it?"

"I think I've driven by there."

"Why don't you follow me, then?" she suggested. Without waiting for a response, she shut the door and went back to her own car. Five minutes later, they were sitting at Fair Grounds, across the table from each other, with grande coffees in front of them.

"So, you're from DOH," Marg summed up. "What is it you want from me?"

"I'm looking into a cluster of tick infections in the area."

"Yes? I still don't see why you want to talk to me. We've all filed population reports and sent specimens in. The only one I know of who caught anything was Berkley. I'm sure he'd be able to give you a lot more information than I could."

"I have talked with Berkley. That's why I went to Bug Bee Gone to look for any more cases."

"Then you should talk to Steve or someone in franchise headquarters."

"I have talked to Steve." Matt sipped his coffee. It was still too hot, but he didn't want to start nodding off in the middle of the conversation. He needed to stay clear and focused. "Sometimes cases can be overlooked. The initial symptoms are just flu-like, so people don't suspect ticks. They write it off as a virus and go back to work never knowing what they have contracted. Sometimes it is years before their chronic symptoms get severe enough to get a proper diagnosis."

Her brows drew down. "I had the flu. But so has practically everyone else in the office. It went through everyone."

"Did you have any other symptoms? Something you couldn't attribute to the flu?"

She rolled her eyes. "I'm not one to complain."

Matt waited, letting her think about it. She might say she didn't have anything to complain about, but she was the one looking for medical leave because of her symptoms. Her eyes widened suddenly.

"You mean my fibromyalgia?"

Matt shrugged. "That's a start. Why don't you tell me about it?"

"I just started having pain in my joints, all the time. Fatigue. I get home at the end of the day, and I just want to lie down and go to sleep." She glanced away from Matt. "Sorry about waking you up like that. You'd think I'd be more sympathetic with how beat I am at the end of the day."

"Don't worry about it."

"That's it, really. Just pain and fatigue. But it's so bad I sometimes can't get through a job. I have to stop and rest. I run behind and don't get to all the addresses I should. And like I say, I get home, and I'm just wiped out. Lay down for a twenty-minute nap and sleep right through supper and don't wake up until the morning. It's dreadful."

"And when did this start?"

"A few weeks ago."

"Before or after your flu?"

"After."

"Have you had any other symptoms with it?"

Her eyes were calculating. She considered his question, scraping with her fingernail at some food dried to the table.

"I never had any rash," she said.

"Most tick-borne diseases come with rashes, but only in eighty percent or so of the cases. Some people never have a rash."

"And I never had a bite, not that I noticed."

"Were you looking for them?"

"Well… no, I wasn't. I always wear my gear on jobs. We're supposed to check our skin and hair for ticks at the end of the day… but you get a little lazy after a while." She ran her fingers through her thick black hair as if combing it for ticks now. She scratched her scalp. "You make my skin crawl. Look at this hair, how would I ever find a tiny tick on my scalp?"

"It's possible you were bitten. How about fevers? Anything?"

"No, no fevers." She made a little grimace. "I don't think so anyway. I've been sort of… I know it's too early for menopause, exactly, but maybe perimenopause… hot flashes."

"Hot flashes," Matt repeated. "Could be a recurring fever. I don't know how hard it is to tell the difference."

She gave an embarrassed grin. "Neither do I, to tell the truth. I've just been ignoring it, hoping it will go away if I don't give it too much attention. Not the way menopause works, I know…"

Matt nodded and took another drink of coffee, his own face getting a little warm.

"So…" Marg was thinking things through. "It's not like we all caught a tick-borne disease from Berkley. And we all go on different jobs, so unless there's a really bad outbreak in this area, there's no way a bunch of us all just happened to get it. I haven't heard about any outbreak. Nothing unusual in the reports we've filed or the samples we've sent. The confirmations come back within normal parameters. So what's going on?"

"I'm investigating the possibility someone might be accidentally or intentionally spreading tick-borne diseases in the area."

"How would they do that?"

"I don't know. It's all speculation so far. Maybe the person lives in an infested area and spreads them on his clothes. Or maybe he intentionally collects them and plants infectious ticks in strategic places."

Marg shuddered. "Plants them? That's sick. But how could you, even if you wanted to? You wouldn't know which ticks are infectious. How would they do it?"

"When I finish my investigation, I hope to be able to answer that."

She shook her head and took a couple of gulps of coffee. Matt sipped at his own, trying to wash away the bad taste their theories left in his mouth. When he looked up again, Marg was studying him intently.

"You think someone in our office is spreading these diseases?"

Matt nodded. "Yes, I'm afraid so."

"Duane Grant."

Matt was astounded. "What makes you think that?"

"He's just the stinking little rat to do it! The way he creeps around, watching everyone, never making friends… he'd be just the guy to do it."

"You think he did it because you don't like him? Because he rubs you the wrong way?"

"No! No, it's more than that. Of course, I *don't* like him, and he *does* rub me the wrong way, and I get my gibes in whenever I can. But there's more to it." She paused, considering it further. "One day I saw him poking around in my locker. At least, I think he'd been in my locker. He was all jumpy when I walked into the room. He was at the wall where my locker is, the complete opposite side of the room from his. I figured he was snooping around, or getting his kicks out of seeing what was in the only girl's locker. I opened the door carefully, to make sure he hadn't put something in there that was going to fall out or scare me. Something juvenile. But I couldn't see anything. Everything looked perfectly normal, untouched."

"There wouldn't be any reason for him to be on that side of the room," Matt said.

"No. No reason at all. The only reason to be in there at all is to get your kit and suit up. And he'd only need to get into his own locker. Not mine or anyone's who is around me. We all have our own kits and gear."

"He couldn't have run out of specimen tubes and needed to borrow some from someone else?"

"No. He would just get them from the stock room. And he didn't try to explain what he'd been doing over there. Just pretended he hadn't been, all red in the face. Little jerk."

Matt swirled the coffee left in his cup, watching the surface. He pictured Grant putting a tick, or several of them, into the inside of Marg's hat, so when she put it on, they would crawl into her thick hair, infecting her instead of protecting her. His stomach twisted. "Any other suspicious behavior? Anything that stands out to you?"

"No. I don't think so. I'll have to think on it some more, see if I can think of anything else. You never know. But right now, no." She shook her head. "I don't like the guy, but I'm not going to make up stories to put a noose around his neck."

"I appreciate that. I don't want to be acting on false information."

They both nodded, confirming this to each other. Matt pushed his nearly-empty coffee cup an inch further away from him.

"Can you tell me what kind of vehicle Grant drives?"

"Why…? Oh, never mind why. Everyone in the place could tell you the kind of car he drives. A cute little red convertible. Doesn't suit him at all, and I don't know how he got it. When he started out at Bug, he was driving a rusting-out beater that couldn't have cost more than a hundred dollars. And believe me, we don't make enough to be buying fancy sports cars!"

"Maybe it was his brother's."

She gave a shrug. "Oh, that's right. Steve said something about his brother dying. Steve figured it was all a scam, so Grant brought him the funeral director's certificate. But I think the car is probably better proof than the certificate! Don't know why I didn't connect that up before."

———

It had been a long day, and Matt was glad to be home to think things through and write up his notes. He would do a bit of paperwork, then take his melatonin and see if sleep came to him. He was tired enough he really hoped it would. He knew what would happen if he didn't get some sleep soon.

When Matt got to his apartment, he stopped short. The door stood open. Matt reached for the handle. Had he been so tired when he left earlier he had forgotten to lock or even shut the door?

But the door hadn't been left unlocked or open. The door frame was splintered. It had been forced.

Matt stood there, not sure what to do. Finally, he reached for his phone and called nine-one-one. The police were there within ten minutes. Two officers approached.

"You didn't go in?" one of them asked without preamble.

"No. I didn't know if someone could still be in there," Matt explained, his voice low.

They both nodded. The first motioned for him to stay put, and made several gestures at his partner. They pushed the door open quickly and entered. Matt's heart pounded. It was just like he'd watched on a hundred TV shows, but he'd never expected to see it in person. He held his breath until one of them came to the door, nodding to him.

"We're clear. Come in."

Matt breathed in, trying to calm his hammering heart. He walked into his apartment, expecting the worst. Everything trashed, electronics gone, wanton destruction of everything the thieves did not want for themselves.

But it looked just like he'd left it. Everything was where it belonged. His lunch dishes were on the counter, and his bed was rumpled. He never bothered to make it anymore. What was the point?

Matt looked around, shaking his head. "I don't get it. Maybe I was wrong. Maybe it wasn't a break-in…"

"The door was kicked in," the younger of the two cops pointed out. "It was a break-in. Nothing obviously missing?"

"No."

"We'll take a look around while you check for smaller items. Jewelry, cash, any other valuables. Do you have a safe or a cash box?"

"No."

Matt wasn't sure what to look for. He went to his bedside table and opened each drawer, looking for anything disturbed or missing. He didn't have any valuables. Just his electronics.

He knew the officers were watching him, so he kept looking. The closets, drawers, even cupboards in the kitchen. Nothing appeared to have been touched.

"The freezer?" one of the officers suggested. "Some people use it as a safe."

"No, not me," Matt said, shaking his head. He opened it anyway. A package of pork chops he had intended to barbecue. More microwave dinners than he cared to admit. A sticky package of fudgicles. The officer grinned.

"Typical bachelor," he observed. "So, nothing? Keys to your car or recreational vehicle?"

"No. I had my car with me. I don't have anything else."

The older cop scratched the back of his neck and spoke up. "Probably what happened is he heard a voice in the next apartment or something that spooked him. He was afraid he was going to be discovered, so he scrammed before touching anything." He gave a shrug. "It happens sometimes. Count yourself lucky."

"Yeah. I do."

"We'll do up a report. Get a tech over here to check for fingerprints. You never know, it could be someone in the system already. You should see if you can get someone over to repair the door, so you feel safe tonight."

———

If Matt had had any ideas about being able to sleep that night, he quickly gave them up. On top of the N24, or insomnia, or whatever he had, he couldn't stop worrying about the break-in. He couldn't just shrug it off like the police. It was his home, his sanctuary. And someone had been there. Someone had broken down the door and had been in his private space.

He kept going back to the thought it had been Duane Grant. While Matt had been sitting in his car outside Bug Bee Gone, waiting for the employees to return, had Grant been breaking into Matt's home?

It was stupid. First of all, there was no way for Grant to know he was under investigation. Or that it was Matt investigating him. Or where Matt lived. Even if he did know those things, he would have no reason to break into Matt's apartment.

From what Matt had seen of Grant in the prison infirmary, and the things he had heard about Grant from everyone else who knew him, Grant didn't have a violent, macho personality. He was a whiner, a sneak, and socially awkward. That wasn't the kind of person who kicked a door down.

Matt hadn't paid for a search of Grant's criminal convictions, so he didn't know what it was Grant had been sent to prison for. But he was sure it couldn't have been anything violent. The death of Duncan had been a freak accident, even if Grant had intentionally infected his brother.

Maybe Matt should have paid for a criminal search. He considered doing one but was too worried about leaving a trail. Was it possible he had already tipped Grant off with the research he had done? There could be computer programs that would send him an alert when someone searched his name. They said nothing on the internet was ever really erased. Maybe Grant was a computer hacker who could trace that back to Matt.

28

There was nothing Matt could do until he could find some hard evidence Grant had deliberately infected people. He had enough he could probably take it to the CDC with the suggestion Grant was patient zero, but he wasn't sure where that would lead, if anywhere.

If there were evidence, it would be at Grant's home. Now that Matt knew where Duane worked and what he drove, there was a simple way to find Grant's domicile. It wasn't through a motor vehicles search as Steve had suggested, but by following him. Grant could have used any address for his vehicle registration. But sooner or later, he would drive home.

Matt felt like a real private investigator waiting on the street outside of Bug Bee Gone. He was surveilling a subject and was going to follow him. He had absolutely no experience in trailing a vehicle and hoped he could keep Grant in sight without giving himself away. He'd seen his share of secret agent and action movies. They always made it look easy. Anybody could do it. But Matt suspected it wasn't as easy as they made out.

He had arrived too early again. None of the bugmobiles had returned to the hive yet. But Matt had armed himself with caffeine pills and was determined not to fall asleep again.

Eventually, the bug trucks started coming back home. Matt wasn't close enough to get a good look at each driver, but he had his eye on the red convertible. The sweet little ride was hard to miss.

The convertible was one of the first cars out of the lot. Matt pulled in behind it and tried to stay far enough back not to be spotted.

Duane didn't drive to a big house on the hill that matched the sports car. It was a little brown bungalow. Grant drove into the carport in the back. Matt drove by slowly to see the slight figure slouch to a basement entrance.

Now he knew. It was like finding a key piece in a puzzle and fitting it into place. He knew where Grant lived, and with a little bit of investigating, he would be able to gather the evidence he needed to prove Grant was the witting or unwitting Typhoid Mary of the Buffalo Head cluster. Matt would be vindicated. They would all know it wasn't just Matt's illness that had made him obsess over the Buffalo Head cluster, but he had really seen something there.

Matt hadn't realized until then how much it had bothered him to have his expertise questioned over the Buffalo Head cluster. He felt like a child who had been patronized by the grown-ups, and now he was going to prove them all wrong.

———

Rather than risk his car being seen by Grant if he looked out one of his basement windows into the back lane, Matt drove around to the front of the house and parked a couple of houses down. He walked to the house, eyes alert, looking for any sign of a dense tick infection or any other clue to what was going on.

It was his intention to check around the front yard and maybe the neighboring back yards. Then he would come back the next day to have a look at Grant's back yard once Grant was safely out of the way. Unless Matt found something he could use in the front. That was always a possibility.

His heart pounded as he walked up to the house. This was the home of his nemesis. Matt glanced back over his shoulder. He felt almost like he had on discovering his apartment had been broken into. Heart racing, a bit dizzy. But this time instead of just a knot of fear and dread in his stomach, he felt something else. A lightness. Excitement. Hope.

The front door opened as Matt walked into the yard and Matt knew he was caught. His brain raced for an explanation as he turned his head to speak to Grant.

But it wasn't Grant.

As Matt had suspected, Grant only rented the basement suite, and it was another man who opened the front door to confront him.

Rich Adams.

Matt braced himself for the anger and accusations. His brain was flailing around for an explanation for his presence. Adams had made it clear he didn't want to meet with Matt. How was he going to react to Matt showing up unexpectedly at his house?

"Hey!" Adams' face was all smiles.

Matt was thrown. He didn't know what to say.

"I'm glad you came here," Adams offered. "I lost your card, and I didn't know how to reach you! You must have called the teacher to find out my address, hey?"

Matt reached out his hand to shake Adams', still at a loss for words. His tired brain processed these details, and he couldn't come up with a proper response. Adams had lost Matt's business card? Adams didn't know how to reach him? Then who the hell had Matt been texting with?

"Come on in," Adams invited, showing Matt into the living room. "I'm sorry, the place is a bit of a mess."

Adams was obviously a bachelor. There was no woman's touch in the upstairs suite. It looked lived-in. Laundry, clean or dirty, sprinkled here and there. A beer can on the floor next to the favorite easy chair.

"It's funny," Adams offered. "I was just getting ready to make a quinoa dish we learned in our class, and I was thinking about you and wondering how I could find your name and phone number. I thought maybe one of the others you talked to might have kept it. Or I could look for the number for your department, and they'd be able to direct me to you."

Thank goodness Adams hadn't done that. Matt wasn't sure what the DOH would have done if they received yet more evidence Matt was continuing his investigation while on leave. He would be lucky if he didn't lose his job. They had clearly told him to leave it alone. Someone else was doing the investigating for the DOH now. They had determined the Buffalo Head cluster was just an interesting anomaly and had put it to bed.

"You lost my card?" Matt said stupidly.

"Yeah, I'm sorry about that. Lost it the day you visited the class. I really should have gotten back to you sooner, but things got sort of busy…" Adams gestured at their surroundings. Matt could see nothing that indicated what busy-ness he had been pursuing to keep him from tracking Matt down in the meantime.

"Have a seat," Adams invited. He paused, looking around the room. "Or would you like to sit in the kitchen while I make some grub?"

"Sure."

Matt settled himself onto one of the kitchen chairs and Adams rattled around the kitchen getting out a pot, a plastic bowl, and various ingredients.

"It's funny; I never had quinoa before I started the class. Now I can't get enough of it. It's high protein, better for you than rice, and so versatile! Have you had it?"

"Yeah, once or twice."

"I'm cooking with it all the time, now." Adams looked over the brand-new-looking measuring cups and implements he had lined up and chuckled. "I'm quite the domestic, now. I cook just about every day, as long as I have the energy. Before this, I barely touched a fork. Microwaved pizza or fast-food burgers. Barbecue. Nothing like this."

"You don't have a lot of energy since your infection?" Matt suggested.

"Since I got this allergy, yeah. I don't understand why I've been so wiped out since I had that allergy attack. I thought maybe I wasn't getting enough protein or iron since I had to go vegetarian, but the teacher said there's plenty in the plant-based diet I've been eating. I think he kind of thinks I'm just making excuses for being lazy and not getting my homework done."

"You have to do homework for the vegetarian class?"

Adams grimaced. "Yeah, can you believe it? It isn't all just cooking, though we're supposed to be polishing up our cooking skills during the week as well. He actually has us writing research papers on different topics and reading them to the class. That way everyone gets educated about all different aspects of vegetarianism. But I'll tell you; I hated writing papers in high school and I hate doing them now. And it's worse now. It's like I'm in a fog all the time. Sometimes I can barely put two words down on paper. So she thinks I'm being lazy about it, but I am really not!"

"Mr. Adams, did you ever get any testing done after your allergy attack? To see if you had a bacterial infection?"

"Rich. No, I haven't had anything like that…?"

"This allergy you have developed. I told you it might be caused by a tick bite. And ticks can carry a lot of other diseases. Rocky Mountain Spotted Fever, recurring fevers, tularemia, all kinds of things. So I was wondering if you had been tested for any of them."

"No. No, nothing. They basically told me 'it looks like you're allergic to meat' and sent me home."

Matt shook his head. He thought they had been doing a better job of educating doctors on the dangers of tick-borne diseases and how to recognize them. The sudden appearance of an allergy to red meat should have been a huge tip-off to Adams' doctor. They should have immediately done bloods and swabs to narrow down which infection they were dealing with, and started Adams on antibiotics. Instead, he'd been dragging around, dealing with malaise and fever for weeks. Who knew what other symptoms he might have that he hadn't mentioned yet.

"They should have been smarter. You should have been treated immediately. You'd be feeling a lot better by now."

"Can they do anything about the allergy?" Adams asked, his voice rising hopefully in tone. "If they treat the infection, will the allergy go away?"

"No, sorry. There is some indication it might fade over the next five years, but I wouldn't be doing a food challenge anytime soon."

Adams sighed and nodded, clinking his dishes as he worked. "I didn't think so."

"Sorry about that. But you could be feeling a lot better, anyway. Can you tell me any other symptoms you have been having? Fever, rash, aching joints?"

"Yeah, all that for sure. They come and go. Except for the aching joints and the mental fog. Those seem to be there all the time. I can barely function at work. Some days they send me home early. I've been making so many mistakes, I'm worried they're going to just give up and fire me."

"I'm sorry to hear that. But there is a light at the end of the tunnel. A course of antibiotics, and you'll be feeling a lot better."

"I hope so. Will you write a note for my doctor or make a call or something? You know how doctor's are. He's going to think I diagnosed myself on the internet and I'm just imagining things. He won't put me on antibiotics, he'll just send me home with a prescription for Prozac."

Did Matt know it. *Just go to bed at the same time every night. Get some sunshine during the day. Don't worry, once you get sleepy enough, you'll fall asleep.*

"Sure, I'll do whatever I can."

"Excellent. You know who's been a really big help? My downstairs tenant, Duane."

Matt's mouth went dry. He swallowed and cleared his throat, suddenly unable to find his voice. "Duane?"

"Duane Grant. It's funny he's been such a support, because before I had my allergy attack... I wasn't very nice to him. Made fun of him a lot. Especially about him being vegetarian. It was like poetic justice I got this allergy. Suddenly I needed his help. I'm getting his advice on the best veggie burgers, instead of making fun of him for eating veggie burgers and not real man food."

"Crazy," Matt agreed.

"When it first happened, I got sick and they told me it was an allergy and was triggered by the venison I had eaten, I was..." He shook his head, trying to find the words. "I don't want to say devastated, but... well, I was. We're all indoctrinated from the time we're little about meat. It's man food. It's macho to eat huge steaks and burgers. Men don't put vegetables on their pizza; they get the all-meat pizza. You know? All around you, you keep getting hit with the message you're not masculine if you don't eat meat. Even though there are vegan weight lifters and triathletes and everything. We just keep getting told you're less of a man if you don't eat meat." He sighed, stirring some vegetables in the pan. "If you can't eat meat, it's like a death sentence to your manhood. It's really been hard for me."

"Yeah, I guess I can understand that."

Adams adopted a cheerier tone. "But Duane's been a big help. He doesn't begrudge me that I used to tease and poke fun at him for being vegetarian. Or anything else I bugged him about. And he's not concerned with getting back at me for acting that way. He's been open to helping me out, whatever I need."

Matt was starting to get the picture. At home, Grant was suddenly above Adams in the social hierarchy. He didn't need to get back at Adams for his bullying, because he had already gotten back at Adams by infecting him. Just the same as he had gotten back at Brad Berkley and Marg and other people at work. He had started removing or reprogramming anyone who caused him grief. Who knows how many of the infected people Matt couldn't yet connect up to Grant had just happened to be in the wrong place, or to say the wrong thing to invoke Grant's ire. People who didn't even know his name. A cashier. A gas jockey. The rude woman in customer service. Grant had gotten back at them.

But how had he done it?

"It's great he's been able to help you," Matt said neutrally, careful not to give away his real train of thought.

Adams nodded. "I've really changed a lot since this happened to me," he commented. "I'm not the same guy I used to be."

"You're better," Matt suggested.

"Yeah. I dunno, maybe all the testosterone or hormones or whatever in the beef made me act like an ass. It's sort of embarrassing to look back now and realize what an idiot and a bully I was being, to someone who never did anything to hurt me."

"Sometimes people just rub you the wrong way."

"Well, Duane did, to start with. But he's actually a decent guy."

Matt decided to take a chance. "You know, I actually know Duane. I didn't realize he was your tenant."

"You know him?" Adams was thunderstruck.

"Yeah, I know him. We met at… the last place he was at."

He saw the glimmer in Adams' eye, and knew the man had heard about Grant's incarceration. Who knew what kind of ideas Adams was getting about how he and Grant had met each other or how well they knew each other. Matt plowed on ahead anyway.

"I actually came here to see whether I could get into his place while he was out. I didn't even know this is where you lived."

Adams laughed. "I guess that explains why you looked so surprised when I came out to meet you. But he's at home now. You don't need to get in while he's out, you can just go down and visit with him." He grinned. "I won't interrupt anything."

"No… I need to get into his suite while he's not home. It's a surprise I wanted to set up."

"Like a birthday party or something?"

"Yes," Matt agreed. "I don't want to tip him off."

"Sure!" Adams was all smiles of approval. "I'd love to help you out. Give something back to Duane for all his help. That's perfect. He's usually home in the evenings. I heard him come in a little while ago, so you won't be able to do it tonight. But if you have any time available during the day tomorrow…?"

"I can be here in the morning, when he goes to work. But don't you have work as well?"

Adams' expression faltered. Then he shook his head. "Not a problem. I'll just give you a key. You can drop it through the mail slot when you're done."

"That would work," Matt agreed. He was pleased. Not only would he be able to get into Grant's apartment with the permission of the landlord, but Adams wouldn't be around to look over his shoulder and ask questions about what he was doing. Matt would be on his own, and he would have all day to go through Grant's suite and figure out what he was up to.

Matt couldn't have asked for a better opportunity.

———

Matt was sure he would be able to sleep. It had been several days, and he could feel his body was ready to give out on him. The previous night he hadn't been able to sleep because of obsessing over the break-in. Now he was working on a break-in of his own. Not really a break-in, because he would have the landlord's key to access Grant's apartment. But it wasn't in the course of an authorized investigation. He didn't have any kind of warrant to search the place. But he did have the homeowner's permission.

Still, he waited for sleepiness to hit and it didn't. Or rather, it did—he kept nodding off for a second or two at a time, but every time he did, he woke up again and was more frustrated than the time before. Lying down in bed didn't help. If anything, his body rebelled and insisted it didn't need sleep. He ended up getting back up again half an hour later, wider awake than before. But he knew his brain was foggy, and he would make mistakes if he weren't careful.

He wished he had tracked the Sandman down and purchased some more of his magic sleeping pills. They would put him to sleep in a few minutes. He might not wake up for several days, which would spoil his scheduled search of Grant's house.

He just wanted to go to sleep and wake up again in eight hours like a normal person.

Like he used to be able to, back before the attack.

————

Morning eventually came around.

Matt was worried. Not having slept for several days, he was experiencing episodes of drifting off for a second or two at a time and then jerking awake. Microsleeps. His brain's way of trying to get the sleep it was starving for and yet prevented him from getting.

He wasn't going to be able to drive. It was far too likely he was going to plow into a light post. Or into another car or person. As the cop who had arrested him had said, sleep was just as much an impairment as alcohol. He was in need of a designated driver.

And he didn't just need a driver, but someone who could assist him in the investigation if his brain didn't cooperate.

He dialed Carol's number.

"Hi, Matt," she greeted, knowing who was calling through the wonders of caller ID. "How are you getting along?"

"Tired," Matt confessed. "And I need your help."

"Sure. I'm happy to help. What can I do for you?"

"I need you to help me with an investigation."

There was silence for a few moments. "Uh, Matt. You're not supposed to be on any investigations. You don't have any authority. Remember?"

"Yeah, that's one of the reasons I need your help. To make this a little more legitimate. But also, because I don't want to fall asleep on the job. That would be bad."

She let out an exasperated sigh. "Really, Matt? I thought you had agreed you would stop. When you were in hospital. Remember that?"

"I remember. But I found out a lot more since then. I found our patient zero."

"What?"

Her voice went nearly supersonic. Matt laughed, enjoying her surprise.

"I did it. I figured out who is spreading the infection. But I need to get the evidence. I need the proof he's doing it intentionally. I have access to his apartment while he is at work today. I'm going to search it. Can you come?"

"I shouldn't get involved in this," Carol warned. But her voice clearly indicated she wanted to. She had to. She needed to.

"Yes, you should. Somebody has to keep an eye on me."

"No kidding!" She laughed. "But I don't know if that excuse will fly with management."

"When we bring this guy down and have all the proof, they're not going to care. They're going to be happy you helped me out. We have to get this guy back behind bars before he spreads tick-borne infections to half the population of Colorado."

"*Back* behind bars?"

"I'll explain when I see you."

She didn't say anything at first. Matt waited for her to make the right decision.

"Oh, all right," she growled. "You want me to pick you up?"

"Yeah. I can't drive today."

"I'll be there in an hour or so, once I can get a couple of things put to bed here."

———

"You look like crap," Carol observed when Matt got into the car.

"Yeah, thanks."

"You're welcome," she said with a wry smile. "So…" she waited while Matt did up his seatbelt and got settled. "Tell me what's going on."

"You remember the two convicts I interviewed at the prison."

"When you got attacked."

"Right."

"Yes, it does stick out in my memory."

"One of those prisoners was named Duane Grant. He ended up with a cocktail of Lyme, Babesia, and alpha-gal, thanks to his roommate who had picked them up in New England and probably transmitted them via a tick infestation at the prison."

"Like sharing needles," Carol agreed. "I remember."

"Grant is now out. He's acting as an exterminator, and a number of the subjects in the Buffalo Head cluster had work done by him before they got sick."

Carol frowned and nodded. She shifted gears as she worked her way through the traffic. "So he's our Typhoid Mary? How do you speculate the infection is being spread? You aren't proposing it's person-to-person, are you?"

"No. He's also infected at least two people at work and his landlord. I can't find a connection with every subject, but I can with a large number of them."

"And how are you proposing the infection is spread?" Carol repeated, not to be distracted.

"I think... it's intentional. He's familiar with how infections can be spread from his experience in prison. He's had some training on collecting and handling ticks through his work at Bug Bee Gone. They regularly send specimens to the CDC. He's got everything he needs to safely collect ticks in his kit."

"So he's collecting ticks at work and planting them on people?"

"Something like that."

"With the number of infections in this cluster... that's a huge number of ticks to plant. You'd have to place at least ten ticks for each one that transmitted an infection."

Matt gave a shrug. "I don't know how he's gotten such a high infection rate."

"You can't weaponize ticks."

"No. Even on a small scale like this... he's not working from a laboratory. He's working from his house. A basement suite."

"How are we getting in there without a warrant?"

"The landlord. He's got alpha-gal, and probably an undiagnosed infection as well. He's agreed to let us in."

"He knows about it?"

"He knows... I know Grant... and he might think we're friends."

"So it's not a proper search."

Matt didn't answer.

"Let's start with the outside," Carol said, as they pulled into the carport. "Maybe there is something in the garbage or in plain sight we can use. Then we can get a warrant."

Matt's heart sank. "I can get us in. Adams gave me the key."

"But he can't do that. The landlord doesn't have the right to entry without notice. Not unless it is an emergency."

"An outbreak of tick-borne infections isn't an emergency?"

"Not yet," she said firmly. "Not without some hard evidence."

Like a sullen child, Matt climbed out of the car and walked into the back yard of Adams' and Grant's house. There was a small patio area. Most of the grass in the yard was neatly cropped. Carol gestured to the back of the lot.

"That's the most likely area to find ticks," she observed.

The grass was long, running up into a series of bushes planted along the back of the lot. Berry bushes, Matt suspected. And the long grass might have been intended to be a sort of a wildflower field, but it had become overgrown with weeds.

"Yeah. Let's do a sweep, see what kinds of numbers we get."

They went back to the car for their gear. Bug nets they would run through the grass and branches and then shake over a white sheet to count the various kinds of ticks and insects. They both put on gloves and hats, made sure their shirt cuffs and lapels were firmly buttoned and their pant cuffs tucked into their thick socks.

Matt watched Carol ready herself, grinning in spite of himself. She looked up at him.

"What?"

"We just look pretty... nerdy."

"Well, we are geeks."

"True. You know... I've always been impressed you are not squeamish around all the creepy crawlies we deal with."

"Because girls are supposed to be scared of bugs?"

"Well, our society does condition them along those lines."

"Most arthropods don't bother me." All geared up, they started to drag the bushes and grass.

"Most arthropods?" Matt repeated, looking sideways at her.

"Most."

"So which ones do bother you? Not ticks or spiders, obviously."

"No."

"What, then?"

"Butterflies."

Matt stopped sweeping and stared at her. "Butterflies?"

"Uh-huh. Pick up the pace; they're going to crawl away."

"I'm not letting it go."

Matt continued his sweep. Then they took the nets over to the sheet to shake out and count.

Even without counting, Matt knew it wasn't anything out of the ordinary. He'd dragged a lot of bushes with denser populations.

"So… why butterflies?"

"My dad took me out camping once when I was little. I was your typical little princess, and I loved birds and flowers and butterflies. Anything on Cinderella."

"I can just picture you as a little girl."

Carol glowered at him.

"Sorry," Matt apologized.

"We were sitting by the tent, resting. There were black and orange butterflies everywhere. They were so pretty, and I thought we must be in an enchanted wood. Dad said if we sat very still, some of them might land near us. Or even on us. So I did. I sat very still, and one landed on me. Then another. I wanted to laugh or talk to Dad, but I didn't want to scare them away. I looked up, and they were everywhere, all around us." She cleared her throat and pretended she was counting bugs from their sweep for a few minutes before resuming. "They gathered more and more thickly. They were swarming us. They started to look like a cloud, a funnel cloud coming straight down to us. They kept landing on me and crawling on me. My skin, my hair, my face. I wasn't trying to be still anymore. I was waving my arms around and trying to keep them off. But they kept landing. I tried to scream at my dad, and I got one in my mouth. I felt like I was inhaling them, they were so thick, and they were clustered all over me."

Matt could feel it himself. The soft crawl of their legs. The flapping of their wings. A swarm of them so close to his face he couldn't breathe.

"It's no wonder you don't like them! What did you do?"

"I screamed. Completely freaked out. My dad ran into the tent and left me outside. I ran away and jumped into the river, fully clothed, to get them off of me. We didn't camp overnight like we had planned. We went straight home."

"Why did your dad leave you alone?"

"He went to get something out of the tent. Bug spray or a blanket, I don't really know what. But he didn't say, he just dived into it and left me there. Like he was abandoning me."

"It must have been horrifying."

"It was. I can't even look at a butterfly without getting choked up. As soon as I see them, I can feel them on my skin, feel myself inhaling them." She cleared her throat again and shook her head. "Uggh."

"We'll drop it. I'm sorry." Matt sighed, looking over the arthropods on the sheet. "I guess we should gather some ticks for testing. Just to see what the bacteria rates are amongst them."

"Makes sense."

They worked in silence, gathering ticks into specimen tubes. They could test them or send them over to the CDC to have them test.

After they were done, Matt walked around the yard once more, looking for anything suspicious or out of place. If they didn't find anything, Carol wouldn't agree to go inside. The day would be a write-off.

"So why did you ask me along?" Carol asked. "Aside from not being able to drive. I mean, you could have gotten a cab to bring you here."

"Aside from that, and missing your company... I didn't want to get inside and fall asleep."

She laughed. "Seriously?"

"You've read news articles haven't you? Every now and then, there's a story reported about someone who breaks into a house and then falls asleep on the bed mid-burglary. I didn't want to be that guy."

"I guess I never considered that."

"Until you've been in my position, you wouldn't, would you? I always thought 'there's the world's stupidest burglar.' Like, how stupid do you have to be not to fall asleep in the middle of a break-in? But now I'm thinking... I wonder if they have a sleep disorder. They've turned to crime, because they can't keep a job falling asleep all the time. Maybe it's narcolepsy. A narcolepsy episode triggered by stress... it could be, couldn't it?"

"I don't really know. I did some research, but not much into narcolepsy. I didn't think that was what you had."

"I'm never going to think someone is stupid for falling asleep ever again," Matt said. "And I'm never going to think someone is lazy because they don't make it to a meeting or sleep in. Or fell asleep at their desk. I have a whole new outlook on sleep now."

"I guess. You look pretty rough," Carol observed.

"I know." Matt kicked at the dirt at the edge of a flower border, his face hot. He bent down and looked more closely. "Hey, Carol...?"

"What did you find?" She stepped closer to him. "Ticks?"

"No. Not ticks..."

Carol looked down at where Matt had scuffed the dirt. "Rabbit droppings." She glanced around. "I wonder if there are wild rabbits around here." It took a minute for her to make the connection Matt had. "Wait... tularemia? You think this is where it came from? Your subject has a rabbit?"

"Tularemia is rare, and I wasn't the only case. If he has a rabbit with ticks, that would explain it."

"Do you think all the ticks came from his rabbit? Maybe he's been spreading them unknowingly. They hitch on his clothes, get spread to other people he's around. Not targeted, just accidental exposure."

"I wondered before whether it was intentional or whether he just attracted them, like some people attract mosquitos and others don't. Pheromones? If he has a rabbit, that might explain why he has so much contact with ticks. But I don't know if it explains everything. Like... how did I get it?"

"I think this might just constitute that emergency you were hoping for."

"Yeah?" He searched Carol's face. "You think so? I know I was giving you trouble, but I want you to be sure. Do you think there's cause for us to go in there?"

"This is pretty good evidence he's the one who is spreading tularemia. Though how he would have infected you, I don't know. You haven't had any contact with him. But maybe when you were interviewing one of his victims or going somewhere he had gone… his office could be crawling with ticks."

"An extermination company? Not likely. Besides, I didn't get there until after I was sick. Maybe it was from one of the subjects I interviewed…"

"If he's spreading tularemia and other bacterial infections around the city, we need to get in there right away. Stop this before it goes any further."

"Okay." Matt produced the key Adams had given him. "I have the key from the landlord, and I have the landlord's permission to enter. We have evidence to support the theory Grant is spreading infectious diseases. We have cause."

Carol nodded. They took off their hats and gloves and shoved them in their pockets. They went to the basement door. Matt's hand shook a little as he fit the key into the keyhole and turned it. They entered the suite. It was dim, and Carol flipped a light switch on. They looked around the little living room.

"Do you smell that?" Carol asked.

Matt did. Rabbit pee. The males especially could produce a very musky smelling urine. Unmistakable to anyone who was familiar with it. He approached the closed door that appeared to be the bedroom.

When he pushed the door open, the smell was almost overwhelming. Matt saw several glass cases lined up along the floor. Not just one rabbit. There were four cages. Unlike a typical rabbit cage, they were not open bars, but glassed in, with fine mesh tops.

"There they are," Carol whispered.

Matt bent down for a closer look at the rabbits. They did not perk up or follow his movements like he expected a pet rabbit to do. They just lay there, unmoving, barely breathing. Glassy-eyed.

"These rabbits are sick."

Carol nodded. "If they've had ticks for a few months, they could be pretty sick."

Matt moved from one cage to the next. "All of them? They're isolated. Ticks wouldn't be able to get from one cage to the other. I don't think even nymphs could fit through that mesh."

"But they are all sick."

There was a white rabbit on the end, lying near the end of the cage

Matt was crouched at. He stared at it through the glass from a couple of inches away.

"They're infected," he said. "Come look at this one."

Carol knelt down beside him. "What am I looking for? Oh…"

She too could see the dark spots through the rabbit's thin, almost translucent white hair. Ticks. Not just a few of them. Not just one or two its owner hadn't happened to notice. But dozens, maybe hundreds of ticks and fleas crawled over and around the listless animal.

"You said I wasn't squeamish about arthropods," Carol said. "But… hold on…"

She left the room, and Matt heard the hollow echo of a bathroom door shutting. He tried to ignore the rest of the sounds that issued forth through the thin wood of the door. The toilet flushed, and she returned.

"You okay?" Matt asked.

"Yes." She swallowed. "I'll be fine. But you should look in the kitchen."

"Why, what's in the kitchen?" Matt knew she wasn't going to tell him. He walked out of the pungent bedroom into the little kitchen decorated largely in green tile. He looked around and spotted what Carol had seen on her way out of the bathroom.

He saw gloves. Tweezers. Rows of specimen jars were lined up on the counter. Most were empty, but a few were stoppered, and when Matt bent down and looked into them, he saw several ticks in each.

"I'd say that's proof."

"I agree," Carol said. "Now we need to figure out who we bring into this. DOH? CDC? Police?"

"I guess DOH would be our first report."

"Yeah." Carol sighed. "I was actually hoping I wouldn't have to explain this to Mavis…"

"Sorry. Use me as a scapegoat if you want. I insisted you come over here. You only came to dissuade me. But when you saw the rabbit droppings and looked in through the window…" He glanced up. "Can you see them through the window?"

"I don't know. I'll check. We should have looked in the windows before we came in."

"Yeah, I guess that would have made sense."

She went back out of the house, and in a minute, he saw her looking through the low window, looking down at the counters. She gave him a thumbs-up. Matt breathed a sigh of relief.

He waited for Carol to come back in, but she didn't, and eventually, he left the apartment, shutting off the lights and closing the door behind him. Carol was standing in the yard talking on her phone. She motioned for him to join her. She said a few words and then waited, grimacing at Matt.

"What's going on?"

She shook her head and didn't answer. But after a few minutes of waiting, she put her hand over the mike of the phone and spoke to him.

"They have to coordinate all the agencies," she explained. "They said to lock up and leave."

"What? We can't just leave."

"They have to get the proper authorizations and warrant and decide whose operation it is. They said it may be a day or two before someone will be here to execute the warrant."

"A day or two?"

"There's a lot of red tape. I don't know. No one sees it as an emergency. Duane is not going anywhere. They're not convinced he's doing it intentionally or will infect anyone else in the time it takes to get everything organized."

"We should have called the police. They would have come straight over."

"Well, they won't now. Not without cooperation from DOH and CDC." She gave a little shrug. "Sorry. It seemed like the right way to go…"

"Not your fault. I was the one who said to call DOH first. I thought they would be all over it. I mean, this is what we do! This is the whole reason our department and the CDC exist in the first place. To identify and contain… outbreaks."

"I could try reporting it to Homeland as a terror threat," Carol said, with a teasing smile.

"All they'd do is throw us in prison. I don't think I want to check out Guantanamo after my visit to the county jail."

"I did have other things on my schedule," she agreed.

Matt looked back at the house. "So we're just supposed to leave everything as we found it. And hope he doesn't infect anyone else before they get around to officially searching the place."

"Afraid so."

Matt swore. He tipped back his head, closing his eyes and trying to calm the anger that rose in him. He had felt so vindicated when they discovered the rabbits and the specimen jars. Carol finally believed him. Mavis and everyone else at the DOH and CDC would see he was right and that they should not have suspended him. Even with his sleep disorder, he was still able to see the pattern no one else had, and to investigate it to the correct conclusion. He wasn't disabled. Just a little... atypical.

"Matt."

"Mmmm?" Matt didn't open his eyes.

"We should get you home. I don't want you passing out on your feet."

Matt forced his eyes open and gave her what he hoped was a reassuring smile. "I'm fine. But you're right... there's no point in sticking around here, attracting attention. We don't need any nosy neighbors calling Grant to say there are people poking around where they shouldn't be. We've been here long enough."

———

They got to the car and untucked their pants from their socks. Matt unbuttoned his shirt cuffs and rolled up his sleeves so he would be more comfortable.

Carol was slapping her legs. She started to swear, brushing at them and slapping some more.

"What's wrong?"

"They're biting me!"

"What?" Matt got out and went around Carol's side of the car. "What is it?"

Carol stopped slapping and pulled back her pant cuff, showing the area of bared skin above her socks.

"Look!"

Matt couldn't see much with his naked eye. There was something moving over Carol's skin. Light brown specks. Carol scratched at the skin with her finger and brought her fingertip up near Matt's face.

"They're nymphs," she said. "Immature ticks. And they're aggressive!"

She again started to slap and brush them off. Matt's own skin crawled when he realized the nymphs were swarming. Such an aggressive swarm questing for blood was rare, but not unheard of. He could almost feel them crawling up his own legs, up past his socks and toward his knees.

Matt slapped at an itch on his leg and belatedly realized it wasn't just his skin crawling. He too was being swarmed by the nymphs. He swore and started to slap and brush at them just as Carol had, pulling up his pant legs and trying to knock them all off. But it only seemed to give them a bigger target area. His legs itched all over.

"Get in!" he told Carol, motioning for her to pull her legs into the car.

"But the ticks—"

"They're coming from outside. Pull your legs in so I can shut the door."

She obeyed. Matt slammed the door shut and ran around to the passenger side and also got in.

"Drive!"

"Where, your place?"

"I don't care where, just away from here."

Carol pulled the car out of the carport and sprayed gravel as she pulled forward down the lane.

"Now they're in the car," she protested.

"Not as many as would be if you left the door open. We were right in the middle of the swarm."

Matt continued to slap and brush at his legs. Carol couldn't do much while she was driving.

"We'll spray the car after we look after ourselves. We've got to wash these off, then go over our legs with a magnifying glass and a pair of fine tweezers."

"Yeah. Your place?"

"I think we're closer to yours."

Carol glanced aside at him. A cautious, measuring look. She had never invited him to her home. They hadn't exchanged addresses. But Matt knew what neighborhood she lived in.

"I suppose."

Carol drove in silence to her house, where they took turns in the shower washing away as many of the nymphs that hadn't attached as they could. While Carol was taking her shower, Matt brought in the spray equipment from her car and sprayed down all the areas they had stepped with insecticide. The session with the tweezers was long and tedious, and

Matt wasn't one hundred percent sure they had succeeded in finding and removing all the tiny nymphs, but it was the best they could do.

"Still itchy?" Carol asked.

"I don't think I'll ever stop being itchy. I don't think I'll ever be able to stop feeling them crawling all over me."

Carol nodded. Matt leaned his head back against the back of the couch and closed his eyes.

29

———————

Duane pulled into his parking space in the back and got out. He stopped at the edge of the paved area, looking down at the imprint in the soft dirt at the edge of it. Someone had pulled too far onto the asphalt pad, their tires sinking into the mud at the far side. He never drove in that far, especially not with Duncan's little car, which hardly needed the whole pad to park on. Those tire tracks were not his, and looking closely at them, he didn't think they were Rich's car's either. Not that Rich would use Duane's parking spot. But he might have if he had just stopped in at the house to pick something up while Duane was gone. If he knew he was just going to be there for a few minutes.

Duane walked slowly into the yard and looked around. Nothing seemed out of place at first, but when he really focused and looked closely, he thought the grass had been trampled, and there were footprints over by the bushes in the back of the yard that looked like a small woman's sneaker. Smaller than Duane's shoes.

He stopped at one of the back windows and looked through it into his suite. He could see his specimen jars on the counter, and the bathroom door was standing ajar. Duane swallowed. He looked down at the dirt and found a few smudged marks in the dirt where someone might have stood.

His heart pounding now, the blood rising in his face, Duane hurried to the door and fit his key in the lock. He stopped for a moment and listened for any sound. He tried the handle without turning the key and found it was still locked. With a sigh of relief, he unlocked it and entered. Still careful. Still wary of any sound and watching for anything out of place.

It was possible he had left the bathroom door ajar. He wouldn't normally, but if he'd been distracted before leaving that morning, it was possible he might have. But he would not have left the bedroom door open too. There was no chance. Duane pushed the door open the rest of the way and turned on the light. Everything seemed to be untouched.

He pulled out his phone and dialed Rich's number. He wasn't home yet. He shouldn't have been home during the day. But there could have been an emergency. A leaking pipe. A running faucet. Rich had a key and as the landlord, he had the right to enter if he thought something needed his immediate attention or there would be damage.

"Hey, Duane," Rich greeted cheerfully.

"Rich. Hey, I just got home. You haven't... been downstairs, have you? To check on something?"

"No, I've been at work. Oh—" Rich cut himself off and didn't say what he'd been thinking.

"What? I think someone has been in my suite."

"It was supposed to be a surprise," Rich said. "He's not... still there?"

"He?" Duane swallowed. His heart felt hard and cold. His chest hurt. "Who? Who was here?"

"Your *friend*. Matt something. He was going to surprise you."

He'd done that.

"He's not my friend," Duane growled. "What did you let him in for? When was he here?"

"I gave him the key. I told him to put it in the mailbox when he was done. What do you mean he isn't your friend? He told me..."

"He's not my friend! He's the DOH! You can't let them in!"

"But... he knew you. He said..."

Duane threw the phone across the room. It hit the wall with a hollow thud and fell to the carpet. No satisfying shatter of glass and spraying parts. Just a dull thud.

———

At first, Matt didn't know where he was. He looked around the unfamiliar apartment and waited for the memories to begin seeping back. He could hear someone else moving around and straightened up, rubbing his eyes. There was a blanket wrapped around him, unfamiliar in pattern and texture.

Carol smiled at him.

"Oh." It came back to Matt in a rush. "I'm sorry. I didn't mean to doze off."

"It's okay. It's not like you were in the way. Did you have a nice nap?"

"Yeah." Matt yawned and stretched. "I'm feeling pretty good now. You wouldn't believe how satisfying sleeping can feel after you've gone a few days without."

"Like eating when you're really starving?"

"I guess so. Sort of like that."

"Speaking of which, can I get you something to eat before we go?"

"Where are we going? I suppose I should go home."

"We're going back to Grant's house. Supposed to be there in about an hour. You up for it?"

"Really? Already? They got it worked out more quickly than expected."

She raised a brow at him and didn't comment. "Do you want something to eat? I could make you a chicken sandwich."

"Yeah, that would be great. I'm not hungry, but I know I need to eat."

Matt tried to stretch out the painful crick in his neck. He rubbed it firmly, and slid his fingers up, feeling the ridge in the bone at the back of his skull.

"If we're going back out, I should spray your car. Just to be sure we don't get attacked again. And let's park around the front this time, not in the carport."

"We'll park around front. You don't need to spray the car, I already did."

"You did? I guess I slept right through it." Matt looked around and saw the spray equipment was, in fact, gone.

Carol puttered around the kitchen making Matt's sandwich. He decided he'd better make a run to the bathroom. He splashed water on his face and looked in the mirror. He had quite a growth of coarse stubble. He didn't remember when he'd shaved last. He thought it had been the day before, but it couldn't have been with that much growth.

"What's the date?" he asked Carol, as he sat down at her sunny yellow kitchen table with the sandwich in front of him.

"The fifteenth. Eat."

"The fifteenth? Then I slept through…"

"You needed to sleep. Your body knew that. I'm just glad you woke up on your own when you did."

Matt took a couple of big bites of the chicken sandwich. Cold chicken, with just the right amount of mayonnaise, salt, and pepper. And something else. Paprika, maybe. It was good. Matt felt like he hadn't eaten in a couple of days. Maybe he hadn't. It filled an empty spot he didn't even know he had.

"So they're executing the search in an hour? Less than that, now? We should head out."

"Do you want to shower before we go?"

"I don't have the time. I'll comb my hair. That will have to do, as far as making me look decent."

He could well imagine how Rebecca would have looked at him if he had made a similar announcement to her. Going out anywhere with her without showering and shaving and making himself look as good as possible? She would leave him behind. There was no way she would be seen with him in the condition he was currently in.

But Carol just shrugged it off. He supposed she didn't much care how he looked. They weren't on a date. It wasn't a social occasion. It didn't reflect on her reputation. But he suspected it was more than that. Rebecca was big on looks. She was a beautiful woman, and always wanted him to look his best to show her to her best advantage. Carol was more like Matt. A bit nerdy. More focused on her research or other work than in looking like a supermodel for work. Not that she wasn't pretty, but she wasn't obsessed with looks.

Matt hurried to finish his sandwich. He didn't want to miss anything at Grant's house. He wanted to be there to see it all go down. It was his bust. He didn't want to take the chance anyone would be there ahead of them.

"Why don't you just take that with you in the car?" Carol suggested. "Instead of wolfing it down without even chewing it. Go ahead and comb your hair and we'll go right now. You can eat on the way."

"Thanks. Yeah. That would be great."

His hair was combed and slicked down in about thirty seconds, and they were out the door. Carol didn't stop to fiddle with her hair or fuss over what shoes she was going to wear. Matt was a little anxious stepping back into the car after the attack by the tick nymphs, but Carol said she had sprayed it, and Carol knew her job. It would be just as safe as Matt's car. Maybe more so.

———

They had to park down the street, and they weren't allowed to get close enough to see what was going on as the bust was finally made.

Matt couldn't see what the big deal was. Grant was at work, not at home. There was no danger any of them was going to get shot unless they shot each other.

Carol took it all calmly. Matt was so tightly wound, he knew he'd better keep his mouth shut, or he'd end up saying something he regretted later.

It was an hour before a policeman finally came up to the car window.

"You can come over now. Crychuk wants to talk to you."

Crychuk, it turned out, was giving various orders to his officers. Any drama was over and done. They had broken into Grant's suite while he was at work, gathered the evidence they needed, and now someone would be on their way to arrest him to prevent him from infecting anyone else.

"Tell me what you saw here two days ago," Crychuk told Matt and Carol.

They exchanged glances. Matt let Carol take the lead on answering the question. He hadn't been there in an official capacity.

"There were specimen jars and collection equipment in the kitchen. And four rabbits infected with ticks in cages in the bedroom."

Crychuk scowled at the two of them.

"You do anything to tip him off we were coming?"

"No, nothing." Carol and Matt shook their heads simultaneously.

"You think he knew?" Matt asked.

"He's gone. Rabbited." Crychuk smiled, showing his teeth in a humorless smile. "Literally."

Carol cocked her head. "He took the rabbits?"

Crychuk jerked one thumb over his shoulder, directing their attention to a cluster of investigators looking down at the ground. His heart tight with worry, Matt moved toward them. As he got closer, he could see the little white patch of fur in the grass. He stayed several feet back. A couple of the men had put on gloves. They watched with amusement as Matt folded his pant cuffs around his leg and tucked them into his socks. He rolled his shirt sleeves down and buttoned them. He took another step closer, pulling a pair of gloves all the way up over his shirt cuffs. He looked down at the dead rabbit.

"That rabbit was crawling with ticks and fleas carrying tularemia yesterday," he advised. "Do you really want to take the chance?"

Everyone took a collective step back and then shuffled back even further, looking at each other.

"How do you know it had tularemia?" challenged an investigator with a CDC ID badge on a lanyard around his neck.

"Because some of the people Grant infected ended up with tularemia. What do you think killed the rabbit?"

One of them reached forward with his foot to nudge the rabbit's body, then thought better of it and drew back.

"Where are the other rabbits?" Matt asked. He looked at the investigators and glanced around the yard for any other bodies.

"The other rabbits?"

"There were four of them."

Everybody suddenly seemed jumpy. They looked around, looking for other bodies or signs of the rabbits.

Carol came up to Matt and put her hand on his arm. "Maybe he took the other ones with him. In pet carriers."

"Why would he take three and not this one?"

"Because it was so sick. Maybe the other three weren't so sick."

Matt looked toward the back lane. "Maybe not," he agreed. "But I can't see Grant putting three rabbits in pet carriers and taking them with him in the car. Carriers aren't sealed like the glass cages. He knows the ticks and fleas could get out and infect him."

"What do *you* think happened to the other rabbits?"

"I think he released all four. One of them didn't make it out of the yard. The others... I guess they made it a little further."

"They couldn't get far," Carol said. "They were too sick. We should look around, see if we can find them."

They didn't wait for anyone to organize a search, but walked out into the back lane. They sprinted through the carport in case the nymph swarm was not gone. Matt looked up and down.

"If I was a rabbit, I would go that way." He pointed at a green space across the lane a couple of houses down. They followed Matt's instinct, walking over to look at it. A small pathway cut down the middle of the green space, down a hill, into a wide park, dense with trees.

"Urban park," Matt observed.

"Good place to breed ticks."

"If the rabbits got down there, they'll spread the infections whether they live or die."

———

They walked back to the house.

"You didn't try to arrest Grant at work?" Matt asked Crychuk.

"He didn't show up at work today. So… no. We didn't." Grant wouldn't have released his rabbits and then gone to work as usual. If something had tipped him off they were onto him, he wouldn't stick around. He would get the hell out of there.

"But you'll be able to catch him, right? You've got a description of him and his car? That car won't be hard to spot."

"Grant could sell it quickly and buy a new identity with the cash. And he's been in prison, so I'm sure he'll have learned how to do it."

"You're not even trying to catch him?"

"Of course I am," Crychuk growled. "He's a dangerous man, if you guys are right about him spreading these infections intentionally and killing his brother. We'll do everything we can to trace him. But he's not going to make it easy on us. I already had them run his credit card. He took out a large cash advance yesterday, and it hasn't been used since. Who knows how much money he inherited from his brother. We'll have to compel the estate to give us that information. Sure, I put an alert out on the car, but you can be sure it's the first thing he'll ditch. If he's smart…" Crychuk shook his head. "He's long gone."

———

They were still there when Rich Adams got home from his job. He looked around at all the people and vehicles in confusion. He waved off questions from the CDC and police, making a beeline for Matt.

"What's going on? What's happening here? Is Duane okay?"

"As far as we know, Duane is fine," Matt assured him. Matt looked at Crychuk. "Is there somewhere we could talk to Mr. Adams in private?"

Crychuk studied him intently. Matt tried to indicate without word or gesture that Adams trusted Matt and would talk to him. Any other investigator or cop was just going to make Adams clam up. Crychuk ground his jaw and nodded.

"Adams lives upstairs, doesn't he? Just go home with him. I'll come by later if I need anything."

"Come on," Matt touched Adams' elbow. "We'll just go talk in your living room, okay? I'll explain everything."

It took some doing. At first, Rich wasn't willing to believe Grant had infected him and had been intentionally infecting others as well.

"But we were friends," he insisted. "He wouldn't do something like that to me!"

"Did you become friends before or after you got sick?"

"Well... after."

"That worked out nicely for him, didn't it? You told me you used to tease and torment him, until you found out you were allergic to meat. Then everything changed."

"Well... yeah."

"So he got you to change your behavior by infecting you."

"But how...? He never came upstairs to plant any ticks. He never put anything on me."

"He was very creative. If he wanted to, he could have found a way to put it through your ventilation or in through the window. Have you pat one of the rabbits."

"His rabbit? What does the rabbit have to do with it?"

"The rabbits," Matt emphasized the plural, "were being used to culture the infections. I don't know whether he started with infected ticks or infected rabbits, or both. But if he did it like I think he did, he would feed the ticks off of one rabbit, then transfer them to another for the next blood meal, until all the rabbits and most of the ticks were infected. That's how he could reach such a high successful infection rate."

"I only ever saw one rabbit. He would take it out in the yard for a walk, on a leash. Sometimes he'd take it down to the park for a walk. I always thought that was crazy. Rabbits don't train to leashes like dogs. And what if it was attacked by a dog in the park? But he said the bunny needed the chance to make new friends."

Matt's stomach churned. "I'll bet he did. Eight legged ones."

Rich sighed and wiped his forehead with his hand. "So he took off after I told him you'd been here. And he's out there now… infecting other people. Makes me think of some vampire story. Except instead of breeding more vampires… he's breeding new vegetarians."

30

Obviously, Matt knew the way to Mavis' office, but Carol escorted him there anyway, giving him an encouraging smile and making small talk along the way to keep his mind occupied. She delivered him to Mavis' door and stood there as if waiting to be invited in.

"Mr. Malloy. Good to see you again," Mavis said crisply. "Miss Stern." Obviously, Carol was dismissed. She shrugged at Matt and retreated. Matt entered Mavis' lair and looked at the chair in front of her desk.

"Have a seat."

He did.

"So…" Mavis studied Matt, putting her glasses on and then removing them again and letting them dangle on their chain. "You've been a busy boy."

Matt lifted his shoulders in a shrug, heat rushing to his face.

"Apparently, you have difficulty understanding what 'leave' means."

"I know…" Matt looked down at her desk rather than at her face. "I know I kept investigating when I probably shouldn't have. But Duane Grant is dangerous. I had to try to stop him."

"As it turns out, yes he was, and it was our duty to gather all the information that we could and pass it to the proper authorities."

"Which I did," Matt pointed out.

"Hmm. I'm not sure you were quite as diligent about passing it on as you were about the investigation part." She tapped the clicker end of her pen on the stack of papers in front of her. "What did you see when you looked at the cluster in Buffalo Head? What was it you saw that no one else did?"

Matt was startled by the question. He hadn't expected anything but recriminations, maybe disciplinary action. He pursed his lips and ventured a glance at her face. Mavis didn't look as angry as he had expected.

"It's hard to explain. It wasn't anything that I could put my finger on. I showed it to you, and Carol, and the others. No one saw anything but a random scatter. But it just... it didn't feel right. It was only slightly above norms. I could easily have written it off. But I couldn't." Matt looked over his shoulder at Mavis' open door, feeling exposed. "It felt like there was something wrong there. Something... malicious."

"Something malicious. How would you know that from a random sampling of infection reports? It's not exactly a checkbox on the form. We haven't ever experienced deliberate infections before. So why would you expect to?"

"I can't say. The reports that I was reading just didn't sound right. Too many things that were unusual and didn't fit together. Rare infections. The geography. I just couldn't get it to fit."

"Well, as it turned out, you were right. I thought you were holding back on your sign-off because you were... impaired. That it was just another symptom that you couldn't handle the work." She forced eye contact. "I was wrong."

Matt glanced away. "It's all right. Sometimes I *was* too impaired. But I just needed a little more time to figure it out."

She doodled in the corner of one of the reports on her desk. He'd never seen her do that before. She was obviously worrying something over in her mind.

"How are you now? How can we work things out?"

Matt was taken aback. He contemplated the question. "If I can work on a modified schedule, that would help. Connect remotely from home. I'm trying to get my sleep under control, but sometimes... there's a few days when I really can't work."

Mavis considered this. "I don't know how to manage that."

"Yeah."

"I'll talk to my manager... and see if there is something we can do."

———

Matt had been hanging around Rebecca's favorite club. Not because he felt like a night out on the town, but because he was hoping to run into her. He didn't think she would appreciate him showing up at her door again. But she couldn't object if she ran into him while he was out. There was no law against him going out clubbing on his own.

He was pleased when he saw her come in. Not just that she was there, but that she didn't walk in the door with another man. That was a point in his favor.

Matt didn't go up to her immediately. In fact, he didn't go up to her at all. He happened to find a seat at the bar in her line of sight, but he didn't approach her. It was a few tense minutes before Rebecca finally showed up at his side.

"Matt! I didn't expect to see you here!"

"Hey, Bec! I didn't know you were here."

"I just got here a few minutes ago. I saw you were here, so..."

"Well, it's nice to see you." He motioned to the bartender and indicated Rebecca with a motion. "What do you want? Margarita?"

"Yeah, sure, that would be nice."

They waited, and Matt sipped his beer. "So how have you been?"

"I'm good. Work is going well..."

Matt nodded. Eventually, Rebecca picked up the slack in the conversation. "How about you? Are things going any better?"

"We figured out what it is I have. This sleep disorder. Actually, it's a circadian rhythm disorder. So that's really good news."

"That *is* good news. So they can give you a medication to treat it?"

"No... I'm trying melatonin and some other strategies. I'm pretty optimistic I can get it under control." That might be overstating it slightly. He wasn't optimistic or confident in the results at all. "It's already making a difference. I'm sleeping at least once in most twenty-four hour cycles now."

"Well..." Rebecca picked up her drink and tasted it. "That sounds good. Good for you."

"Since I'm doing better now," Matt said, as if the thought had just occurred to him. "Maybe you and I… we could try again. See if things worked better now."

"Uh…" Rebecca looked around the room. She took another sip of her drink. She smiled brightly. "Actually, I'm seeing someone else now."

Matt's hopes came crashing down. The beer turned sour in his stomach. "Oh. I see."

"There he is now." Rebecca waved across the crowded room to attract her new boyfriend's attention.

The man, a tall, light-skinned black man, slid through the crowds to get to Rebecca and Matt. Without looking at Matt, he embraced Rebecca and kissed her soundly, pulling her tight against him. Not until after that, with Rebecca giggling breathlessly, did he look at Matt.

"Oh, hello."

Rebecca giggled again. "Landon, this is Matt. An old friend of mine."

An old friend. She didn't even refer to Matt as an ex. It was like their relationship had never even happened.

"Nice to meet you," Landon said politely, looking over Matt's shoulder. He tossed a bill on the counter to cover Rebecca's drink, nodding to the bartender. He took her by the arm. "Let's go get a booth."

"Okay. See you, Matt. It was nice talking to you again."

———

"Are you ready for me?" Carol asked.

Matt smiled and opened the door the rest of the way for her, sweeping his arm to invite her in.

Carol entered. She paused to look around. Matt held his breath to see how she would react. The entryway was dim, lit only by a few candles on the side table that he had lit on his way to the door.

"Is this part of your therapy?" Carol asked, sliding her jacket off and handing it to him.

Matt hung the coat in the closet.

"Yeah. Blackout after six o'clock. The only acceptable lights are candles or red lights.

"It's romantic," she said, smiling.

Matt breathed a long breath out and in again, trying to relax the tenseness in his stomach. "I hope so."

She gave him an uncertain look, then another smile. Matt took her arm and led her into the kitchen to keep her from running into anything in the dimness. The table was set, and more candles shone on the table. The flickering flames made the china and silverware glitter and gave them a rich sheen.

"It's all very lovely!"

"Glad you think so. Now, I'm not much of a cook, so I'm relying on the candles to make everything look better than it really is to fool your brain into thinking it tastes better."

"Sounds good!"

Matt pulled the dish out of the microwave and indicated the cold salads. "There's lots here, help yourself and feel free to go back for seconds."

"It all looks great."

"That's what I'm counting on."

The dinner went even better than Matt could have hoped. They retired to the living room afterward, where there were red lights rather than candles.

"One thing I learned is I can't have candles unless someone else is over," Matt said. "So I have red lights in here instead. With the candles, if I fall asleep, I could burn the place down. And my landlord probably wouldn't be too happy."

"No," Carol agreed with a small smile. "He probably wouldn't. I promise if you fall asleep, I'll blow out the candles."

"Good. I'm counting on you."

"So is it helping? All this stuff?"

"Cold shower first thing and bright lights for three hours in the morning. Blackout and mega-dose melatonin before bed. A bunch of little things. So far… yeah, it's helping. Not perfect, but I'm at least sleeping for a while each night, and that's better than I was doing before. I'm hoping I'll be able to come back to work before long, on some kind of modified schedule."

"I hope so. I miss having you around."

"I miss being there. I enjoy working. It's weird kicking around here with nothing to do all day except make sure I go to sleep and get up at the right time."

"I guess. It sounds boring. Though you can get caught up on your reading…" She nodded to the stack of books on the side table.

"No blue screens before bed. So no computer or TV. I'm getting a lot more reading in than I ever was before."

Matt sat down on the couch and indicated the space next to him. Carol sat down and snuggled up with him. She scratched her arm, wincing and frowning.

"What are you reading now? You want to read some out loud to me?"

"That sounds like heaven," Matt agreed.

And it was.

EPILOGUE

Duane looked down the hill from his little house to the green swath of parkway and pathways. He held the new little bunny, soft and sleepy, in his lap. It would be a great area to go for walks.

He would be more careful this time. Operating in Matt Malloy's hometown had been a mistake. Duane had been sloppy, assuming that no one would be able to trace him. Duncan's death had been unusual and might have drawn attention to his name.

Duane had agonized over whether it was better to choose an area with low tick infection rates, where the doctors and CDC were less likely to diagnose them properly, so that no new patterns would be noticed and investigations launched. Or in an area with higher infection rates, where a few new ones were not likely to attract attention.

In Colorado, he'd been indiscriminate in who he infected, not weighing the significance of their infractions or how likely an infection was to correct their behavior. This time, he would be more careful, targeting those who were most likely to be reformed by an infection or brand new alpha-gal allergy.

With a new home, new job, and a new name, Duane was untrackable. He could continue his mission.

As long as he was careful, no one would ever trace the infections back to him again.

He smiled, stroking the rabbit's fur.

Did you enjoy this book? Reviews and recommendations are vital to making a book successful.

Please leave a review at your favorite book store or review site and share it with your friends.

Don't miss the following bonus material:
Sign up for mailing list to get a free ebook
Read a sneak preview chapter
Other books by P.D. Workman
Learn more about the author

Sign up for my mailing list at pdworkman.com and get Gluten-Free Murder for free!

PREVIEW OF SHE WORE MOURNING

ZACHARY GOLDMAN MYSTERIES #1

CHAPTER 1

ZACHARY GOLDMAN STARED DOWN the telephoto lens at the subjects before him. It was one of those days that left tourists gaping over the gorgeous scenery. Dark trees against crisp white snow, with the mountains as a backdrop. Like the picture on a Christmas card.

The thought made Zachary feel sick.

But he wasn't looking at the scenery. He was looking at the man and the woman in a passionate embrace. The pretty young woman's cheeks were flushed pink, more likely with her excitement than the cold, since she had barely stepped out of her car to greet the man. He had a swarthier complexion and a thin black beard, and was currently turned away from Zachary's camera.

Zachary wasn't much to look at himself. Average height, black hair cut too short, his own three-day growth of beard not hiding how pinched and pale his face was. He'd never considered himself a good catch.

He waited patiently for them to move, to look around at their surroundings so that he could get a good picture of their faces.

They thought they were alone; that no one could see them without being seen. They hadn't counted on the fact that Zachary had been surveilling them for a couple of weeks and had known where they would go. They gave him lots of warning so that he could park his car out of sight, camouflage himself in the trees, and settle in to wait for their appearance. He was no amateur; he'd been a private investigator since she had been choosing wedding dresses for her Barbie dolls.

He held down the shutter button to take a series of shots as they came up for air and looked around at the magnificent surroundings, smiling at each other, eyes shining.

All the while, he was trying to keep the negative thoughts at bay. Why had he fallen into private detection? It was one of the few ways he could make a living using his skill with a camera. He could have chosen another profession. He didn't need to spend his whole life following other people, taking pictures of their most private moments. What was the real point of his job? He destroyed lives, something he'd had his fill of long ago. When was the last time he'd brought a smile to a client's face? A real, genuine smile? He had wanted to make a difference in people's lives; to exonerate the innocent.

Zachary's phone started to buzz in his pocket. He lowered the camera and turned around, walking farther into the grove of trees. He had the pictures he needed. Anything else would be overkill.

He pulled out his phone and looked at it. Not recognizing the number, he swiped the screen to answer the call.

"Goldman Investigations."

"Uh… yes… Is this Mr. Goldman?" a voice inquired. Older, female, with a tentative quaver.

"Yes, this is Zachary," he confirmed, subtly nudging her away from the 'mister.'

"Mr. Goldman, my name is Molly Hildebrandt."

He hoped she wasn't calling her about her sixty-something-year-old husband and his renewed interest in sex. If it was another infidelity case, he was going to have to turn it down for his own sanity. He would even take a lost dog or wedding ring. As long as the ring wasn't on someone else's finger now.

"Mrs. Hildebrandt. How can Goldman Investigations help you?"

Of course, she had probably already guessed that Goldman Investigations consisted of only one employee. Most people seemed to sense that from the size of his advertisements. From the fact that he listed a post office box number instead of a business suite downtown or in one of the newer commercial areas. It wasn't really a secret.

"I don't know whether you have been following the news at all about Declan Bond, the little boy who drowned…?"

Zachary frowned. He trudged back toward his car.

"I'm familiar with the basics," he hedged. A four- or five-year-old boy whose round face and feathery dark hair had been pasted all over the news after a search for a missing child had ended tragically.

"They announced a few weeks ago that it was determined to be an accident."

Zachary ground his teeth. "Yes…?"

"Mr. Goldman, I was Declan's grandma." Her voice cracked. Zachary waited, listening to her sniffles and sobs as she tried to get herself under control. "I'm sorry. This has been very difficult for me. For everyone."

"Yes."

"Mr. Goldman, I don't believe that it was an accident. I'm looking for someone who would investigate the matter privately."

Zachary breathed out. A homicide investigation? Of a child? He'd told himself that he would take anything that wasn't infidelity, but if there was one thing that was more depressing than couples cheating on each other, it was the death of a child.

"I'm sure there are private investigators that would be more qualified for a homicide case than I am, Mrs. Hildebrandt. My schedule is pretty full right now."

Which, of course, was a lie. He had the usual infidelities, insurance investigations, liabilities, and odd requests. The dregs of the private investigation business. Nothing substantial like a homicide. It was a high-profile case. A lot of volunteers had shown up to help, expecting to find a child who had wandered out of his own yard, expecting to find him dirty and crying, not floating face down in a pond. A lot of people had mourned the death of a child they hadn't even known existed before his disappearance.

"I need your help, Mr. Goldman. Zachary. I can't afford a big name, but you've got good references. You've investigated deaths before. Can't you help me?"

He wondered who she had talked to. It wasn't like there were a lot of people who would give him a bad reference. He was competent and usually got the job done, but he wasn't a big name.

"I could meet with you," he finally conceded. "The first consultation is free. We'll see what kind of a case you have and whether I want to take it. I'm not making any promises at this point. Like I said, my schedule is pretty full already."

She gave a little half-sob. "Thank you. When are you able to come?"

———

After he had hung up, Zachary climbed into his car, putting his camera down on the floor in front of the passenger seat where it couldn't fall, and started the car. For a while, he sat there, staring out the front windshield at the magical, sparkling, Christmas-card scene. Every year, he told himself it would be better. He would get over it and be able to move on and to enjoy the holiday season like everyone else. Who cared about his crappy childhood experiences? People moved on.

And when he had married Bridget, he had thought he was going to achieve it. They would have a fairy-tale Christmas. They would have hot chocolate after skating at the public rink. They would wander down Main Street looking at the lights and the crèche in front of the church. They would open special, meaningful presents from each other.

But they'd fought over Christmas. Maybe it was Zachary's fault. Maybe he had sabotaged it with his gloom. The season brought with it so much baggage. There had been no skating rink. No hot chocolate, only hot tempers. No walks looking at the lights or the nativity. They had practically thrown their gifts at each other, flouncing off to their respective corners to lick their wounds and pout away the holiday.

He'd still cherished the thought that perhaps the next year there would be a baby. What could be more perfect than Christmas with a baby? It would unite them. Make them a real family. Just like Zachary had longed for since he'd lost his own family. He and Bridget and a baby. Maybe even twins. Their own little family in their own little happy bubble.

But despite a positive pregnancy test, things had gone horribly wrong.

Zachary stared at the bright white scenery and blinked hard, trying to shake off the shadows of the past. The past was past. Over and done. This year he was back to baching it for Christmas. Just him and a beer and *It's a Wonderful Life* on TV.

He put the car in reverse and didn't look into the rear-view mirror as he backed up, even knowing about the precipice behind him. He'd deliberately parked where he'd have to back up toward the cliff when he was done. There was a guardrail, but if he backed up too quickly, the car would go right through it, and who could say whether it had been accidental or deliberate? He had been cold-stone sober and had been out on a job. Mrs. Hildebrandt could testify that he had been calm and sober during their call. It would be ruled an accident.

But his bumper didn't even touch the guardrail before he shifted into drive and pulled forward onto the road.

He'd meet with the grandmother. Then, assuming he did not take the case, there would always be another opportunity.

Life was full of opportunities.

She Wore Mourning, book #1 of the *Zachary Goldman Mysteries* series is available now at pdworkman.com

ABOUT THE AUTHOR

Award-winning and USA Today bestselling author P.D. (Pamela) Workman writes riveting mystery/suspense and young adult books dealing with mental illness, addiction, abuse, and other real-life issues. For as long as she can remember, the blank page has held an incredible allure and from a very young age she was trying to write her own books.

Workman wrote her first complete novel at the age of twelve and continued to write as a hobby for many years. She started publishing in 2013. She has won several literary awards from Library Services for Youth in Custody for her young adult fiction. She currently has over 70 published titles and can be found at pdworkman.com.

Born and raised in Alberta, Workman has been married for over 25 years and has one son.

———

Please visit P.D. Workman at pdworkman.com to see what else she is working on, to join her mailing list, and to link to her social networks.

———

If you enjoyed this book, please take the time to recommend it to other purchasers with a review or star rating and share it with your friends!